THE FORESPOKEN

BETTY LEVIN

THE
FORESPOKEN

MACMILLAN PUBLISHING CO., INC.
New York
COLLIER MACMILLAN PUBLISHERS
London

FOR ALVIN

LIBRARY OF CONGRESS CATALOGING IN PUBLICATION DATA

Levin, Betty.   The forespoken.

Third vol. of the author's trilogy, the 1st of which is The sword
of Culann; the 2d, A griffon's nest.

SUMMARY: An ancient sword hilt draws fourteen-year-old Claudia
back through time to the nineteenth-century Orkney Islands. [1. Space
and time—Fiction.   2. Orkney Islands—Fiction]   I. Title.

PZ7.L5759Fo   [Fic]   76–15575   ISBN 0–02–756400–2

Hard, passing hard is the treasure here,
Even my sword in its sheath of bronze:

.   .   .   .   .   .

[These] have made tryst with darkness.

—From the Metrical Dindshenchas in
The Book of Leinster

PART ONE

ONE

Claudia sat for a long time before raising the stone from the hearth. She was close and snug and no longer scared.

Once the old man sat up. He drank some soup. Then he struggled to stand. She helped him, noticing how damp and warm he felt, but unworried because soon there would be people here who would know what to do for him.

Colman managed to get to the door, and then she helped him again, letting him use her like a crutch to get down the step. She understood he wanted privacy, but she only ducked inside for a moment. The flame in the lantern hissed and blazed, brightening the tiny shack, showing cracks and patches and black rot.

After Colman was back inside and asleep again, Claudia stoked the fire. She sat hunched under the sleeping bag, wide awake. She was listening for the sound of Ernie Gray's lobster boat. Maybe they'd send something bigger. Maybe even the Coast Guard.

Finally she crawled over to the hearth and lifted the loose stone. There was the metal figure with its wild face and stumpy knobs for arms and legs. How worn it looked, how queer. If she hadn't known, she would never have guessed that it was the hilt of an ancient bronze sword. She glanced toward the dark corner where Colman lay wheezing and snoring. She knew he wouldn't mind if she took it out; he had always shown that it was as much hers and Evan's as his.

She crept back with it, drew up her knees, and propped the bronze man against them. She rubbed its coldness into her palms till it seemed a part of her, inert, waiting.

She remembered being afraid. That seemed a long time ago, not today, not this morning.

This morning in town she had waited at the wharf while Phil, her stepfather, was getting something drilled. Winter had transformed the place, making it bleak and strange to her, the town skeletal, the harbor naked, the boat yard crammed with unrecognizable shapes propped under canvas like prehistoric monsters dug up from the past. A few men had stopped to talk. There were no women, no sailboats riding the harbor moorings. There was no sun.

This past year two college tuitions and a lot of work had kept the family from its usual summer routine. The house in Maine had been rented, the boat too. Then in January word had come about roof damage, and Phil had decided to take a few days and camp out in the house with the two younger kids. But Evan had come down with flu, so Claudia had found herself Phil's sole partner on the repairs, helping with measurements and holding things and fetching from the boat yard and from Vernon's Variety Store.

At the wharf this morning, she had overheard talk about the old man on Thrumcap Island who might be sick or anyhow too weak to get away on his own. The men were thinking of doing something about him, though no one seemed to know where he belonged or even who he really was.

Claudia had volunteered the information that he was from Grand Manan. "We've always called him Mr. Colman," she had told them, "but it's really his first name."

At first that had silenced them. That meant he was Canadian; he wasn't their responsibility. They could inform the authorities. Only they guessed someone ought to check in on him anyhow. After all, he'd been going to Thrumcap Island as long as any of them could remember. Him and his old man. There were stories about the old fellow, a seiner who had talked funny and lived funny too. And now the son, an old man himself. This was the first winter he hadn't taken himself off the island for the mean months.

"You'll have one hell of a time getting that guy off of there, if he is alive," Ernie had observed. "Told me once he'd just as soon die there."

"But if he does die, who's cleaning up after? And they'll say we left him to die. They'll have us for neglect."

"Hell of a time getting him to move, I can tell you."

And then Phil had thrown out a remark about how well Claudia and Evan had gotten along with the old man in past summer visits to the island. The others had looked at Claudia. Most of them had known her since she was not much bigger than her orange life jacket. They'd looked at her and nodded. Kids sometimes talked to people when others couldn't.

Before Claudia could understand what was happening, Phil had offered her to Ernie Gray and the others, a useful, capable girl of fourteen who might be able to accomplish what none of them would have any idea how to do.

At first she was only uncomfortably aware of how different this was going to be from a summer vacation jaunt. But back at the house, when Phil had let her know that she was really needed out there on the island, she was unnerved. She had rehearsed excuses: She had homework to do. She wasn't quite over her period yet. What if she was carrying Evan's bug? They had all sounded pretty lame when she spoke them. "Well, what if Mr. Colman's really sick?" she had blurted. "Really, really sick?"

"You can hold his hand and keep him from feeling deserted till more help comes."

She had watched with growing dismay as Phil stopped at Vernon's for soups and cereals and a box of disposable diapers. "You never know what kind of a mess he'll be in," he had muttered. He'd thrown in a roll of paper towels, a few more cans of stew and beans.

"But we won't be there overnight," she'd protested, following him down to the harbor, resisting the whole premise on which sleeping bag, clothes, and food were included.

"Here." Someone threw another blanket into Ernie's boat. "Won't hurt to have some extra along. Just in case."

In case of what? she had wondered, her stomach already clenched against the greasy, putrid smells from the boat.

Later, shoving the supplies in under cover, she'd heard one of the men talking about heavy weather and those tides they'd been hearing about over the radio.

"What tides?" she'd asked, and they were surprised she didn't know that right now, in the beginning of February, the tides would be higher than they had been in anyone's memory, higher than they would be for another seventy years.

Phil had started to explain about the alignment of the sun and moon and the moon's closeness to the Atlantic coast, but the explanation had been swallowed up by talk about repairing the wharf during the low tide's extreme. "But watch your mooring out there," someone had reminded Ernie Gray, whose answering grunt indicated that he didn't need anyone telling him about these things.

TWO

THE sky had crouched like a predator over the dull bay, over Ernie's boat. The timbered islands looked nearly black; the bare ones, stained by birds, were brown. On the eastern horizon the clouds and waves were already locked together.

The boat had slammed down against each wall of water, shuddering and thrusting on. Its teeth-shaking engine had produced more heat than they'd needed. And still Claudia had felt shivery.

"He might not recognize me," she had shouted to Ernie.

"What say?"

She had shouted louder.

Ernie had shrugged and wiped the cracked windshield.

Thrumcap Island. There was Mr. Colman's double-ender at its mooring, the cove the same, the trees and islet the same, and the shack certainly not visibly different. It was their mission that seemed unreal. Thrumcap Island meant the time and timelessness of summer; it meant encounters *through* time, gripping and in the grip of Mr. Colman's man-shaped hilt.

Claudia could recall her wonder the first summer when that bronze man had led her and Evan back into its own past; she could recall the intensity of her anticipation the next year when they had returned to Thrumcap; she could also recall the dread that had grown until it had finally submerged her eagerness to follow where the bronze man led. And yet she had always followed, because what led her was compelling beyond any ordinary force.

But it was a year and a half since Claudia and Evan had last returned the bronze man to its place under the stone in Mr. Colman's shack. Life had gone on; she and Evan had grown apart. Though there were still times when Claudia thought of the hero Fergus and the Hound of Culann, of outcast Nessa and the Icelander Thorstein, they had receded into the realm of special memories. Even Mr. Colman, with his bronze man and his crusty old crow, had faded from her world.

So she couldn't understand being scared, unless it was of sickness and death. She couldn't understand the sense of unreality, unless it was that the real world had never really intruded into the world of Thrumcap Island, not for long anyhow, and not to wrench its hermit dweller from the solitary life he had made for himself there.

But once they were inside Mr. Colman's shack and Ernie Gray had given up trying to get the old man farther than the doorway, everything had begun to settle into place for Claudia. She was too busy grappling with immediate problems to notice the damp cold and the slimy filth that had collected both inside and out. Ernie, never talkative, had begun a monologue that seemed to take Claudia into account without expecting any response from her. She thought maybe Ernie was talking to hide the awful sound of Mr. Colman's squeaky breathing. But if Ernie was worried about the old man's condition, his slow, deliberate actions gave no indication of it.

His only real conversation with Mr. Colman was about the fire for the stove. Colman had warned against wood; Ernie, skeptical, had broken up the kindling. Then Colman had pointed to Claudia and declared with surprising clarity that she would know where on the islet there was turf for burning.

"So you do remember her," Ernie had responded, giving Claudia a shove toward the old man.

But Mr. Colman had subsided into sudden sleep, or possibly unconsciousness.

They had gone around by boat to the east side of the islet, where Mr. Colman's turfs were stacked under rock-laden plastic.

It was strange coming to Thrumcap's islet like this. Usually she and Evan had crossed to it when the tide was low enough to walk over the connecting bar. But even when they had approached from the sea, it had always been to uncertainty, to mystery, not to stiff black plastic and frozen lumps of turf.

Back again, it had taken a long time to get the stove going. Ernie had used a lot of kerosene. The shack, beginning to warm, had become unbearable. To the kerosene fumes were added innumerable odors of rot and filth. Ernie heated water to wash the old man, stripped him, and sent Claudia down to the beach to burn his clothes.

She had never seen Mr. Colman so scrubbed. Bare skin showed through his hair, with scabs and discolorations. The fresh clothes may have been as old as his others, but they hadn't shaped themselves in layers to his naked frame; they were like a wrong shell.

Claudia had lifted Mr. Colman's head, spoken to him, and tried to feed him some soup. When he opened his mouth, she had poured a little in, but it had dribbled down his chin and onto the clean wool shirt. What if he died? she had wondered. What if he died while she was here alone with him?

"What if he dies?" she had whispered to Ernie.

"We can't carry him. Not down there. Not without killing him probably. We'll do what we can, is all. I'll have to get help."

A moment after he'd left, he was back. "Wind's making up some."

Claudia had eyed him.

"If there's a delay . . . ." He had pointed to the food, the blankets; he had pointed to the chunks of turf drying beside the stove.

Claudia had nodded, afraid that if she opened her

9

mouth she'd cry out, beg to be taken. She didn't know anything about sick people, about old people, about people dying. She was just fourteen years old and she had homework to do. "I forgot my books," she'd heard herself reply. Phil would have heard the plea. She could feel the tears begin.

"The door," Ernie had instructed. "Keep it open a little. Needs air in here."

She'd blown her nose on a paper towel. Ernie had been right. The shack was filled with smoke. It would make Mr. Colman cough. It would make anyone's eyes and nose run as if they'd been crying.

A long time later she heard Mr. Colman roll over onto his side. He was looking at her. "The boy," he said. His lips hardly formed the words; they were like paper. His face was a mask.

She made him tea and put lots of sugar in it, telling him all the time about Evan, hating herself for talking to him as though he were a child. Or feeble-minded. "It's only flu. Evan will be fine soon. Like you. You'll be well after they get you to a doctor. They'll have you in the hospital in no time."

He sucked the tea through his gums, coughing afterward, a deep rumbling from the core of his body. Removing the cup gave her an excuse to get away from him.

He mumbled shreds of thoughts, nothing whole, nothing connected. He would not leave this place. Wouldn't leave his crow. Nor this place.

She fed a chunk of turf to the stove. "When they come back, I'll look for your crow." She wondered if she should refill the lantern. But the kerosene was outside.

Maybe Ernie would be back before she needed any more. "And the bronze man," she added. "I'll be sure they take it with you."

This set the old man babbling again. Coughing hoarse phrases, he started to rise. She ran to him, offering to help if he had to go out, trying to press him back before he fell. She was surprised at his strength; she understood that he was insisting that the bronze man stay. That he, Mr. Colman, stay with the bronze man that had brought his father and him, and with the crow that belonged. She tried to soothe him. She hated his deafness; he seemed only to hear what upset him. There was nothing she could do that was right.

She wished she could make him shut up. He was holding on to her now. This weak, sick old man was actually shaking her. They swayed there together, and now she was revolted by him and furious at Ernie for leaving her and with Phil for sending her and with Evan for having got the flu.

"Brought him," she heard. "Brought him who'd follow. And follow I did. With my daddy looking, then . . . alone. And ever . . . ."

"You'll come back when you're well."

That made him laugh, but his laugh was frayed air. He was coughing again. He clutched her while the coughing shook him and shook her. He seemed to be drowning. Then he sank back onto the heap of his bed.

She felt choked herself. The stove was smoking badly. She tied a rag around a leaking joint in the stove pipe, then took it off, suddenly fearful of fire. She found a box of cookies and fished one out. It tasted of sour smoke. For a moment she considered looking for the

11

crow. Maybe if he had the crow with him he would be more willing to be helped, more resigned to leaving. But how could she hope to find it? It was pitch dark outside.

She guessed that no one would try coming till daybreak. She made a bed of the sleeping bag, then felt something jabbing her leg and pulled out the bronze man. Mr. Colman didn't want it taken from the island. She remembered all he had told her about how it had led his father from far away to this very island. And farther still through time. At first Mr. Colman had warned her and Evan about that, warned them that if they followed it through the half-light of the mist they might be caught by the sun. That first summer, and the next, they had been caught, but always to return with the following tide. Only Mr. Colman's father had been caught one time after another, and always farther and deeper, always following.

Mr. Colman had followed it too, but warily, baffled, till he learned finally to follow it, he claimed, without even crossing over to the islet, just going and coming to the Other Place with his eyes half closed.

She recalled how hard it used to be to tell his sleeping from his waking, his pale eyes scarcely opening, yet catching at her, challenging her, warning. She had never understood his attachment to the bronze man, except that it seemed to have nothing to do with love or hate. She supposed they were linked, one to the other, as tides to the moon. Or as the man-shaped hilt was attached to the blade from which it had been separated over the centuries.

She wondered what would become of it when Mr.

Colman was taken away. She couldn't believe he'd live. She wished they had left him alone, let him die where he chose. Then she thought of that coughing and how it might get worse. That was awful. She pictured a sweet young nurse wiping his brow. Maybe they'd send for some long-lost relative in whose arms he could die, reconciled at the end. But these were television images. Looking across at the sleeping man, she knew that he would be alone.

Well, she thought, closing her eyes against the burning smokiness, maybe he can be buried with it. And her fingers slowly curled away from the figure till they were barely touching it.

three

CLAUDIA opened her eyes, dimly conscious of her surroundings. She could hardly see Mr. Colman. She could hear him, though, his harsh breathing muted, perhaps by his arm or a fold of the blanket. The shack was thick and sour with smoke, full of shadows that quivered when the stack shook in the howling wind. She thought of the sheep that wintered on the island; she supposed they were huddled deep in the ravine, tails to wind, noses low. She dozed.

The next time she started to open her eyes they were smarting so badly she kept them half shut. This changed her perceptions; she had a sense of things rearranged. She wasn't even curious. Then she came to realize that smoke was concentrated in the middle of the floor. She stirred, thinking of the fire hazard. But if those two women weren't concerned, it hardly made sense to fuss about it. Besides, the smoke rose from a small, smoldering heap in front of a low, separate wall. A black pot hung from a chain attached to a straw rope. The rope glistened black. Sludge dripped from the sloping blackness above.

Off in Mr. Colman's corner there was a groan, then a weak voice calling. The two women looked at each other. One sighed and shuffled over to the corner. A moment later she reappeared.

When the women began to speak, Claudia tried to strain forward, but she couldn't move. She felt bound by the whorls of smoke that coiled around her and drifted everywhere in blurring tangles. Then she realized it wouldn't have helped to draw closer. Each time the bronze man had led her to a glimpse of the Other Place, she had found herself like this, held back from the things she saw and heard and smelled. It was only when she was caught in that time and place that she became a part of it and visible to its inhabitants; it was only then that she would speak as they did and know their language.

So she sat there, her eyes half closed, feeling herself suspended in the blue-gray smoke of Mr. Colman's shack and the blue-gray smoke of this room. And she listened to the women's muted tones and strange inflections, hoping that somehow she would begin to sense their meaning.

After a while she was able to tell that they were tending someone in the dark corner where she had believed Mr. Colman to be lying asleep. She understood that they were waiting for someone. There in the drifting smoke she was slow to realize the significance of that much understanding. Checking herself, she listened intently till she recognized a word, an entire phrase. One woman was asking the other whether something or someone called the gripper would be there before nightfall. It wasn't exactly English as Claudia knew it, and yet that much had come through.

The two women continued in low tones, but most of their conversation was still unintelligible to Claudia. She became aware of other figures, someone hunched and silent across the room, a calf tied to the wall. Above her, fowl roosted in the eaves. And farther into the darkness something huge rolled over. Suddenly the straw around it was seething as though with insects uncovered by a rock. The seething was charged with a desperate energy. Then Claudia realized that these were piglets scrambling to fasten themselves to the upturned belly of a sow.

One woman went to the door. "It's coom on a filthy dab o weet." She pulled her shawl tight over her shoulders.

The open door admitted a gray half-light and enough wind to scatter ashes across the earthen floor. The woman inside prodded the smoking heap. The one at the door spoke sharply. "Dunno darin the fire or thoo'll hae it clean oot."

Claudia wondered about Mr. Colman. Was he off in that dark corner? Then she stopped thinking, for the

15

woman at the door turned. "She's cooman now, the gripper," she announced. "She and Jock and Davie. And . . . and sommat. An unkan." Then she called, "Sibbie, what for are thoo staan oot there baiverin' i' the wind?"

The doorway was suddenly crowded. Voices filled the room with sounds of discord and indignation. Finally one man's voice broke through as the others fell silent. Claudia was astonished at the ease with which she could understand him. Even though he spoke with an accent, she could follow almost all his words. He was a friend of someone here who had died. He spoke of a dying husband's last wish, of Annie, of gifts.

Someone seemed to object. Others spoke all at once. "I've carried them all this way," the man shouted over the din. "First home, though. I came just as ever I could, carrying them still. He set great store by the knife. And said the skin was for the child." His words were drowned out again.

Someone reminded the women that the stranger had traveled far and was worn from the journey.

"Yes," agreed the visitor, "it was hard. The hungry. And on the ship to Glasgow they sickened. Many . . . ." The man staggered.

The men helped him toward the door.

"The knife now," he called back to the women. "The Eskimos said it had powers. James believed that. It's for the child too. I should have come straightaway," he added brokenly, "but there was passage home. Do you hear?"

After the men had led him away, a woman who had arrived with them pulled a sodden shawl from her head. It was she they had called Sibbie. Claudia saw her face, ravaged and gaunt, but of haunting beauty. Claudia stared at bones too prominent, hair streaked gray, eyes so deep and dark they were like eye sockets on a skull.

Immediately Sibbie took charge. She spoke too rapidly for Claudia to follow, but single words stood out, especially words repeated, like *knife* and *Bible*. Issuing orders, Sibbie wrung out her soaking skirt and shawl, then toed aside the thing the stranger had dropped on the floor. One of the women shook it and held it up for inspection. It was a silver gray skin mottled with dark splotches. Sibbie gestured, and the woman carried it past the sow and piglets and crammed it high up in a niche under the roof. Sibbie nodded approval and smiled, showing a few discolored stumps for teeth. Then she carried the knife and a black book off to the place where someone lay groaning in the depths of the house.

At the sight of that toothless grin, Claudia shrank back against the wall and squeezed her eyes tight shut. She invoked sleep; she sank away into a darkness of her own.

When she was next aware of anything, it was of another commotion at the door. For an instant she wondered where she was. But then she saw the open fire and the little wall behind it; she saw the drab, long-skirted women; she saw the sow asleep, with the piglets leachlike over its legs and against its nipples. The hunched person seemed to be gone, but the calf started up. It humped its back, lifted its tail, and squirted a brown liquid onto the stone floor. One of the women took a wooden bucket from a stone shelf and sloshed the droppings toward the door. No one in the doorway seemed to notice.

"Thoo'll get no blide-meat the day," shouted the other woman.

"Let him hae a look on the frothe then," a man insisted.

Sibbie stepped out of the darkness with a bundle in her arms. She seemed different now. She wore an apron. Her hair was caught back under a white cloth bonnet. Claudia wondered how much time had passed. It was more than minutes later; it could be hours, perhaps even days.

The stranger staggered forward. Sibbie drew back.

"Wait noo. He nivver catched a glim o' it."

Sibbie clutched the bundled infant. "What are thoo gleeran at?"

"Nothing. It's that I feel so . . . queerly. Ah, so let me have a look then. And did you know of his da's intention that he be named Callum after myself?"

All three women screamed at him. Claudia saw bafflement and then a kind of stubborn outrage in his eyes. He turned toward the men who had befriended him, but even they seemed caught in some kind of horror.

The stranger looked from face to face. Slowly he brought his hands to his eyes. His face was glistening with sweat. The others fell silent. "I meant no harm," he muttered. He was shivering. His hands were shaking. "No harm. Only it's a true thing, the naming, and I came . . . came a way for . . . ." He faltered, sensing their disapproval, then blundered on. "And just in time

18

too. For the fine, fine bairn. Yes, of course he's a fine lad. I can tell."

The horrified stares seemed to hold him briefly. Then he seemed to fold over onto himself. He slumped almost soundlessly to the still-fouled floor. His arm moved as if to swim, and as the sleeve bunched up, they could see the deep red splotches that covered his pallid skin.

The men bent to raise the stranger, preparing to carry him out. One of them hesitated. "Thoo's best ha' a look, Sibbie," he suggested, but she refused to go near. She seemed to be telling him that it was enough to be tending the poor mother, "all blessy-like," and the "puir wenyarn bit o' bairn." Then she jerked her head toward the near corner and its heavy round stones. "Tae off the stane," she ordered. The man rattled off an answer. With her free hand she grabbed the tongs and picked up a lump of peat in them. She gestured with it, warning him to keep watch everywhere about, not just in this house.

From the dark corner came a feeble cry. They all turned to that darkness. Sibbie raised the smoking peat. "Tae off the stane," she repeated, sweeping the turf as if she could cleanse with the burning ember the words the stranger had uttered. The men withdrew.

Now that the door was closed, the cottage was clogged with smoke again. Sibbie went to Annie in the dark corner. The infant emitted a thin wail. One of the women fanned her apron at the fire. "What a fuggis o' reek's i' here," she grumbled. "The wind's surely geen round noo," the other answered. She went to the door to let in some air. As she stooped to set a stone beside

19

the door, something wild and black hurtled through the opening, dashed against the opposite wall, swooped high, and set the chickens in the eaves into a cackling storm. Feathers flew, white and brown floating on the smoke, while excrement and the black sludge from the roof hole splattered on the floor.

Claudia drew herself in from the mess and uproar. The women shrieked and raced after the black thing. A dog that had not stirred before leaped up and barked. Only the sow wouldn't be aroused; it flicked its ears and snuffled irritably. One woman seized a broom and swung it above her head; a hen tumbled squawking to the floor. From off in the dark corner a harsh guttural voice seemed to scrape itself from the blackness. For an instant the women froze. Then Sibbie moved swiftly to the door, flung it wide, and gestured the others back.

The crow walked out of the darkness, wings dragging. It stepped unevenly, unhurried, more or less toward the open door.

The wind whirled the feathers. More seemed to drop from the chickens, all suddenly silent, heads foolishly cocked, eyeing from their roosts the arrogant intruder below.

The crow took its time. Just at the threshold it paused to extract one white chicken feather from its own plumage. It was in the act of dropping that white feather when the woman holding the broom swung down. Black feathers scattered. The crow took flight like a broken machine.

The door slammed. The two women looked to Sibbie, who gazed stonily at the shut door and wouldn't meet their eyes. Slowly she raised her hands, her fists clenched before her. Claudia could hear her muttering under her breath and was able to understand that she spoke of the danger lurking in the midwinter darkness, of how the trows would surely grind the stones against the sun and steal the child, forespoken now and naked to all peril.

The feeble voice, half query, half plea, called to Sibbie from the far end of the room. Sibbie wheeled in response. In the instant before she strode to it with soft, angry tread, her piercing look seemed to penetrate the smoke and scan the shadowy blackness where Claudia sat huddled, petrified.

The remaining women exchanged uneasy glances. The one with the broom began to clean up the mess. She took special care to collect all the black tail feathers; these she fed to the fire with deadly intent. But when the feathers burst crackling into flames, the sweeper jumped back, dropping the broom. She watched the feathers burn from across the room. Her companion, eyes never leaving the fireplace, sidled along the wall toward the sweeper until they were joined in a kind of trance of dread.

The feathers took a long time to burn. They made a smell that Claudia would never forget.

FOUR

CLAUDIA woke with a jolt to a sour smell of burning. But when she glanced toward the stove, she saw that the fire was out. She jumped up to start it.

"Might be at the door yet. The crow."

Claudia didn't even turn around. She knew that if you didn't blow just right, a single downdraft could douse the fire. She said, "It's safer outside."

He seemed displeased by her answer. "Hurt. Belongs."

The tiny flame crept round a live ember; blue tentacles encircled the turf. She almost laughed out loud because she had answered him from a dream. Of course the crow would be safer inside. Outdoors was a winter storm; outdoors were predators. She said, "I'll see if it's there in a second." The smell still lingered. Maybe a nest from last summer had stuck to some of the turf, maybe even some feathers.

"They'd kill it," said Mr. Colman.

"I know," she told him, turning and seeing that he meant to get up again. She went to him, but he tried to shake her off. "I know they'd kill it," she chattered, thinking that if she kept on agreeing with him he'd stop struggling. He swayed. She supposed he was embarrassed by her presence. She hovered behind him, guiding him to the step, where he nearly fell. She heard the trees moaning and the sea crashing on the rocks below. She said, "I'm closing my eyes," steadied him, wishing he'd hurry up and pee and let her take him back inside. He just stood there, battered by the wind, unhearing. "Look," she screamed, "you go in, and I'll go look for the crow." She shoved him toward the door.

There in the howling night he turned and without raising his voice warned her, "Don't let those damn fool women get ahold."

She could only ignore what was obviously the raving of senility and sickness. She pushed off against the wind. Any bird that hadn't huddled down into a crevice would be blown inland. Probably the crow was sitting out the storm in the woods, burrowed down in a thicket, untouched by the wind and perfectly safe from marauding sea birds. But she was drawn to the leaping sea, to the islet she knew so well.

She only made it part way, cowering under the slashing wind. Waves hit the rocks and exploded into beads of phosphorescence. Drops clung to her lashes and magnified the brilliance. She felt drenched in colors. Then, staring through the stinging blur of water and tears, the colors faded greenish gray. She was on a slope more gentle than before, halfway between a cluster of stone buildings uphill and a stretch of water below.

She was watching people launching a boat with another tied and dragging behind. The second boat carried a long box. Out in the turbulent channel were more boats in pairs, each carrying a similar burden. Still staring, she was hit full face by a drenching wave. She turned, running blindly, the wind supporting her now and thrusting her up the slope.

She banged into the shack, feeling the smelly warmth

in her nose and eyes and throat. She felt like yelling with relief because she was inside and safe. She grabbed a fistful of paper towels and scrubbed it over her face and head. Her teeth were chattering. She started to giggle.

"Didn't see him," Mr. Colman declared.

She nodded, unsure whether it was an accusation or a question. She wished she could tell him she'd had a hallucination, a wild hallucination. Her skin tingled and felt good, even though her teeth wouldn't stop clicking. Her eyes were swollen from the salt.

She put the soup back on the stove, standing close so her clothes would dry. Mr. Colman was sitting on the bed heap; he seemed to breathe more easily when he was sitting up. She handed him a cup, squatting down in front of him. She searched around for something to say, while her mind grappled with the hallucination and some part of her wanted to break into laughter at the macabre vision of the coffin boats. She asked him to tell her about his life on Grand Manan; she reminded him about things she already knew, about how his daddy had come there from across . . . across from where? Once he had told her.

Mr. Colman nodded, content to hear her recitation of those distant events. And he had the bronze man, she prompted. It was because of the bronze man. "Yes," Mr. Colman supposed, "and other things too."

"What things?" She straightened the tilting cup in his hand.

He sucked some soup into his mouth, but the swallowing set the rumbling cough going. "After something," Mr. Colman finally explained. "Looking. And following." He peered across the cup at Claudia. "No one but him and me. And now you two." He nodded. "You going out like a damn fool." He sucked in air like soup in little spurts that made him lose his breath altogether.

"But I went because you asked . . . told me. . . ." Claudia didn't want him getting agitated about the crow again.

He was shaking his head and wheezing in what might have been mirth. She smiled at him, taking his cup before it spilled, hoping to share his joke, to agree. If only he'd stay put until help came.

But even as her smile spread into as much of a grin as she could manage, she saw his mouth work and realized he was far from mirth, trapped in the agony of suffocation. Saliva swung from his lip. His pale eyes strained toward her. She couldn't erase the grin she had adopted for his sake, though tears streamed down her cheeks and fell on her hands, already wet from his dribblings.

"Crow," he croaked. The sound he uttered embodied the thing he named. Then he whispered, "You."

She nodded through her tears.

"Fire," he rasped.

She looked helplessly toward the stove. The fire was fine now. She had it going beautifully.

While she stared at it, he clutched her. His fingers pried at her shoulders, plucked at her sweater in random spasms. Stumbling to her feet, she pulled free. The contents from Mr. Colman's cup scattered, a mess of noodles and diced vegetables. She looked around, relieved to have something to do, and found a shovel

25

with a broken handle against the wall. As she swept the mess toward the stove, she turned to find him gaping at her, his mouth stretched as if to scream. She stopped, staring back, filled with disgust and a crawling sense of wrongdoing. But what was wrong? She was only sweeping. . . .

He gestured toward her. She was too close to the stove; her pant leg was smoking. The scorched denim smelled bitter, like burned feathers. Mr. Colman was still gesturing, not warning her as she'd first thought, but fending her off.

She shook her head. She was Claudia, not a woman in long skirts on a floor of dirt and stone in a cottage somewhere in some other winter, some other time altogether, some other place. But she was as speechless as he. If he died now, she thought, it would be with this last terrible vision. She flung down the shovel and grabbed her foul weather gear, a wad of paper towel, a candy bar, the bronze man. She knew that if she was to find the crow and bring it back to Mr. Colman before it was too late, she would need to cross the wind and water where they joined at the bar and gain the islet on the other side.

Five

WHAT had been black before was dense and still
dark, but down along the water she could see more of
the contours of the shoreline. It looked as though the
ocean had washed gray over the land, leaving a thin
residue of light in its wake. The waves still splintered
on the rocks, but they were farther off, duller. The
ocean had receded; she would have no trouble crossing
to the islet.

Usually water edged the abrupt seaward sides of the
islet where a cliff stood off from a narrow stony beach.
But now, as she made her way along the slippery bar,
she could see footholds and walking spaces right around
to the cliff. She remembered that this would be an ab-
normal tide. It might be possible to approach as though
from the sea. If Mr. Colman's crow was out there on the
islet, she'd have a better chance of catching him that
way; she might only have to clap her hands and chase
him inland and back to the shack.

She had to bend away from overhanging ledges, but
the wind helped, pushing her landward. Spray pat-
tered on her hooded head and back. It wasn't bad at
all, only queer that everything was so different. It
looked as if the ocean had been peeled away from a
layer of the islet she had never seen before.

She could tell, without turning, when she was near the headland. Soon the footing would improve as she reached that shallow beach below the cliff. But the wind was fierce out here and across her now. There was a declivity where she reached for a handhold, so she dragged herself onto a kind of shelf and then lay on her stomach for a small rest before having to climb the cliff and call the crow. The tail of a wave slapped across her dangling heels and she drew them up. Then she shimmied farther in and twisted around so that she was nearly sitting. But there wasn't enough head room. When she grazed her forehead, she sprawled again, and found herself lying on the base of a triangular hole. She waved her hand, discovered space under the rock.

Did she dare go in? She had to remove the bronze man from her belt. She couldn't crawl with it jabbing her ribs. Then she was up on her hands and knees. There was a shelf to the left, another, really a platform, to the right. That was where she dragged herself.

Evan would want to know all about this cave. They'd never suspected— But suddenly she recalled the day they had been moored out beyond the islet, the look of the cliff from the sea and how the dark hollows and striations had seemed cavelike to her. She wished Evan was with her now.

She had to shrink from the incurving wall on her right. Below was emptiness, but she could see the vertical rock face glisten and guessed that the tide would fill that hole.

It was a while before she realized that the wetness up on the platform was from her. She could rub her fingers on crumbly dirt. She smelled the dirt between her fingers, then froze. The same kind of smell, sour, birdlike, and something, almost like singed feathers, that made her stomach clench. She forced herself to be sensible. She might have brought the smell in with her, like the wetness, on her clothes. Or else maybe birds had sheltered here when the tide was low.

She concentrated on looking ahead. To her surprise the cave seemed lighter. She crawled on till she was close enough to see that the light was no supernatural emanation, but the place below a crack through which a green-gray light filtered down. Another opening to the cave would surely explain that bird smell.

Satisfied, she began the laborious return backward. She felt more confident now that she was on her way out. She could almost let herself slide down the sloping rock. She paused where the head room improved. It gave her a chance for another look now that she was more accustomed to her dark surroundings. Across on the opposite shelf was something she hadn't noticed before, but now its solid black body was set off by the dim light outside.

Was it a crow? It was black, and there in the half-light she could see how ungainly it was. And wouldn't a wild bird take off as soon as it saw her? The bird took one unsteady step and stretched a scraggly wing.

"Crow," she called. Now she could get back to Mr. Colman. All would be in order by the time it was fully light and Ernie Gray showed up with help. She called softly several times, but each call sent the bird back in the darkness. She knew that Mr. Colman would have sworn at it. Halfheartedly she tried to copy him, but she didn't feel like swearing. It didn't work. Suddenly she felt it was all too much. Just getting herself back seemed hard. Near the opening it seemed to be lighter, but the wind cut into her; spray lashed her legs and soaked her sneakers. And on the other side of the cave the crow kept edging away.

She decided to give it a moment to get used to her presence. At the same time she could give her neck and back a chance to relax. She pulled herself back in, just out of the pale cold mouth of the cave. She stuck the bronze man back in her belt and dropped her head in her hands; that felt better. She closed her eyes for a few moments.

When she raised her head again and realized she had actually dozed off, she was filled with alarm. Had she let the crow get away? She turned warily, craning to see, and began to snake her way out once more. As soon as she caught sight of him, she began to speak. She told him that Mr. Colman was sick, probably dying, and wanted him. She promised that everything would be all right. And all the time she talked, she was feeling her way toward the small opening, waving one foot, then the other, and scraping the side, the top, the empty drop to the other side that separated her from the bird. "He thinks that I'm that woman with the broom, that I chased you, burned. Well, yes, I chased you now, before, when I first saw you. But I wouldn't hurt . . . won't hurt you." She tried to offer her candy as a lure, but only dropped it. She tried reaching across the chasm. It wasn't far to the bird's side, but she had to lunge at it to keep from falling.

The bird squawked and flapped its wings in great futile strokes. Then it scrambled over her fingers and shuffled out into the light. Her instinct was to dash after it, not let it go, and as she drew back to get free of the rocks, she slammed against the overhang. Then, as in slow motion, she sank feet first out of the darkness.

When she opened her eyes, the first thing she was conscious of wasn't the brilliance, nor even the bird, but a queasiness that made her want to hold perfectly still. Then she saw the bird. Gladness surged and was promptly overcome by the other feeling in her head and stomach. The bird was black, all right. It was ungainly. But it wasn't any crow; it was a half-grown shag.

She let this fact sink in slowly. It seeped through her senses, through what her eyes blinked against and her nose drew from the sun-filled air and her ears caught from the hissing sea. She had dropped some distance down onto a flat tablestone. She saw now that she could make her way to a broader step at the edge of the water. Beside her, rising like steps, were shelves of flat pinkish rock splotched green and black from the sea and birds. For another few seconds she kept her eye on the motionless bird hovering in a rock shadow. Then she began to mount the steps.

She half-turned to reconfirm the existence of the scrawny shag. She told herself that birds nested and raised their young in the spring. By midsummer, fall at the latest, the fledglings were off. Everyone knew that. There could be no fledgling in the middle of winter.

By the time she had absorbed what this meant, she was high enough to see most of this small bare island, the steep land beyond to one side, the sloping green across the water to the other, and halfway down the hill, low and solid in the grass, a number of gray buildings and walls.

Just beyond the continuing edge of cliff a sheep

31

scrambled up from a gorge. Another followed, then another. They stared at her incuriously, then dropped their faces to the moist green clumps that sprang from every crevice.

six

Looking back, Claudia saw the flat pink tablestone far below. Gulls sat silent on a patch of dark water, but beyond them, startling on the level sea, a chain of wavelets spread away toward the high headland across the channel. She was almost certain she had seen that headland before.

She started off toward the gray buildings. Weeds grew all around the walls, but narrow paths were worn from one to the other, and the ground along those paths was covered with sheep droppings. From a farther cluster of buildings, all roofless, though surrounded by what had once been a stone enclosure, a thin column of smoke pointed straight to the sky.

She saw no one. One sheep emerged through an opening in a turf wall, waiting, sun-drenched, for its tiny stilt-legged lamb. The ground cover grew finer. She was on a road that led to a gateway in the stone enclosure. Inside were more weeds, debris of all kinds, more sheep lying against the buildings, eyes closed. Sud-

denly a gull flew up with a wail; all around her others
flapped and circled, and then one by one they returned
to their hidden nests. Their clamor had no effect on
the sheep. No one appeared from around a house; no
voice called or inquired.

The building that had the fire was in the center of the
group. She had to clamber over rubble to get into it,
but as soon as she was inside she had no trouble rec-
ognizing where she was. The half wall behind the
hearth was nearly buried. The small fire had been
built in the corner instead. But she remembered the
corner, the stone shelves and niches. And there was the
wall where the calf had been tied to a protruding stone.

She began to explore. On one stone shelf she felt a
sack of potatoes. Next to it, wrapped in cloth, were
some round flat loaves or biscuits. She backed away from
this corner and looked around. Up above, where only a
fringe of thatch remained, the hens had roosted. There
beside the fire the sow had nursed her squirming piglets.
And at the other end, once dark, a woman named Annie
had given birth. There was no trace of any furniture but
the stone bench or table. She caught sight of something
rolled and shoved in under the beam, and that reminded
her of the higher recess in the corner where the woman
had stuffed the skin.

She had to climb and lean over the banked fire, the
heat causing her clothes to give off a terrible stench. She
would have to wash that cave smell out of them. If there
was time. She thought of Mr. Colman in his wind-blown
shack. She tried to tell herself that even if she seemed to
delay here, wherever here was, the time would be different at home and she would return no later than the next

tide. But how could she be certain of this? Nothing else was the same as before. And Mr. Colman was so sick; he was dying.

She pulled at something heavy that was set inside. As she tugged, it began to slide forward, dust and filth scattering before it. She yanked, leaned back, and let it fly out beyond the fire. It landed with a wet thud. Whatever it was, it was no skin. She reached once more, heaving herself onto the upper stone shelf and bracing against the other wall. Her fingers grazed something else that felt like bark. Once she dislodged it, it came away quite easily, and she was able to swing it farther than the first bundle, which she decided to replace at once. But that turned out to be harder than getting it out. It exuded a sour milky liquid that ran down the front of her and soaked into her sweater. As soon as she could, she tried to unroll the other object, which was less like bark once she had parted the stiff outer layer to reveal the hairy skin she remembered. It wasn't even very dirty, and it looked warm enough to serve as a covering while she washed her stinking clothes.

She found a stretch of pebbly beach with stones strewn over it and with one long flat rock jutting out at an angle that offered some protection. Across the channel she could see a number of farmsteads, cows in walled enclosures, even a few people about in the sun. She glanced behind her. If she nestled in under the low foreshore, she'd be more or less out of sight; if she stayed close to the big rock, it wasn't likely that she'd be noticed at all.

First she washed out all her clothes and set them with the bronze man under the shallow turf overhang. Then she dragged the heavy sealskin down to the water's edge. She drew a deep breath before plunging all the way in, but the water wasn't so bad. She came up tingly and already feeling cleaner. She spread the sealskin across the rock so that the sun would warm it for her, and ducked back into the water. She scrubbed herself, suddenly feeling hurried, anxious to be out and covered. One more dive to rinse off the sand, and she came up, blinded by salt. Her fingers grabbed at the rock, groped for the skin. They touched something soft-hard, yielding. Her eyes shot open. She was clutching someone's foot. With a gasp, she pushed off, submerged, came up again, and shook the hair from her eyes.

A boy stood on the rock. A slow grave smile attended his intense scrutiny. The smile bore wonder and pure, amazed triumph.

"Come out now," he told her.

She spit out a mouthful of water. "Go away."

"You'll come." He stood his ground.

"But not without— Not like this." Treading water, she hunched down, though in the clear water she was hardly invisible. "Go on, go away," she yelled at him, indignation and helplessness making her flail about.

"You'll have to come out sooner or later," he returned. "You'll not get far the day." He showed her the skin. "Not without this."

"I'll come out if you get away from here."

He shook his head.

"I'm cold. I've come a long way. I'm cold and hungry."

"Come out then."

She swam back to the rock and looked up at him. "At

least let me have the skin when I come out." Her teeth began to chatter. "Please."

"Only if I'm onto you first."

She directed him to close his eyes. With an ostrich-like reflex, she squeezed her own eyes tight. She felt him grab her wrist and heave her up. A second later she was crouched shivering under the skin, her wrist still firmly in his grip.

Once they were on the turf, she told him he could let go of her now, but he paid no attention. She tried pulling free; he held firm. She followed along glumly, anger and anxiety welling in turn, until, at the entrance to the cottage, he pulled his own shirt over his head and gestured toward the fire. "Now," he instructed, "the skin. I'll have it."

The shirt felt scratchy, but it was long enough to cover her, light enough for comfort, and warm. The boy had ducked out of the house, dragging the sealskin after him, as though he had no further concern about her. By the time he returned, she was beginning to feel like herself. He stood gazing at her. She returned his look, trying to appear cool and insulted by his insolence. Her stomach growled emptily and the boy nodded in acknowledgment. He was wearing another shirt like the one he had given her. He had loose trousers that stopped well above the ankles; his bare feet were streaked with grime. His thick black hair nearly hid his eyes.

"I'm Thomas," he said to her. "We'll have a bannock." He reached over the smoke to extract one of the round flat loaves from the sack. It broke like a biscuit and he extended half to her. "It was to last two days," he confided. "Do you eat the like?" He grinned. "Or will I have to catch you a fish?"

She bit into the bannock, which was grainy and coarse. "It's bread," she mumbled, her mouth full.

Thomas slid down till he was propped against the rubble. "It's made from the bere. Is this your first eating of it?"

She nodded. She wondered if he had anything to drink.

"It's a bit skurmy," he warned, watching her swallow the dry crumbs.

Claudia settled down with her back to the fire; she was facing him. "Where is everyone?" she asked.

"There's only me. And you now." He paused. "Only the herd boy and you." His face began to crease into a smile, then held. "Give me your meg then," he demanded, extending his hand.

Hesitantly, hoping this might be some form of greeting, Claudia reached out her own. He turned it palm up, examined it, then ran his finger lightly over her skin. His smile had vanished. "It's smooth," he remarked with a kind of awe. "Smoother than . . . than any I know of." He spread her fingers one at a time.

She had to force herself to remain still. She looked up at the sky. "But where are . . . ?" She tried again. "The roofs . . . everything . . . gone." She looked toward the corner where Annie had been. "Where's the bed?"

Thomas dropped her hand. "You've been here before? To Eynhallow?"

She nodded.

"It's empty. All these years. Did you know my mother? My father?"

"I . . . I didn't really know anyone," she answered carefully. "Only I saw . . . saw . . . ."

"You mean you didn't stay before. Well, but you will now."

"Oh, no. I can't. You see I'm looking for . . . something. A crow. Are there any crows around here?"

He seemed to consider this a trivial question. "They're mostly hoodies here in Orkney," he said, dismissing the subject. "And what name will I call you? You must have a name now that you're here to stay."

SEVEN

LATER that day, at Claudia's insistence, they moved up the hill to one of the stone barns that still bore part of its slate roofing. Here, she reasoned, they could share a fire and shelter and at the same time manage a little privacy. Thomas said little. He seemed bemused and fascinated by her bossiness, but he loaded the deep carry-basket he called a caisie and slung it onto his back.

Claudia worried about a toilet site; there was nothing like an outhouse anywhere. Once Thomas disappeared for a moment behind one of the walls; he didn't go very far. Claudia decided to wait a while before instructing him in basic sanitation practices. Anyone who would deliberately choose to camp out in a roofless house when there was a barn offering a bit of cover must be a little slow to grasp things.

Soon the sky clouded over; the wind sprang up. Claudia was glad they were already settled. Here they could sleep on either side of the stone partitions on the remains of bedding that was crusted over with age but not without resilience. She chose the little stall opposite a square opening in the wall. When she demanded the skin for a blanket, she found that Thomas could be as stubborn in his silence as he had been compliant about the move.

"Where are you going? What are we going to eat besides potatoes and that smelly cheese? Isn't there a lamp? You can at least answer me about that."

"The lamp's for trouble. There's little oil. I've a ewe coming on to lamb. You can fetch up some gull eggs if you like. The nests are marked that'll be fresh."

"Where will you be?"

"Over to the North Graand, past the Point of Grory where I found you." He pointed toward the eastern end of the island. "Where the crus are for holding the sheep; I've closed her in one already."

Claudia waited till he was gone and then returned to the beach for her things and the bronze man. She had only to think of the sealskin to realize that she could take no chances with these. Now that she was here, on this island he called Eynhallow, she had no way of knowing how long she would have to stay. The important thing was that she wouldn't be able to get back to Thrumcap without the bronze man. Whatever time of year it might be here, she was sure that once back there nothing would be changed. She would need her clothes.

She found a cranny in the round end of one of the barns and stuffed clothes and hilt in together. She wished she could wear her sweater, but didn't dare.

She rummaged through Thomas's bag of clothing and found a knitted jacket and a kind of vest. The wind had a bite to it now. Maybe if she did something considerate like bringing him the vest to put on, he would give her back the sealskin.

The high island to the north loomed dark across the angry race. To the south, the green fields were no longer dappled and bright; they seemed to shrink into blackness. The sheep were beginning to bunch together against the turf wall. Looking all around her, Claudia was again struck by the familiarity of the landscape. Memories and impressions closed around her: the headland she had climbed with Nessa, and, farther to the east— But here the difference was profound, for there was no massive round tower at the curving promontory. She could only set aside her confusion and concentrate on now.

The stone pens above the shore had different kinds of sheep, some small and scraggly, others larger, with finer heads and denser fleeces. One of these scrambled to its feet, dislodging a lamb from its back. Claudia stopped short while the lamb collected itself, shook, sought out the wild-eyed ewe, and pawed at it like a child tugging at its mother's coat. But the ewe would not lie down again. It stood eyeing Claudia.

"It's going badly," Thomas called to her. "Give us a hand."

Moving cautiously, Claudia told him she'd brought him something warm.

He tossed his hair from his eyes. "I'd sooner take my shirt off." He rubbed his sweaty face against his sleeve.

The sheep lay stretched on its side, its eyes fixed and

40

sightless. Thomas reached under its tail and grabbed at something, but when he pulled, he dragged the prostrate sheep right with him.

"Hold on to her," he directed.

Claudia gulped. She stashed the vest against the incurving wall and stooped down. She didn't know what to hold on to.

"Brace your feet," Thomas instructed.

They faced each other, bare feet to bare feet. She clutched greasy wool and skin. Thomas pulled. A long grinding moan issued from the sheep.

Claudia cried, "Oh, don't."

Thomas paused. "She's near dead anyhow." He looked at his hands and told her they could change places. He made her sit where he had been and showed her the thing he'd been pulling.

She stiffened with revulsion. "It's dead, dead," she babbled. She tried to twist away.

He seemed oblivious to her panic. "Put up your sleeves."

She saw that his own arms were streaked with blood and yellow-brown mucous. "I can't," she protested. Nothing would make her touch the tip of the muzzle with its swollen black tongue.

He was behind her, his arms guiding her hands. "Use your fingers like this." He forced her fingers under the lamb's chin. His breath came hot against her ear. "You'll pull down, see. Yes. Now find the feet. They were out once, but I slid them back."

She closed her eyes. Her fingers felt something small and harder than the muzzle. Once during the minutes that followed she opened her eyes because one of the

41

hoofs had slipped from her grasp. The other was there just below the hideous tongue; it was like a yellow knuckle, more pliant than hard. It had a kind of embryonic softness that was strange, but not repulsive; she was able to imagine it belonging to something real, something living.

But the pulling was terrible. Her arms burned. She was certain she was tearing the lamb apart. Thomas shouted at her to keep on. And the ewe, which had ceased moaning, was totally inert. Claudia guessed it was already dead.

She lost all sense of time. She felt connected to something rooted, like this island, beyond sight and knowledge. Her shoulders ached and her wrists grew numb. Just as she withdrew one hand to rub her arm, the warm wet mass beneath it twitched, and she brought the head ripping down with her. The rest came rapidly. Thomas was with her now, his hands stripping away the bloody casing, his fingers plunging into the mouth and nostrils. Then he swung the limp, dead-looking thing into the air, flinging it from one side to the other like a slab of meat.

Claudia couldn't move. Her arms trembled and her back seemed locked. She watched him slap the sodden thing, watched and watched in unbelief as it snuffled and bubbled and then uttered a faint blat.

Thomas plopped the lamb down beside Claudia and fetched a tin cup from the wall. He pulled at the ewe's teats till one yellowy viscous drop emerged, then another. When the bottom of the cup was covered, he handed it to Claudia and told her to get some of the thick liquid from the tinnie onto her finger and into the lamb. She obeyed automatically, dipping, smearing, forcing the tiny mouth to close on her finger, till suddenly she felt that mouth clamp on and draw her in.

Thomas carried the lamb, Claudia the clothes and cup, slopping now with milk taken from the ewe in the other pen. Inside the barn he poured a bit of oil into a hollowed stone with a reed in it. The oil sputtered and smoked and gave light. They would eat, he told her, before he showed her the way to the well.

Claudia said, "But don't you want to wash off first? You can't sit here all gooey."

He saw nothing wrong with being gooey. What did she expect at lambing time? Where had she put the potatoes?

But Claudia wouldn't show him the potatoes till he had washed. They trudged down to the shore together, heads bent to the wind. Claudia had brought along the extra clothing. They would wash their shirts, then put on something clean. Thomas was aghast. Tomorrow he'd have to bury the ewe and no doubt mess with another lambing, or at least he hoped so, for he intended to smear the afterbirth of the next lamb on the orphan and get it adopted. They argued, until Claudia, exhausted and defeated, moved away to remove her own shirt and scrub it and herself. She rejoined him wearing the jacket, which she had to hold together with one hand.

After they were back in the barn, with the fire going, he brought her a straw rope to tie the jacket closed. They ate some salty wet cheese while they waited for the potatoes to roast. He showed her how to make a nipple with a milk-soaked rag. He informed her that if she had bothered to gather some gull eggs they could have had some eggalourie with a bit of the sheep's milk.

It was hard to feed the lamb, for the stronger it got, the more frantic it became, butting at her hand and missing the cloth unless she held its head tight against her. She stroked its stiff hairy ears and wiped the drippings from its chin. Where her jacket parted, her skin felt sticky; bits of bedding stuck to her midriff.

"So much for washing," Thomas observed.

She snatched the jacket closed, fumbling with the rope of straw. "Hang my shirt by the fire," she snapped.

He took his time before doing what she asked. He didn't actually hang it up till he had pulled out the potatoes, scorching and crisp. He handed her a wooden dish with a handle. "The one bummie for the two of us," he declared, kneeling anxiously while she drank the clotted milk and meal. She wasn't sure she liked it, but it quenched her thirst and filled her. Afterward, munching the sweet inside of the potato, she relaxed at last, leaning against the stone partition. He took the bummie before it spilled and slurped noisily from it. The lamb lay asleep in her lap, its drying wool curling and stiffening where the milk had dribbled. Half asleep herself, Claudia was just barely aware of Thomas's hand reaching over to feel the lamb's thin sides. His hand brushed against her own and paused, then explored as it had earlier the texture of her palm. She was too drowsy to react, and in the next moment he pulled away.

Much later she heard the lamb stir and felt Thomas lift it from her lap. Relieved to be able to shift her position, she toppled over onto her side and was instantly and soundly asleep.

44

eight

SHE woke once; it was just dawn. Thomas was speaking to her. He laid the lamb down next to her. Somehow she understood that she was to feed it, but then Thomas was off and she was asleep again.

A long time later the lamb woke her, its nose butting against her arm. When she sat up, it stepped out toward the stone partition, seeking with its muzzle. Finding her again, it dropped to its knees, still butting, until it nuzzled down to the straw rope and began to suck it.

The lamb followed her when she went outdoors; it bumped against her legs. She remembered that she hadn't established a toilet area with Thomas, so she just ducked down against a sheltering wall. Back inside, Claudia found the tinnie, already refilled, and settled down with the rag and milk and lamb. She was still feeding it when Thomas appeared in the doorway. He had a funny, puzzled look.

"Any sheep lambing?"

He shook his head. "I've been making a hole."

"Oh, yes." She'd forgotten that he'd have to bury the carcass.

"There's something," Thomas blurted, "something I . . . you'd better see."

She shook her head violently. "Not me. You do it alone."

45

He looked surprised. "I can manage all right. It isn't that."

She set the lamb aside. It tottered over to Thomas, who ignored it.

"There's something . . . strange up over," he said. "You'd best come."

He led her along the turf wall and through the gap. He scowled at the tiny black lamb sheltering there. She could see nothing wrong with it. "The first lamb," he explained as he turned downhill. "If the first lamb's black, it'll go bad after. Now one sheep's lost." Some of the sheep he tended were his uncle's, were Davie's; most of these were the small short-tailed sheep, he explained, the old bussie broos. The big ones, the Cheviot-Leicester crosses, belonged to the farm, to the proprietor. "It's bad luck, that's all, but they'll blame me."

Claudia pitied the small unwelcome lamb, the little black bussie broo. She said no more for a while.

Thomas led her to a fresh hole not far from a stony area. He pointed down. Claudia, half expecting to see something gruesome, peered from a distance and saw nothing but the broken surface of a flagstone. He beckoned her closer, lay down on his stomach, and fished inside the hole. He brought up a length of battered, rusty chain. Claudia sank down across from him. He was reaching in the hole again. "Sometimes when I bury sheep," he said with a grunt, "I find elf arrows in the ground. They're good luck, elf arrows." He drew something up and rubbed off flakes of dirt. "I saw this." His voice was hushed. "Felt it, I mean." He swallowed. "I didn't want to . . . . Well, but it's just a queer-looking . . . thing." He shrugged. "It's all this happening at once, the black lamb coming first, and then getting you here, and the ewe dying, and now. . . ." He fell silent. Suddenly he threw the object from him. "I oughtn't to have touched it. That's what Mr. Lindsay always tell us, tells Sibbie and me. Save it for him, he says."

Claudia's heart was pounding. She forced herself to keep from staring at the thing he had thrown into the grass, though she knew, without another look, that it was a bronze man he had uncovered, one just like Mr. Colman's. "Who's Mr. Lindsay?" It was hard to keep her voice level.

"A gentleman who talks to Sibbie. Took me into Maes Howe, the great mound, when they were digging." He leaned toward Claudia. "I could just put these things back, couldn't I? Cover them up?"

"No, wait." Claudia flung herself between him and the bronze man, but she didn't touch it. "Does Mr. Lindsay know about this place?"

Thomas didn't know. "But he finds graves and things, or folk find them for him. Then the gentlemen come, and you can't do a thing, can't drag the plow across or sow the oats or bere, can't do what needs doing, even if it's your own strip of land. You must keep the pig off it too. I saw it done on the beach across from the Brough. They found a skeleton down inside one of those stone boxes they call cists. The gentleman came and carried off the stones and things and wrapped up every bone. Even the whole head of someone."

"Is that what you're scared of finding here?"

He shook his head impatiently. "I'm never scared." He shrugged helplessly. "That's a bad thing too."

She was baffled. "What's wrong with being brave?"

47

"I'm not that either. I don't know what I am. Nor what I'm to do. I'm not like my father who jumped into the water where the ice was to save someone. That was brave." He stopped to see if she was following. "It wasn't out of foolishness he did it. Likely he was scared." Thomas's voice dropped. "If I had my wits I'd be scared of all sorts of things." He gestured toward the hole. "In there. Bones and who knows what. I'd have been scared in that room of stone with the writing on the walls, there in the howe. And when they lower me down the cliffs on a rope." His light eyes seemed to darken. "Why do you suppose it's always me, when they daren't send one of the men but must have the eggs? And them above playing me like a fish. And then," he finished dully, "wanting me away."

Carefully Claudia said to him, "Thomas, I think maybe you should wait and not cover anything. I mean, let that Mr. Lindsay know. In case it's important." When he didn't respond, she went on. "If you don't mind leaving something like this. If you really aren't . . . don't mind."

"If I had my wits," he told her slowly, "I'd be scared of you too." His eyes met hers. "Only Sibbie has ever looked at me straight. Till now. And she's different, because she can unspell a cow and take a pain away from your stomach. Of course, she had me with her in the beginning when I was sickly and my mother dead and my Aunt Minnie after her. No one wanted a child forespoken by a stranger and spelled by the trows. It was only Sibbie could raise me up, trowie and all."

Claudia frowned with embarrassment and disapproval.

48

"I know. There's many don't believe that. Mr. Lindsay doesn't. Mind you, he writes down what Sibbie says. In a book with yellow paper. And red lines from top to bottom." Thomas stood up. "I've the sheep to bury still. You look out for a laboring ewe. If we don't get another birth before the day is out, we'll have a bad time of it with the lamb." He held out his hand. "I'll take the thing."

Claudia swiveled round; her fingers closed over the bronze man. The impulse to keep the hilt was unsettling. She was here because she had tried to find Mr. Colman's crow. She hadn't meant to follow the bronze man all the way through time. Mr. Colman needed the crow; he needed her. This hilt, which felt so familiar in her hand, lured her from her purpose. Why couldn't she just hand it over to the herd boy and forget it? Her grip tightened; she couldn't let it go.

The first time she had followed Mr. Colman's bronze man, she had come to it when it was part of the entire sword, beautifully burnished and feared by almost everyone but the warrior who carried it. She had served that warrior, had served the sword itself. Much later, when the hilt was attached to a new, false blade and then severed from it, she had continued to follow until she herself was separated from its protector. Even then the hilt had glowed as from an inner flame. Never, until now, had she found it like Mr. Colman's, pitted black and crusted green, and cold as stone. It made her feel queer, as if time had contracted and the distance she spanned between the one hilt and the other was shrinking.

"I'll take it back for you," she offered. "And the chain.

49

We'll keep them safe." But from what? she wondered. For how long? How long would she be here before she found a way back to Thrumcap? "They'll be safer in the barn," she told him, "and it will disturb things less in the hole. And maybe you should fill it just a little. In case of rain. So nothing else gets . . . changed."

He said he had to bury the sheep first and started down toward the stone pens. She fell into step beside him. Puffins fluttered overhead. "Tammie-norries," he called them. "They've a mind to land."

"Do they nest here?"

"A few. More will go on." He pointed across the water to the headland and its sheer cliff. "There and to the Brough of Birsay. But a few will stay." He turned to her with a smile. "It'll be gull eggs with our potatoes and meal till then. Unless. . . ." His smile died. "Until Davie comes across from Evie."

"What will Davie say when he finds me here?"

Thomas didn't answer right away. The thought seemed to have just occurred to him too. "I'll show you a cave you can stay in when he comes," Thomas finally told her. "You won't mind that. You must be used to caves."

She was startled by this, and he noticed.

"They'll not see you. Not till I can make more . . . sense of things." Suddenly he drove the spade into the turf. "And why did you make me move from the house? Sibbie said . . . ." He glared at her.

Claudia backed off, thrown by his veering moods. "Because of the roof," she replied nervously. "We're . . . you're better. . . ." She broke off.

"Are you here to mock me?" he demanded. "To hinder or to help?"

50

Claudia felt the blood rush to her face. "Why would I want to hurt you?" she threw back at him. "You're the one who made me go with you. And I helped you with the lamb. How can you . . . ?" How could she answer him when she couldn't fathom his reactions to anything she said or did? She looked down at the bronze man clenched in her fist. "The lamb will be hungry again," she whispered. Without looking up, she turned and set off across the island.

NINE

THAT evening one of the sheep near the houses went into labor. Thomas managed to corner her at the end of the main building.

Meanwhile the orphan lamb had grown insatiable. Barely had Claudia finished one feeding than it was demanding the next. Thomas told her she would make it sick. Let the lamb stay hungry; it would attach itself more firmly when it was taken to its adoptive mother.

The wind rose, and with it the sea. Each time Thomas returned from the lambing he would plop down, start to talk, and then, mid-sentence, drop off to sleep, his face fallen onto his knees. When the lamb was born, he roused Claudia. Outside, the wind slammed into her. Thomas, the orphan lamb in his arms, started to run. It was like pushing against a wall.

Abruptly they reached the shelter of the house.

Thomas had set a lamp on a stone shelf. There in a kind of room at the end of the building the ewe stood muttering to its baby. Thomas acted swiftly. He smeared the orphan with strings of afterbirth from the newborn lamb, then dunked it in the remaining fluid. The lamb struggled and bleated. The ewe turned her head anxiously, approached the messed-up little thing, snorted, and butted it away.

"Hold her," Thomas ordered, but it was he who had to catch the ewe and pin her to the wall. "Now." He pointed to the orphan. "Bring it to her nose." Again the ewe pushed it away. "Try the tail then. Tail first."

The orphan's rump was coated with slimy filth. The ewe sniffed, blew hard, then sniffed again. It nibbled, beginning to clean off the slime. Thomas made Claudia take his place. He brought the ewe her own lamb, which butted hard and then sprawled under the ewe's head. Quickly Thomas held the orphan to the udder. The sucking lasted a few seconds before the ewe twitched, kicked out, and Thomas had to pull the lamb to safety.

After that Thomas let the ewe have a rest with its own lamb. Then they repeated the introduction, the nursing. The newborn lamb was steadier; it found and lost its mother's udder over and over again. It was time for another pause.

While Claudia and Thomas sat hunched down, the orphan lamb asleep between them, Thomas leaned back and eyed the little room. "Think," he murmured, "of living here and never knowing it was a chapel."

"This?"

"Yes, an olden one." He yawned, then suddenly turned. "Sibbie may know about you." He waited, as if for confirmation. Then he continued with his own fumbling thoughts. "Next to her, and Mr. Lindsay, no one ever looked straight at me." After a long spell of silence he spoke again. "If I'd my wits about me, I'd fear this place."

"Why?"

"Because . . . because it's holy and there would be gamfers and—"

"I don't know what gamfers are, but if people lived here when they didn't know it was a church, I don't see what difference—"

"In a chapel the devil himself might come. Sibbie said if I passed the night here the devil might come. And scare me back to my senses. The devil could come in any shape, she says, and make me do . . . do what I shouldn't want. Like . . . ." His voice dropped. "The way you made me move to the barn."

Claudia held her breath. Instinct told her to be careful. Several times she had been on the verge of blurting out questions about what year this was and what country; such questions could only lead to ones from him that she wouldn't know how to answer. She could see that he was full of strange notions. There was no point arousing unnecessary suspicion or hostility. Hoping she sounded meek and artless, she murmured, "I only thought we'd be more comfortable there."

"Anyway," he told her, "I'm not afraid." His voice was tinged with sadness. "Not of you, not of what may be down in that hole. Nor even here where it was so bad the folk had to be sent away."

"Why were they sent away?" She was relieved to ask such a straightforward question.

"When the fever came on them, there was death in

every house. My mother was the first. Then Aunt Minnie. Oh, and the stranger," he added. "The man who brought me this all the way from my father in Greenland." Thomas brought out from under his loose shirt the queerest knife Claudia had ever seen. The blade was thin and worn and uneven; the handle, of pitted bone, was shaped like an elongated C with a round extension at the end. She'd had a glimpse of it before in that smoke-filled cottage, in this very house, in fact. She couldn't take her eyes off it. Her hands and neck felt clammy and cold. Just because she recognized the knife? She didn't think so. Something else, something beyond that recognition stirred in her. "The man that brought it," Thomas went on, "it was him my father saved. They were together at the whaling."

Claudia's mind raced. If Thomas had the knife, wouldn't he also know about the sealskin? Was that why he insisted on keeping it? She wanted to ask, yet didn't dare. Now that Thomas was telling her so much, it was likely that he would come to it on his own.

But Thomas never mentioned the sealskin. The gifts he spoke of were more like curses. The stranger who had brought this knife had brought the fever as well, Thomas explained, and it was the stranger's careless greeting, exposing the infant to the perils of the unblessed, that had condemned Thomas to the fate of the forespoken. "So those were his gifts," Thomas finished, "a child lost, a mother dead, and after her so many of the others."

"But maybe he didn't realize he was sick," Claudia protested.

For a moment they eyed one another, then turned

from the uneasy confrontation to prod the lamb into nursing again. The lamb was more sleepy than hungry. Without its drive for nourishment, it seemed more vulnerable. The ewe bashed at it with her head and sent it toppling.

Claudia wanted to give up and wait for another ewe to lamb, but Thomas maintained that the best mothers were always hardest on other lambs. Once the orphan was truly accepted, the ewe would be able to care for it and its own lamb without neglecting either. The orphan stood blinking and sleepy for a while, then settled down again between Thomas and Claudia.

Suddenly a thought occurred to Claudia. "Thomas," she blurted, "do the people who moved away from here . . . do they blame you because . . . ." She couldn't finish without admitting that she had some knowledge of his birth.

"Because," he finished for her, "the stranger failed to bless me?" He considered. "Sibbie says it's more than just the forespeaking, more than the fever. See, Thomasmas Eve, when I was born, is close to Midwinter night, when the trows do their worst mischief. They'll steal the children then and do all kinds of harm to folk who must live on what they harvest each year and not much more. That night only Sibbie seemed to realize the danger. Davie and his mother and Minnie wouldn't bother to remove the grinding stone to keep the trows from turning it against the course of the sun and spoiling everything to come. And so the harm was done. And more, though Sibbie won't tell me what. All I know is that when the stranger came just before I was born, and when he came again after that and spoke of me without a blessing, the trows did come and took my right self away into the hill. And my mother to her grave. Then the others, till the houses were so full of death that none could live here. That's when they found that this very house had been a chapel. When the roof was taken off it."

"Why was it taken off?"

"The proprietor had it done. To keep folk from coming back. Oh, he saw them settled, mostly over in Rousay, a few on the Mainland, like Davie on the Evie farm. It's only sheep and cattle live here now."

"And you, Thomas."

"For a time, yes. Though I'm far too old for a herd boy now."

"Maybe they keep you at it because you do it so well."

Thomas flinched and darted a look at her.

She understood that she had hurt him, but couldn't imagine how, unless he assumed that she was mocking him. To cover her confusion she asked him where he lived when he wasn't herding, then realized as he answered that she had only added to his humiliation. Davie was his Aunt Minnie's husband, and all the family he had left. It was Davie who worked for the big farm, but he only wanted Thomas now and then. Sometimes he was sent off to Sibbie's. Sometimes, like now, to the herding.

Gradually Thomas began to feel Claudia's concern. His voice grew less constricted. He leaned back, not playing for sympathy, but no longer harsh and raw. "When I was little," he told her, "only Sibbie would have me." He spoke easily, almost lightly. "She cares for me still, does Sibbie, and never minds that I'm

56

trowie." He smiled. "Though she does try now and again to set my wits to rights. Once put a fish in my bed when I was just a little fellow. To scare me back, she said."

"That's awful," Claudia exclaimed.

"Well, it didn't work. That fish flapping wet. Flopped right onto the floor. And then the cats got it and Sibbie walloped me for losing it, a fine fish from Hundland Loch for our pot. She was so angry she forgot to mind I wasn't scared back to my wits."

Claudia couldn't help laughing. "So she thought maybe this place might do it?"

He nodded, then cast her a strange look. "Claudia," he said. "Claudia. Now that's a funny sort of name. I've never heard anyone called that before."

"Where I come from," she answered, "it's no funnier than Thomas."

He rose, picking up the lamb. "I'm named for the night I was born. Sibbie says there was another name. She says that if ever I find my wits and learn to fear, I'll have the name as well." He hauled the ewe up and presented the orphan's rump. "The name was part of that night's harm. For the stranger said it right out, the name my father had chosen." The ewe made no effort to resist the orphan. She even blew around its face and nibbled at its milky chin. "Said my name for the trows to hear, and they everywhere waiting in the dark. The trows will always take a name if it's spoken before the baptism, the name and the child itself."

Claudia bent to the lamb. She wanted to tell Thomas that she didn't believe in any of that superstitious nonsense, that there was nothing at all wrong with him except that all his life people had treated him as though there was. She glanced up at him. She remembered that he had been up most of the night before feeding the orphan and letting her sleep. "Thomas," she said, "I'll stay here. I slept so well last night. You go on up the hill and get some sleep."

He rubbed his face. "No. I'm the herdie boy. I'll stay the night."

The orphan lamb picked its way over to the newborn one and pawed at it. Then it folded itself against the other. Across from them the ewe looked on, then closed her eyes.

"Come on, Thomas. They're all right. Let's just go to bed."

Thomas shook his head.

Claudia pressed him. He'd fall asleep anyway, she pointed out. He might as well get the most of what was left of the night. Even if the ewe didn't let the orphan close, it would manage till morning, especially snuggled like that with its new brother. She saw Thomas weaken. He was groggy, exhausted. She kept at him until he went with her up the hill.

The wind pushed them to the barn. Thomas prodded the embers, set on another chunk of turf, and stumbled to his bedding. Claudia lay awake, full of all the things he had told her. She tried to piece the bits together with what she had seen in the smoky cottage. Why hadn't Sibbie told Thomas about the sealskin? Or the crow? Claudia rolled over, but kept her arm under her face to keep a distance between her nose and the sour bedding. The wind sound changed, as though sending a great bundle of fallen leaves against what remained of the roof. It spattered on the slates, ceased, then hit again.

But how could there be leaves here where there were no trees? She listened to the drumming. Sinking into sleep, her mind sprang awake for an instant, just long enough to realize that what she heard was rain, rain-laden gusts flung like leaves onto the moldering slates. She curled tight so that her body would become another barrier against the onslaught, and the rain drove her deeper into sleep.

TEN

THEY both woke late. Thomas stirred up the fire. He would start the potatoes and look over the other sheep while Claudia checked the lamb.

Entering the house, she approached the walled end cautiously; she didn't want to alarm the ewe. She peered around. The ewe stood in the middle of the enclosure, its rain-parted fleece still soaked. Its own lamb had settled on a pile of stones to keep dry, but the orphan hadn't been so smart. Claudia saw it asprawl right down on the muddy ground. She caught her breath. The lamb was lying in a puddle, its hind legs spraddled out behind it, its muzzle dipped into the brown water.

Claudia climbed over the barrier. Her bare feet squelched in the muck. The ewe advanced and placed herself between her lamb and Claudia, who leaned over the orphan and shoved her hand under its head. The lamb was rigid. Claudia felt its mouth, which was open and cold. She couldn't close it.

Back at the barn she was greeted by the sweet smoky potato smell. Her stomach lurched. She made for the wall.

Thomas found her with the water bucket trying to slosh away her vomit. She told him about the lamb in hoarse angry gasps. He stood there with a kind of dumb scowl on his face watching her waste their fresh water. "And that's your idea of a good mother," Claudia rasped at him. "Some mother."

He said, "One Cheviot had twins. Both fine. Another coming."

"Good," she retorted. Her throat burned. "You're the herd boy. Leave me out of it."

"Where did you put it?"

"Go see for yourself." She stumbled away toward the high end of the island. She'd had enough of this place. She'd look for that cave she'd come out of under the cliff. She'd go back in and wait till something happened. Anything. She wanted to go home.

But she was forced to slow down to avoid stepping on baby gulls. Thomas only gathered eggs from gulls around the houses and barns. Here, everywhere she looked, there were babies. She bent down, her face close to the shiny black eye of a chick; it didn't stir.

She went on down the rocks. Shags and black guillemots and gulls took off at her approach. They circled and returned. Out beyond the breakers eider ducks rode the swell. A puffin settled above her, its accented eye and colorful parrot beak cocked sideways at her.

She found that she could think about the lamb without her stomach heaving. She supposed things like that happened all the time, only mostly you didn't know. She guessed it was better not to know. Thomas would be used to it. Probably he was only worried about what Davie would say. She thought about that for a while too, about Thomas out here, alone, accepting her almost as though he had dreamed her up. Someone to help and to talk to. Someone who would look right at him the way Sibbie did. Claudia almost giggled. Maybe Thomas thought she was a figment of his imagination. But that idea stopped being funny as soon as it reminded her of the way old Mr. Colman had looked at her in his shack. There was too much of the same sort of craziness. Thomas had been raised to believe in apparitions. It was as simple as that.

The tide was rising. Instead of making her way farther down the cliff, she had to draw back to avoid the spray. Overhead the clouds tumbled, spilling their shadows on rock already wet. On the opposite shore the island Thomas called Rousay stood up to the clouds, its brown hill solid and high, dark to dark. Again Claudia thought she recognized that island hill. But when she turned toward the Mainland, which Thomas said was the name of Orkney's main island, she grew uncertain again. Bemused, she knew she couldn't begin to look for the cave, for a way home. Not only was the tide wrong, but she had neglected to bring the hilt.

Besides, in all her previous experiences she had only managed to return through time during special days that marked the old divisions of the year. She didn't know when the time would be right any more than she knew whether she was here because of the crow or because of the newly found bronze man. Still, she couldn't help feeling that before she left this place, the bronze man Thomas had dug up would become one with the burnished hilt her memory kept alive.

She thought about staying. She supposed she could get used to the discomfort. At least she could take off like this and watch the island birds and get to know their ways. On the water below her, black guillemots seemed to be weaving a chain of themselves around a pair of slow, solemn puffins. While Claudia watched, the chain suddenly broke; the guillemots, scattering like beads, submerged, their bright red legs paddling furiously.

Birds were fine, Claudia thought, and Thomas was all right too. Only she longed to get back to Mr. Colman. Thomas was all right when his stubbornness reflected a kind of inner strength, even if it irritated her. But when it seemed to mask bewilderment as raw as pain, as deep as desolation, all she wanted to do was run. And she could go no farther than here.

She gazed down into the shallows. The two puffins swam in small, endless circles. They seemed no more aware of having been deserted by the guillemots than they had noticed being surrounded before. Claudia wondered if they were blind or merely stupid. She was startled when the male puffin, wings whirring and head jerking like a wind-up toy, overtook the female and fluttered onto her back. The coupling looked impossibly precarious; only the male's violent wingbeats seemed to keep him from toppling over backward. Within seconds they separated, preened, and resumed their circling, again solemn, again remote.

So much for blindness, she thought. So much for stupidity. When would she stop viewing everything here in her own limited terms? She turned and picked her way to the green foreshore. The clouds were thicker, the wind sharper. If she wasn't getting back to Thrum-cap soon, she told herself, she'd need to wear more than an oversized shirt that barely covered her knees.

She saw Thomas coming along through the nest-strewn turf. He paused to watch a different pair of puffins facing each other, their bills crossed. Claudia noticed a third puffin emerging from a rabbit hole. Like Thomas, it drew up in apparent fascination, craning toward the billing pair. Claudia nearly hooted at the spectacle. Then, without warning, the male withdrew from the female and lunged at the intruder, which scooted back into the rabbit hole. Thomas also retreated. The male puffin retained his outraged stance, beak agape, neck feathers ruffled.

Thomas saw Claudia and forgot the puffins. He gestured with an arm from which something hung. Had he thought about warmer clothes without being asked? Claudia broke into a smile of welcome and gratitude. As he would share his warm clothes, so would they share what was good in this day, the funniness of the puffins, their intensity, the quickening all around them. She pointed out past the breakers where the black guillemots had formed new lines. Thomas looked, smiled. "Courting already, the tysties. These tammie-norries too," he observed, glancing back at the puffin pair.

As he drew near, he held the thing he was carrying behind him as though he intended to make a presentation. Fine. She would show him how pleased she was. It would wipe away the ugliness from before.

Her smile broadened. His hand shot out, proffering the gift. She reached, then stopped short. Dripping pink over the grass between them was a fresh lambskin, its curly wool fairly clean except for smudges and the blood that gathered at the edge. She stood stock still.

"You'll find hill-bark for the tanning." Thomas held a stem with a greenish yellow bud, silvery leaves. "Only you must be sure to get the roots of it. This is only to show you." He couldn't seem to stop. "You can use my knife for the scraping. I've never let . . . ." Finally his words trailed off. There was no sound but the wash of the sea and the mewling of the gulls. "What's wrong with it?" he demanded. "I took it all in a piece, didn't I?"

"It . . . it's that lamb."

He seemed on the edge of exploding. "Do you think I went and lost another then?"

Claudia shook her head. "The one I fed."

"What's the use," he declared thickly. "There's no pleasing you. What's the use of you looking and . . . and then looking at me like this?"

She couldn't speak.

"Well. . . ." He threw the skin down onto the rocks. Within seconds the gulls were at it, ripping it, tearing at the integument, the blood. In an instant the puffins had disappeared into rock clefts, into holes in the turf. The black guillemots rose in disarray. A few were chased viciously by gulls who could not get close to the offal. Everything was shrill and frenzied.

"And I thought you'd be hungry," Thomas muttered, a potato in his hand.

"No." She was famished, but she couldn't eat anything he had touched.

"I'd best show you the cave for hiding then."

"I was . . . looking . . . down here. . . ."

"There's a better one in the big geo beyond the Bow-cheek." He started off quickly, concentrating on the nests and never once looking back at her.

Catching up to him, she tried to explain to him that she needed clothes. "Like yours. Breeches or trousers." She was breathless, but determined to get them talking about something else, something different.

"It's not fitting for a girl to wear the like," he returned. She barely caught his words. He pointed to a line of rocks on one side of a chasm. "We'll go down here."

For a while they were busy climbing down to the cave. A slopping wave caught them both and soaked them. "You can even land a boat in there," he told her. "Inside you can get back of the water." They were clinging to the farther rock face. Claudia slipped. Thomas reached back, steadying her and drawing her up the sloping floor of the cave. They stood in water, in dimness. Farther in and around to the right she saw a fine needle of light from a slit in the ground above. It made her think of the much smaller cave she'd discovered on Thrumcap.

"If you must hide and the tide allows," he instructed, "this is where I'll look for you."

She didn't bother to ask him what she should do if the tide prevented her coming. As they climbed back out, she was thinking that she might as well retrieve her underwear from her cache of clothing. She wished she could wear her dungarees, but even rolled up tight they would surely show. She felt like telling him that his notions about what was fitting might do for him, but she was too cold this way. She felt like telling him that he'd better start treating her like someone real, someone with real feelings. She felt like telling him all kinds of things, but they were high up now, and the way he strode off, setting a pace that left her breathless as well as indignant, made her decide not to speak another word.

She was brought up short by the sudden flapping of an eider trying to lead them away from the shelter of a rocky cairn. The duck's extravagant display was somehow unsettling. Even Thomas seemed a little unnerved. Anxious to show the duck that they were neither dangerous nor stupid enough to believe in its wing-dragging trick, each of them swerved, giving the nest site as wide a berth as possible. Quickly, almost eagerly, they took advantage of this rift to part without further talk.

ELEVEN

OVER the following days the constraint that had risen between them never wholly dissolved. Sometimes at night they chatted a little before falling asleep. Occasionally Thomas asked Claudia for help. Once she stayed up alone the whole night to assist a weak twin at its nursing. By morning she ached from the crouching in the chilling dampness, but she returned to the barn so exhilarated by her success that before she flopped down to sleep she launched into a thorough housecleaning, throwing everything out to air. By the time she awoke the invariable shower had begun, and when, later, Thomas appeared, soaked and filthy, she was still vainly trying to dry things out over the smoking turf.

By now Thomas expected her to undertake those chores that were properly a woman's. No longer did he keep the fire going and prepare their monotonous meals; it wouldn't have been any more fitting than letting her wear his breeches or his long trousers. She figured that as long as she was stuck here with him she should try to get along, even if she couldn't be whole-hearted about everything. So she collected fresh gull eggs more readily than she ate them, explaining to Thomas that she didn't care for their strong taste and conceal-ing from him her revulsion at the mere sight of the greenish yolks.

Thomas seemed to be waiting for her to recognize something in their relationship implied in the role he defined for her. Whenever she felt herself sharing more than the task itself, she would resist and try to hold her-self more aloof. But almost at once something else—a lamb or sea bird or Thomas explaining one of his strange terms for a plant or a certain light in the sky— would draw her out of her wariness, and she would for-get that she had meant to be reserved.

Only the appearance of a solitary gull, with a glower-ing cloud bank behind it and a pale, hard light glinting off the steely surface of the water, would stop her in her tracks. For an instant she would see black, black wings, black body and head, and her heart would beat wildly. When, in the next moment, the gull wheeled and she could see that it was not a crow, she would continue to stand and stare, arrested by surprise as much as by dis-appointment. She realized then that she was still looking, still waiting for the crow, as Thomas was waiting, it seemed, for her.

Claudia was amazed that her presence hadn't been noticed. Once a boat sailed close enough for Thomas to shout a message for Mr. Lindsay, but she wasn't seen. It was easy enough to make out people on Rousay and in Evie, especially when they were in the fields that sloped to the shores.

"What are they all doing?" she asked Thomas after she had watched the figures bend and rise and move slowly up and down the rows.

"Setting the potatoes." He pointed to the smaller figures. "Everyone will be at it. Men and women preparing the fields, the children with the sets after them."

"I should think Davie would want you—"

He cut her off. "No. Not for the planting. Not for the potatoes or turnips, nor the oats or bere." He was mending the caisie; for a few moments they both stared at his fingers tugging at the raveled straw ends of the basketry. "But for the lifting," he added. "Oh, yes, then it's safe."

Claudia said no more, though she wondered why they let him see the flock through lambing, until she realized that this too was a form of harvest.

Meanwhile each day passed very much like the one before, and usually wet. One northeast gale even pelted the island with snow and hail. But there were still spells of sun and timelessness when Claudia would perch motionless on the cliff, starting up only to scare off a predatory gull or an arctic skua harassing the smaller seafowl.

That was where Thomas found her when their solitude was abruptly broken, the waiting over. She was hunched down out of the damp flow of an easterly, musing idly about the various words Thomas used to describe the weather, especially bad weather. The cliff, spattered with guano and stained by algae, drew its colors into the stone as the mist seeped down. Hearing Thomas running and breathless, she assumed there was a lambing emergency. Reluctantly she turned.

"He's here. Across where the hole is. Davie didn't stay. I don't know what to do." Thomas broke off.

"The man you sent the message to? Mr. Lindsay?"

"But it's not," Thomas blurted. "And I don't know what to do." Thomas waited for her to tell him, and when she only looked blank, he gestured helplessly. "A gentleman, all right. Only not . . . not like Mr. Lindsay."

Claudia sighed. "What's wrong with that? Maybe Mr. Lindsay couldn't come and asked this man to come in his place. Just show him—"

"He's . . . ."

"What? What's the matter?"

Thomas shook his head. "I don't know. I promised Mr. Lindsay. Sibbie made me promise. And he . . . he isn't a friend of Mr. Lindsay's."

Claudia hesitated. Right now she would have preferred to retreat to the cave. But this was different. Thomas needed her. They started off.

The long-beaked oystercatchers filled the air with their plaintive cries. Thomas called them scolders; he waved them off, but they kept up the din halfway across the island.

"He's not like Mr. Lindsay. Mr. Lindsay makes you want to show him things."

"How long is he staying?" she asked, slowing down.

69

One oystercatcher sailed by, turned, almost level with her eyes. She couldn't see any nest, but was afraid of trampling one.

"Not staying." Thomas pointed down toward the long rock on the shore. "Davie left him off in the rowing boat, and I'm to take him back this day. While we can yet see across. And get back here."

"Well then. It doesn't matter. He'll just look and be gone." She stared off toward the gray horizon. She didn't mention the bronze man.

"He seems used to having his way," Thomas muttered. And because he didn't speak of the bronze man either, the complicity of their silence brought them closer than they had been for many days.

They strode down together toward the rocky promontory where the first grave for the ewe had been prepared. The oystercatchers had left them, had ceased their mournful accusations. Claudia raised her hand as if to stroke the falling mist. "Thomas," she asked, "is this what you call a mizzle?" She caught a glimpse of a pair of eiders hunched down in the grass. Ducks and drakes were pairing all over this end of the island now. She supposed it was their kind of day.

Thomas considered. "Or a dister. More of a dister, I think." He drew a quick breath before plunging on. "That night now, that bad night, was a baffin. That was a baffin, that wind and rain."

At first she thought he was speaking of the snow. But his voice was charged with urgency. He was trying to tell her something else. "A baffin?" she repeated to give him time.

"The lamb we lost, the poor kiddy," he explained.

70

"The rain washed the shackle off it. And all the smell we'd put to its back. A baffin can do that, wash everything clean off."

Claudia nodded gravely.

"A baffin," he declared in the slow, distinct manner of instruction. "And this . . . this would be a dister." His hand, like the careful word he formed, like Claudia's brushing the mist, opened to the fine gray texture.

TWELVE

THE gentleman was leaning back on his heels as though he could count on gravity to prop him up. Everything about him was bony and long and gray, but for his dark round hat and the gold chain that spanned his gray waistcoat and showed when his long gray coat parted.

He took Claudia for Thomas's sister. He had nothing to say to her. He told Thomas there wasn't time for a thorough investigation of the site. "If you would just clear out the loose rubble. Down to that slab you remarked." He wiped some mud from his trousers.

Claudia was fascinated by his accent, till it dawned on her that probably she, like Thomas, spoke in the dialect she had heard in the smoky cottage, which meant that the gentleman's accent must be closer to ordinary English. And his suit was almost modern, old-fashioned modern.

The gentleman was impatient with Thomas, who lay flat on the ground, groveling in the hole and handing up chunks of filling to Claudia. Finally Thomas muttered something under his breath about Mr. Lindsay.

"Mr. Lindsay holds no lien on this or any other site," the gentleman informed him. "I know something about that man, and while I would refrain from calling him a charlatan—"

Thomas lifted his head. "Mr. Lindsay belongs to that society in Edinburgh."

"Which does it no credit. Nor is he, alas, the first such member. I can't imagine what he has done to impress a crofter lad with his importance."

Thomas tossed out a clump of sodden turf.

"And I don't know," continued the gentleman, "what he may have done to foster such misplaced confidence." He pursed his lips. "No doubt he gave you sweets."

Claudia saw Thomas's neck redden under the streaks of dirt. He kept his head bowed, intent on the scooping. "He's not a small boy," she heard herself retort.

Without a glance in her direction, the gentleman added, "A few pennies then."

Claudia's response was swift. "He's given Thomas an interest. In what could be buried here, or anywhere."

"If the lad is interested, there are ways for him to become informed and to learn within the limits of his position. And ability. How much schooling do you have, lad?"

Thomas drew himself up, his grimy hands on his knees. "Only into the fourth form, and that not regular. But I can read. And write some things."

"Then you must study your books."

"Sir, there are no books. Only the Bible, and that's full of words I've never heard spoken. Mansie had some pages from a Poetical Reader. But they're nothing like what Mr. Lindsay has told me . . . us about. Nor like the books I've seen in school."

"And what does Mr. Lindsay tell you?"

The curt interrogation was too much for Thomas. He could only stammer.

"Speak up, lad."

Claudia charged in. "If Mr. Lindsay hadn't shown Thomas how important buried things could be, you'd never have learned about this place. He taught Thomas to respect old things, even some rusty chain that otherwise he might have used and then forgotten about. There would have been a dead sheep rotting in this hole."

To her astonishment, the gentleman seemed to consider her outburst. After a moment he declared, "Lindsay may well have inculcated more respect for antiquities in this herd boy than he himself has displayed." He turned to Thomas. "You deserve commendation for your alertness. If you develop a sense of judgment and discrimination, you may find yourself called upon for careful excavations. But you mustn't let yourself be used by the unscrupulous—"

"Mr. Lindsay has always—"

"Let me illustrate. Some years ago a monument of supreme importance was investigated on the Mainland. Mr. Lindsay appeared, claiming to be there on behalf of Mr. Farrer, who directed the excavation. He took advantage of the foreman, gained access—"

"Sir, Mr. Farrer is a friend of Mr. Lindsay's. They

73

were together there on the beach across from the Brough of Birsay. I was just twelve, but I recall it. It was where we boys used to slide. The men took away the sand from our mound. I'll not forget that." His eyes shone with what he had discovered. "How I watched. The bones and the stone box that was like a square coffin, only in pieces. Mr. Lindsay stopped to explain, to show what was buried there where we used to slide."

"Now listen," the gentleman returned. "I know what you refer to. That hillock was so badly mutilated we shall never know what we might have learned from a proper excavation. If what you say is true, it might explain the bungling and absolve Mr. Farrer. I also realize that there might have been other objects there. I have often wondered about that bronze bell buried so close to the ruined church on the Brough. Sir Henry Dryden will be measuring that ruin this summer. And the chapel on this island too. These buried objects must be preserved, the sites preserved, if we are ever to understand how, for instance, an ancient church bell of Irish design came to be placed in a grave. And Mr. Lindsay has done harm to other sites as well. There is even some opinion that he is responsible for the effacement or removal of rune stones from Maes Howe."

Thomas gasped.

"So you know about Maes Howe. Of course you would. It looms large in the local beliefs, as Lindsay knew when he played on those superstitions to accomplish his end."

Thomas gazed open-mouthed at the gentleman.

"I hope you are not speechless with terror because of that foolish notion about the hogboy of Maes Howe."

"Sir," said Thomas, his mouth working.

"Well?"

Thomas brushed his hand across his eyes. "Sir, will you be staying the night after all? We have no real house. If you must get across to the Mainland, we'll need to get off soon, or we won't see our way."

The gentleman looked through the graying atmosphere. "Has this spot a name?"

"Yes, sir. Monkerness."

The gentleman nodded thoughtfully. He peered into the hole. "And you found nothing but a length of chain?"

Thomas and Claudia exchanged a look. Claudia shook her head in warning.

"Now, lad," the gentleman intoned, "was there anything else in here?"

"A bit of metal, sir."

"What kind? Of what shape? Where is it?"

"I already promised Mr. Lindsay it. I always—"

"Have you attended what I have been saying?"

Thomas nodded.

"Then perhaps you will come forth with—"

"But, sir, the misting. It's not safe to cross the channel—"

"The fellow who left me said you would have no trouble finding your way, even if we must wait till evening. They are burning the hill heather tonight. There will be fires on Costa Hill and in Aikerness, he says."

"Then it'll be the eve of May Day," Thomas exclaimed. "Fires for the hill planting." Thomas turned to Claudia. "Mr. Lindsay calls them Beltane fires from the time when folk called back the sun. Calls them that even though he knows they're for the hill planting."

"Call them what you like," the gentleman declared, "so long as they are beacons to guide us."

"But those fires are never very high," Thomas remarked. "They aren't like the Midsummer bonfires. They smoke, but if you count on flames to guide us—"

"Enough." The gentleman sounded suddenly weary. "I have been too patient with you. Collect what was taken from this site. Fill the hole a little. I'll make one or two measurements. Then we'll be on our way."

Thomas looked to Claudia. Maybe she could go back for the chain and the other metal thing while he checked out some ewes.

She gave herself time to mull everything she had heard, but her thoughts were all at cross-purposes. Maybe this gentleman was right. Maybe Mr. Lindsay had been taking advantage of a lonely boy. She remembered what Thomas had told her about being inside a hill where he should have feared but couldn't. Everything swam together in her mind: the hill, the bronze bell, the hilt itself. She said aloud, "Byrgisey," the name of the home of the Orcadian earl from long ago. Then she said, "Birsay." She listened to the sounds of the island that answered her, and the two names became as one. It was like walking through the gray of timelessness. The headland beyond was almost hidden, a blur on the horizon. All at once she was convinced that this was the Holy Island rescued from the mists. Here Colm and his monks had built their round stone huts in an earlier age. And somewhere near the spot where Thomas had dug the hole a small stone oratory had once stood, the bronze man hanging on its wall, and a tongueless bell on which the hours had been struck. . . .

Inside the barn it was so dark that she found a ready excuse for failing to produce the metal object the gentleman had demanded. She only happened to stumble into a section of the chain. She could show him a bruise if he doubted her. And while she rehearsed all of this, she took the rope that Thomas had made for closing her jacket and tied the bronze man around her waist under her shirt. Just in case, she thought, and then instantly wondered what that case might be.

As it turned out, the gentleman merely expressed determination to get the metal object reasonably soon. He was hurried and preoccupied. He waved her into the boat and sat far back in the stern, leaning as she had first seen him, as though propped from behind. He questioned Thomas about the perilous current. Thomas, trying to push them off without getting the gentleman wet, glanced off to the east. The sea wasn't rough; what troubled him was the easterly and the fog it carried. He made Claudia lie low; the bronze man dug into her ribs.

As soon as they were afloat, Thomas back-watered with one oar, rowed with the other.

"What are you doing?" came a sharp demand from the stern.

"Sir?" Thomas, having turned them in a complete circle, began to pull on the oars.

"I saw you turning to the right," the gentleman told him. "You know we need to hurry. There's no time to indulge in such nonsense."

"Yes, sir. It's a habit."

"If you intend to improve yourself, you'll have to outgrow the old superstitions. Turning the boat to the right is simple sun worship."

After this exchange, there was a long silence. The oars plopped and the water slapped against the boat. Occasionally Thomas turned to peer over his shoulder. The gentleman broke the silence.

"The fellow who brought me out said you were a stout lad and would get me back." He paused. "I was surprised you were not . . . bigger."

Thomas explained that he was trying to gauge the thrust of the flood to keep them on course. The gentleman shifted on the thwart and tried to make out the Mainland shore. No one mentioned the fires. Claudia tried to think of something to say that would distract the gentleman and free Thomas from his anxious scrutiny. She pulled the chain away from her leg, rubbing the imprint on her flesh, and asked the gentleman what he thought would be done with it.

"The museum in Stromness first."

"And then?"

"Depends. Depends when. . . . I think we're coming up against something here. Just off."

But it was only a rock, freshly awash, its fringe of weed sucked by the flood into a swirl of darkness.

Claudia tried again. "Will you find out what it was used for?"

"What? Oh, the chain. Perhaps." He straightened. "Therein lies the difference between a man like Mr. Lindsay and responsible antiquarians. All such finds must be catalogued so that they are available to other scholars. For those in the future too. That," he finished, "is why you must learn to place your trust with caution."

"But aren't you all looking for the same things?" asked Thomas.

"If a man be clumsy as well as vain, then he will put his own gain ahead of the general good. Whatever his motives, lad, you may be sure that none of the objects you have helped him to collect have been offered for the perusal of better minds than his own."

Thomas leaned on the oars, lost in thought.

"Now then, lad, are we to drift any old way?"

Thomas resumed rowing. Claudia huddled down inside her heavy shirt. She had begun to doze when the boat scraped bottom. She sat bolt upright.

Thomas pulled hard, then leaped from the boat and tugged it up the beach. The sand was almost white; the water at its edge looked milky green. They had missed the jetty. Thomas pointed. It would be easy to climb the embankment here and walk straight onto the road.

The gentleman hesitated. "Perhaps you should come too. The visibility is much worse. It's no condition for setting out."

"Davie said . . . ."

"He couldn't tell it would become so thick. Be sensible, lad."

The gentleman sounded genuinely concerned, but Thomas stubbornly refused to leave the boat. He would rest awhile, then start back. This day especially he knew he would not be welcome at any house in the parish.

The gentleman stood, holding the chain away from his gray trousers. "Perhaps I'll see you again. When you locate that other object."

Thomas did not reply.

"I'll probably return with Sir Henry Dryden," the

gentleman pursued. "But if not, I trust you will lend yourself to his worthy effort."

"I'll do that sir, if I'm here. Or there."

The gentleman started to climb the embankment. Halfway up, he turned. "Look, lad, if you have ambition as well as interest, do not hesitate to come to me. I'm in Kirkwall from time to time, and I can always be reached in Stromness through the Natural History Society. Ask for Dr. Cameron. You're no ordinary crofter lad. I can tell that. Mind what I've told you. You may have a future. Within reason," he hastened to add. Then he struck out in the direction Thomas had shown him.

ThirTEEN

CLAUDIA was too cold to stand still while Thomas sat resting on the gunwale, slouched over his knees. She wandered along the beach, then inland. Here the sand changed to shale, hard and sharp under her bare feet. Her skin prickled with vague, uneasy recognition. Clutching her arms, she raised her eyes and stared up into the dripping gloom. There, she thought, a massive tower had stood as if risen from the sea. A stone bulwark had followed the line of a great ditch and its encircling wall.

She stared, stared at nothing but grass and some

stones, the usual birds of the shore, and above, where she clambered for a fuller view, only the gentle mound of a small hill worn smooth by weather and time. Sheep nibbled at its lush wet grass.

Back with Thomas, she had to wake him. She pointed to the mound. "What's that place called? Was there ever something . . . are there walls, foundations?"

Thomas shrugged. "Time to go," he said.

"But what is it?"

Thomas glanced where she pointed. "Nothing. A mound."

"But could there be something inside it?" she insisted.

"Likely there is. Mansie's grandfather says the trows can be heard at their hammering in some of those mounds. He says they'll come out at certain times, like now in the grimlings, when it's neither light nor dark. But Mr. Lindsay told Sibbie there could be dwellings in some mounds, the houses of the Picts that lived here long ago."

"Do you believe Mr. Lindsay?"

Thomas rowed into the raw gray space. He spoke haltingly, as though he was not quite sure where his answer would take him. "When I was little, the others used to be afraid of the grimlings time, and their folk could make them do anything with the threat of trows and the like. They might not believe, see, but in the half-light you can sometimes . . . see things. Especially at certain times of the year, May Day and Johnsmas at the Midsummer and Midwinter Eve . . . ." His words trailed off, then picked up again. "I was never scared like them, but I always knew why." His voice dropped.

81

"It was the first thing I was ever to know, that I was trowie."

"But if no one really believes in trows any—"

"Sibbie told me. And she's wiser than anyone hereabouts."

"Including Mr. Lindsay?"

Thomas frowned. He thought for a moment. Finally he said, "He can study what she knows. And write things down. But it's not the same as curing a cow or signing the boats at Hallowmas or setting the Bible and the knife into the birthing bed for protecting the mother and baby and . . . . Well, she makes things that many folk still want even though a fellow comes round regularly with ointments and camomile pills and the like." Thomas shook his head. "Still, Mr. Lindsay knows . . . more than he knows too."

Claudia was too baffled to respond.

"Like the hogboy the gentleman was talking about. Mr. Lindsay learned about it from Sibbie. That's why he took me into the mound. And because Sibbie told him I wouldn't bolt, not for all the tales of a hogboy in it. Took me at night, after they had stopped the digging and all gone off."

"The place the gentleman talked about? Maes Howe?"

Thomas nodded. "You know, Claudia, inside it was darker than any night, except where the sky lit one part. Mr. Lindsay had a paraffin lamp with glass around it. It burns ever so bright. He showed me all the stones that made the walls of the big room. We kept stumbling over piles of dirt, not looking down at all. Staring. For everywhere, like hundreds of spider webs, and crooked like the legs of the spiders, were the lines, some this way, some that, even as rows in a kale yard. He took my hand." Thomas let go the right oar for an instant. "This hand."

Claudia grabbed the oar just as he did. His fingers, hot and calloused, closed over hers on the oar. "You're cold." He uncovered her hand.

"Go on about Maes Howe." She drew her hand to her lap. "What did Mr. Lindsay do then?"

"Lifted me up on a heap of stones they'd been clearing from one of the smaller rooms. Lifted me so I could touch those spidery marks—runes, they're called. They were words he had me touch with my finger tips. They said a treasure was buried away west by north. Mr. Lindsay said one day I might help him find that treasure. That I must pass the night with those words that told of the treasure so that I would always have them with me. He left me then."

"Alone under the mound?"

"It wasn't long, for it was not much past midsummer. Just before the sun rose, I did as he told me and climbed out. Didn't head for Birsay either, but went along the road toward the Bridge of Waithe where the people cross who come from Stromness. Some of those coming to dig would not go back to work, though the foreman himself showed them that I was only a crofter lad, not the hogboy, and that it was a trick of the grimlings that made it seem other." He fell silent.

Claudia couldn't begin to unravel the threads of credulity and deceit in his account. But she saw that he was bound by those threads like a spider's prey. Webs of writing scratched in stone had closed around him.

And he who longed to fear had not been afraid, but had traced the message of hidden treasure with his grubby hand.

She noticed that his strokes were becoming uneven. Sometimes the oars went too deep and were almost pulled from his grip. She suggested taking a turn, but he told her that wasn't fitting. Instead, he would rest a little, he said, and then pull harder to the west. He swiveled on the thwart; soon they might be seeing smoke from the Ward Hill on Rousay.

After that Claudia tried to look for him, though she didn't really know what she should be seeking. Blurs like land masses seemed to hover over the water, sometimes dissolving as soon as they were apprehended, sometimes shifting into almost recognizable shapes. She knew about false horizons and mirages; she wondered what Thomas thought when he saw those shapes on the fog-bound sea.

At times he talked, but mostly he was silent. Claudia, staring into the dripping void, kept falling into a kind of trance. A word from Thomas would rouse her briefly; she would discover that she had been clutching herself for warmth. Her clenched jaws worked stiffly; she could barely speak.

Then she saw a seal so close to them that she could discern the hairs on its face, the quivering of its dilated nostrils, the liquid brown of its eyes. She touched Thomas's leg and pointed. Together they watched the seal tip slowly backward and sink. Thomas darted an anxious glance at her. Claudia thought of Nessa and the seals that had surrounded the monks' island long ago. Mulling all of this, she murmured wonderingly, "The color . . . the skin . . . ."

"Does that make you grieve?"

She was so astonished at the question she didn't know how to reply.

"The way that selkie looked," he remarked, "as it would know you."

Thinking still of Nessa, she felt herself alone in this vast bleak sea of fog. He didn't know where they were. She was sure of that. How long could they go on like this? Instead of answering him, she asked, "If we don't make our landing, will we get to some other island?"

Thomas told her they might fetch up on Wyre or even Gairsay, which was a good deal higher and could probably be seen. Last fall at the end of the fishing he and Davie and some of the others had landed on Muckle Green Holm when the selkies were hauled out for the calving. They'd waited out the fog surrounded by the newborn pups, white as snow. "We could have taken any number then, but we didn't. Not one. Davie wouldn't let us. For he knows. All the older folk know." Thomas kept glancing at Claudia but avoiding contact with her eyes.

"Know what?"

"Who the selkies really are." Thomas heaved back on the oars with renewed vigor. "Anyway, there's always Rousay if we slip past Eynhallow, and if the current takes us east we're bound to see Gairsay. Besides, I haven't tried to use my biter yet. Maybe it's time." He brought the knife out from beneath his shirt. "Past time," he amended, stroking it with pride.

Claudia felt like retorting that it was time for some good hard rowing, not for fooling around with a knife. "You keep pulling to one side," she observed after he

85

had started rowing with the knife in his hand.

He nodded, unperturbed. "The blade will help now."

"What?"

"They say that long ago Eynhallow belonged to the sea folk; it used to disappear as soon as any man approached it. Finally one day there came a man who held steel in his hand and kept his eyes fixed on the island all the way to it and took it from the sea folk. There are still islands, they say, off to the west. No one knows quite where. Some say they are under the ocean, some that if you sail through the fog or the grimlings, you may land on their shore. Davie says if you be lost, always rely on a bit of steel to guide you." He rowed on, but two strokes now with the left oar to every stroke of the encumbered right. "And too," he said, "this biter is special."

Claudia found herself nodding in silent assent. It might well be special. Who was she to judge? As she sat stooped over, the bronze man gouging at her, a new idea found its way into her thoughts. It was chilling, like the fog that collected at the ends of her hair and trickled down inside her loose shirt. The smoke that Thomas craned to see was from fires made to clear the land, though Mr. Lindsay regarded them as leftovers from an older time when the Feast of Beltane was celebrated. And the ancient Feast of Beltane split the year, and through its open seam any one or thing might pass just as she and Evan had once passed from the time of the ancient sword to their own. Thomas believed in the power of the knife; he couldn't know that the bronze man might lead them through the fog into another time and place. Maybe soon they would fetch up on an island, only it might be Thrumcap, with sick, old Mr. Colman waiting through the winter night for his crow.

She waited for Thomas to pause, then spoke to him gently, trying to suggest that he be prepared for the strangest sights, for anything.

"I know that. Don't you think I know that?" His voice was sharp, on edge. "Only I've sheep to tend on Eynhallow," he added with a little frown of worry.

"If you do find yourself in a strange place . . . ." She faltered. How could she convey the difference in time; he might still get back to Eynhallow before this day was over. "Where you land, the time may seem . . . longer. . . ."

"I know. It's that way in the hill too. Of course time's different. Only I keep thinking of the ewes I penned this morning, three of them, with nothing but the weeds that grow between the stones."

"How long do you think we've been?"

He shrugged. "A fog like this makes night and day all one. And I can't tell from the tide. It was slack when we left. It should be pulling hard now. But . . . it's not."

The circle of fog was growing lighter. Claudia thought she could see a real demarcation between the water and the sky. Land?

"The water is flat." His face looked strained.

"It's been smooth all along. You even said we were lucky—"

"We are somewhere," he concluded, his voice deepening with forced confidence. "A cove maybe. Soon you'll be warm."

At this point that was almost all Claudia could think of. Shelter and fire and dry clothes. Suddenly she caught sight of something massive looming in the fog. A huge rock? Was Gairsay that steep? Thomas veered away from it. It was too high out of the water, he said. Besides, he didn't like the look of it. It was too sheer to land on. And anyway he knew of no cliff anywhere so ghostly pale as that.

A moment later they saw a shoreline. They beached on pebbles which crackled under them. Claudia could make out a rocky cliff to her left, nothing to her right. She tried to orient herself to Thrumcap's coastline. She thought of the beach where she and her brothers and sisters had tried to build a shelter. Well, it didn't matter now that they were here. They would pick their way to the high-water mark, secure the boat, and then she would gain her bearings. She hoped the fire hadn't gone out in the shack. She hoped Mr. Colman would be fast asleep.

The stones were icy underfoot, but then she realized that this was winter again, not May Day.

Thomas warned her to stay close. He was puzzled, anxious. "It could be the other side of Rousay. I don't think I know—" He pointed.

Claudia looked. She was just coming to terms with what she saw, with grass that couldn't be green on Thrumcap in February, and with what that meant. Disappointment dulled her perceptions. She had been so certain that this had to be Thrumcap. What difference did it make what side of Rousay they were on? She wanted to be home. What was the good of following Thomas's various conjectures as he pointed to and started toward the little farmstead huddled against the hill?

"We must wait in the byre till someone is about. See, Claudia, it's one of the old steadings made from turfs. You don't see many of them in Birsay and Evie."

She stood waiting while Thomas explored a small outbuilding. Then he beckoned her into the blackness where there was at least something dry on which to curl and wait. Her fingers were numb, her skin shriveled, her muscles all sore. She was too cold to sleep. She listened to Thomas breathing deeply and thought of the stove at Thrumcap, of their little fire on Eynhallow, of any fire.

Suddenly she needed to go out. She felt her way to the small opening and squatted down in the shelter of the wall. It was lighter than when they had arrived. She could look down to the stony beach. There was the boat lying aslant well up from the water. The water itself was darker, though still gray. Soon, if the fog continued to lift, there would be color again on the sea.

Her gaze swept from the jagged cliff across to where the fog still hung. And there, not so immense as it had seemed from the boat, was the thing from which Thomas had veered. It was hard to know just how big it was. Too sheer, Thomas had asserted. Yes, only not so ghostly now that the surrounding atmosphere showed sky and water and land. In fact not ghostly at all, but absolutely solid and dense and dead white.

The cold drove Claudia back to the shelter. She could see enough now to understand how Thomas had settled down to sleep in a stone stall almost exactly like the one he used on Eynhallow. There was nothing here to provoke uneasiness in him. Even the tie holes matched at successive levels to accommodate the height of the bedding. And the bedding itself was fresh and deep, though only two calves were kept at the back. Thomas slept from exhaustion and in peace. He had probably never even seen a picture of an iceberg. How would she prepare him for what he would find when he rose from his nest of nearly warm straw?

PART TWO

FOURTEEN

CLAUDIA shrank from the rough intrusion. "No," she grumbled, her arms locked over her eyes. Thomas pulled at her, demanded that she shake off sleep this instant. But even after he had hauled her to her feet, she could only stand bewildered by the brilliance of everything beyond the doorway. She shaded her eyes against the intensity of light, the blue expanse of water, the high mountains down which frozen streams glittered like jagged cracks, the utter whiteness of the distance.

Thomas wanted to be off. He had already explored the farmstead and had found some dried fish. The people would be waking soon. He didn't want to be caught.

Reluctantly Claudia followed him to the rocky beach, to the water, tranquil enough but studded with icebergs. Thomas wouldn't even discuss their course until they were well off land. He had stolen; the first order of business was to disappear.

He rowed hard till they had rounded the point of the cove. Above the rocks, which rose straight up from the water, a green plateau stretched back a few hundred yards before rising sharply to a rocky peak. Two more farmsteads were sheltered here under the crags, a cluster of buildings like outcroppings of sod and thatch.

Beyond this plateau the watercourse divided, one way leading into a river jammed with ice. As they rowed across the river mouth, the frozen air clamped round them; the river hissed and creaked. They saw the pack ice part as an iceberg tipped and rocked, grinding the flat surface, piling up the ice layers. Suddenly, like an explosion, the ice cracked. Water spurted up, spraying the churning river with huge white shards. The iceberg was sliced clean through. Its spawn tumbled, revolving and rolling all the way over. When it surfaced it was transformed, smooth, blue-green, shadowed.

Suddenly they realized that the wake was racing toward them. Claudia scrambled to Thomas's side and grabbed an oar. They were able to turn the boat so that it wouldn't be caught broadside. Then, as the wave lifted them up, they rowed with all their strength. Down in the trough into which they plunged they were drenched, but not swamped. They kept on rowing, using the momentum to pull themselves out. They kept on after that, never stopping till they had passed the mouth of the ice river and were in another and vaster arm of the sea. It was a while before Thomas made Claudia return to her place in the stern.

They gnawed on the dried fish. It made them thirsty. Soon, Thomas promised, they would land somewhere and find water. Or eat some snow.

Claudia wondered when he was going to comment on this place. Thinking about Thomas helped put off coming to grips with her own alarm. He didn't seem beset by the helplessness that engulfed her, though she could tell that he was puzzling over everything he saw. He spat out fish bones and pointed to an occasional newborn lamb on the mountainside. "Lambing has only begun," he ventured finally. "Early." He had reduced this one observation to his own known terms. "Lambs before their time seldom make it."

Just then they caught sight of a ewe standing over a lamb, trying to fend off an attack by crows and gulls. Thomas remarked that if the ewe didn't clean the lamb off fast enough, that sort of thing happened at home too. "They go for the eyes," he said, speaking of the blackbacks, the crows. "They just keep on."

Claudia was horrified. She saw the ewe stamp and toss its head. She saw the lamb lift its muzzle; a bird dove in and covered it. Gulls attacked the rear of the ewe, and when it lunged around, it nearly slipped from the narrow ledge. Suddenly Claudia couldn't stand it anymore. She stood up in the boat; she waved her arms and shrieked. Thomas stared open-mouthed at her. The birds were making such a racket they couldn't possibly have heard her way up on the steep rock face. But she couldn't stop till she was hoarse and blinded with tears.

Crumpled on the thwart, she sensed that Thomas had stopped rowing. She rubbed her face. He was staring still, but not at her. "I would never have thought," he whispered. Claudia looked up. "It must have heard you."

The bird, crow or raven, flapped steadily toward them. Claudia rubbed her eyes some more. They were crusted with salt. "It's the crow," she rasped. Closer now, the bird looked bedraggled, almost helpless.

A streak of brown catapulted out of nowhere. The crow swerved and plummeted. Claudia staggered to her feet again; at least this time she would have a chance to beat off the attacker.

"That's a bonxie," Thomas exclaimed. "They come down from Shetland now and then. They're worse than the baakies for killing."

The crow dove for the boat, the bonxie so close that it was able to strike the crow sideways into the water. Thomas waved an oar. Claudia leaned over; the icy water slipped in along the gunwale. The bonxie descended again, its massive wing striking for a kill. Thomas swatted, but the oar just glanced off it. It worked, though. With amazing speed the bonxie pulled itself upward, circled once bewailing its loss, and slid across the sky toward the mountain.

Thomas pronounced the crow so close to death that the rescue was probably pointless. Claudia held the limp, cold creature. Deep inside its saturated breast plumage was a white feather that didn't seem to belong to it. Forgetting the white gulls on the cliff, Claudia's mind fastened on the chicken feathers flying about the cottage where she had last seen this or some other crow. She tugged at the feather, expecting it to be unattached, but the crow had recovered sufficiently from its frozen plunge to make its objection clearly felt. She had to let go. And that wasn't like Mr. Colman's crow, which had always liked to be handled. Still, she reasoned, this crow had heard her, had sought her out. She couldn't imagine any other crow doing that.

Thomas was rowing again. On the farther shore they could see someone driving cattle onto a grassy hill above a settlement. Thomas considered crossing over. They saw more people now, smoke rising from thatched roofs, boats. But it was a long way to that side. They peered up the closer shoreline, shielding their eyes from the glare. Thomas thought he saw more smoke;

he took up the oars again, though he kept glancing back at the other shore, the walls and buildings, the small stand of dwarf trees under the hunched shoulders of the hill. Claudia watched him stealing those glances and wondered if he was deliberately refusing to notice the ships at anchor, each long and low and easily recognizable to Claudia from the time of Nessa and Thorstein, though they carried more beam than Viking ships of war.

Finally, with hard swift strokes, Thomas landed their boat on a narrow strand below a single steading. Claudia grabbed the crow, which began to protest and then, still exhausted, subsided into acquiescence. Thomas made for the house, pushing aside a skin which hung over the doorway. A few hens rushed out. They smelled and heard the bubbling over the fire before they could make out the round pot, the iron chain. Claudia begged Thomas not to steal again; she didn't want to have to flee. So they just held out their hands to the fire and shook out their salt-stiff wet woolens and waited for someone to come and offer them a share of food.

Claudia had just sat down on the earthen floor to raise her feet to the fire, when the dimness in the house darkened and a deep voice spoke. "There you are. I saw you come while I was taking the cow up the hill. Then when I got down I thought you might have gone. No sign, not a sound. Till I saw the boat. Now that's a different sort of boat, that one. Well, but you're here, and that's what counts, doesn't it? You and the bird. Lik-Lodin will be glad of that."

As the man spoke, he moved toward the fire and the light came after him again. His face was creased with smiling and deeply lined. His hand tipped Claudia back. She looked up at red hair, a bushy red beard, bright-dark eyes, and was conscious of the acrid smell about him. "All wet," he said. "And you, lad?" Claudia heard Thomas say that he was all right, but that she would need clothing. The man's answer filled the small low house. "We'll pick a fine dress of wadmal from those unfortunate folk whose bodies Lik-Lodin has just now taken to the church in Gardar for burial. There are sealskin cloaks as well, but they might be warm for—"

"No," Thomas retorted. "No sealskin."

The man regarded him with surprise. "These are fine skins, and clean, you understand. Everything is. Lik-Lodin always washes the clothes of the corpses before he sells them, and these—"

"Clothes of corpses?" Claudia shrank away from the huge man.

He looked from Claudia to Thomas. "Don't you . . . . Didn't Lik-Lodin direct you here to wait for him?"

"We . . . we don't even know where we are," Thomas blurted.

"I see." The man pulled at his beard. "I see. You mean you just happened . . . happened here?"

Thomas nodded.

"I see," the man kept on murmuring. "Then it will come as a surprise to Lik-Lodin. It is all happenstance. His leaving the clothes too, since he would have to return for his new blade. So. He said he was hoping someone at Brattahlid or Gardar might have seen you. Hoping the crow might recognize you for him. So. And it did. I'm surprised he let it get away." He paused. "Are you certain you didn't see Lik-Lodin on the fjord?"

Thomas said, "We saw no one. We don't know where we were. We don't know who you are either," he added bluntly.

The man laughed. "You sound tough as walrus sinew. No wonder your master thought you could have made your way and traveled this far. Well, now that the crow has found you, you needn't wander any farther. Unless Lik-Lodin decides . . . well, but that is for Lik-Lodin to consider, not Bjarne. Though I will find some work for you till Lik-Lodin returns. And wadmal for the maid."

"What is in the pot?" Thomas asked quickly, adding, "Are you Bjarne?"

"I am Bjarne, and I will fetch the dress, and you two may share the morning meal with me."

"We don't want to trouble you," Claudia put in. "Maybe a little bread—"

"Bread." The big man shook his head. "I'm a smith and have no time to reap the wild beach corn, as do some who must have their ale. There's little bread in this land, even at Brattahlid."

"But we saw stacks," said Thomas. "We saw straw in a byre."

"The season is too short for reaping," Bjarne explained gently. "Head and stalk are used together for the winter fodder, the remains for bedding with the ash. You'll get no bread, but a fine liver stew this day."

Once he was gone, Claudia and Thomas waited in uneasy silence. Claudia felt the bronze man under her shirt. She realized that Thomas thought the knife had brought them here. "I think, Thomas," she said, her voice low, "we ought to stay close." Thomas nodded. Was he thinking of his knife?

Bjarne returned. "This should fit. It's from a maid not much bigger than you."

Claudia peered at the thing hanging over his arm. "It was on a dead person?"

"I have just said."

"I don't think . . . . Actually, I'm beginning to dry—"

"Tell your sister," said Bjarne, turning to Thomas, "the gown is twice washed. A fine homespun, the wadmal that merchants carry away for sale. The Greenland cloth is highly prized."

"Where we come from," said Thomas, "folk are buried in their own clothes. It would be thievery—"

"Lik-Lodin earns little for his labor. If he didn't find the corpses of the shipwrecked and the lost, who would see to their final rest in consecrated ground? No one has traveled so far into the snowy wastes of the northern hunting grounds for so little reward. This family lay frozen all winter. Now they will be buried by the church. Do you think they would begrudge him what they wore?" He dropped the dress at Claudia's feet and strode out into the sunshine.

"You'd better put it on," Thomas told her.

"I won't. Why should I?"

"You put it on. I'll go out and . . . . I'll thank him for his kindness."

Alone beside the fire, Claudia pulled the shirt over her head. The dress was heavy, even coarser, but it smelled a good deal fresher. She pulled the dress into place, fumbling until she could figure out how it was shaped from strips of woven wool sewn together.

She stepped outside. The crow, blinking at the sudden brightness, followed closely. She wished she could see herself, but the house had no windows at all and

99

only a flap of skin for a door. She tried twirling; the red and brown skirt belled out. She looked into the first building she came to, wanting to show the dress to Thomas, but there were only bins and sacks and iron bars against the wall. The next building was the byre. From its darkest corner a shaggy black calf gazed out at her. Around behind the other side was a shed, half open, and there, with their backs to her, stood Bjarne and Thomas.

"Look." She hadn't meant to shout. Thomas whipped around; Bjarne turned more slowly. She grinned at them. "Look," she commanded, spreading her arms.

"What?" Thomas spoke dryly, distantly.

"Look at me," she pronounced, and then felt clumsy, foolish.

"No." Thomas stepped aside. "You . . . you look."

She saw a stone anvil, an immense stave bucket, the tools of the smithy resting here and there. Then she noticed the knife on the stone, its new blue-gray blade, the creamy white handle smudged black. It was a crude replica of the bronze man. She turned to Thomas, who looked cold, and she recalled her own uneasiness when he had first shown his knife to her. Only now she understood the chill that had struck her. Thomas's hand was at his side. She guessed that his fingers were hard against the C-shaped handle of his knife, his touch confirming that it was as if the hilt on the stone had lost an arm and a leg from one side, leaving the other to form a C like his, its knob at the end a smooth round head.

"So this shape is known to you," Bjarne observed. "Had I doubted before when I saw you with the crow, I would certainly doubt no longer."

"Doubt?" questioned Claudia, stalling, resisting. She wanted to flee before she was caught up in this curious extension of the bronze man and its world. But glancing at Thomas, she knew it was already too late. He would not forget or pretend that he had not seen this hilt. He would never deny the resemblance between it and his own, between it and the bronze man. And anyway, where could she have fled to?

"That you are the thralls, the lost thralls. It is what the Icelander intended, or anyhow hoped. And told to Lik-Lodin."

Numbly Claudia's mind registered what he was saying and, unready, veered away from its meaning.

The smith raised his arms. "The sun is scarcely high, and already the day has brought great good." His hands fell to their shoulders and he drew them after him, one on either side in his exuberant embrace. "Now we will eat," he announced, his voice carrying like a fanfare up the side of the mountain.

High above them the cow lowed a plaintive croon. "Never fear," he shouted up to her, throwing back his head, "your small one will get her share. No one will hunger this morning."

FIFTEEN

W<small>HILE</small> Claudia filled Bjarne's basket with seaweed from the shore, the crow spread its bedraggled wings and sunned itself. It was so lethargic that when she struggled back uphill, the crow merely opened one eye to mark her going. Here, protected from the wind and in the full mid-morning glare, the air was soft and warm.

From time to time Claudia heard the smith's voice, heard ringing blows from the forge, but mostly the tiny farmstead seemed swallowed by the surrounding vastness. Icebergs drifted slowly on the tide. The village of Brattahlid across the fjord seemed to belong to another world. In the small field where she spread the seaweed, her bare feet sank through tender grass studded with yellow and white flowers. The upper surface of the surrounding wall was hot, but lower down in the shadows of the stone, snow still clung to the seams and gaps.

The sun had burned through the crust of the hill; just under the lush turf the melted earth oozed and sucked her every step. Before she was done, grass and blooms were crushed, and her skirt dragged heavy and wet. She wondered what time it was. Then she wondered about the time here in the larger sense. What made this place confusing was seeing Thomas so remarkably at home.

Her head was beginning to ache. She didn't want to ponder the time or the knife hilt or the things Bjarne had told them. She knew what time it was, she thought: time to go home. Now that she had the crow, she needed to concentrate on getting it and herself back to Mr. Colman. As for Thomas, it was enough that he had that knife and would sense its connection with the bronze man. Let him do what he liked with them.

She could barely keep her eyes open. Everything she looked at seemed to be rimmed with red. She set the basket on the wall and made her way, wavering a little, toward the house.

A loud squawk brought her up short. She watched a hen run crazily, casting a few feathers; others took up its alarm. Then she saw that the crow had come up from the shore and was flapping and dropping to the ground again. She was too dazed to go to it, but as soon as it saw her it made for her skirt. She could feel its wings beat against her muddy ankles. Only then did she see the man who had been chasing it. He lunged and fell sprawling at her feet.

"That's my crow." He glared up at her. "I brought it all the way from Iceland, and it's not getting away again." He grabbed, and the crow scooted between her legs. The man pulled back, still on his knees. "You give it. Bjarne knows it's mine. Bjarne will tell you."

Claudia backed away. She stared at his long face, his prominent teeth and deep eye sockets. He wore boots to his knees, a long, belted shirt of leather over skin leggings. His light brown hair fell in a tangle to below his shoulders. He had no beard or mustache; his cheek was so badly scarred that it pulled his nose to one side.

103

His face was that of a youth not much older than Thomas.

Claudia had backed to the wall. Still the young man advanced. When he stood just in front of her, she mumbled, "Excuse me," and dashed past him. The crow tumbled with her, nearly tripping her. Aiming for the byre, she was blocked by Bjarne, who caught her. Limp with relief, she allowed herself to be held, while Bjarne, scarcely seeming to notice his burden, rumbled with laughter and explained things to the bewildered young man. She supposed the crow was all right because it had stopped complaining. She heard Thomas ask a question. Bjarne touched her head and berated himself for failing to give her a head scarf. Then he carried her into the house.

The three voices wove a pattern in the cool, dim house. Bjarne's was the warp through which the other two sped, the young man's slow but droningly insistent, Thomas's short and full of heat. Thomas brought a wet cloth for her burning face. "Did he touch you?" he whispered, bending over her. "Did he hurt you, that Lik-Lodin?"

Claudia shook her head. "Wanted the crow." Her lips felt parched; she closed her eyes.

As from a distance she heard Thomas speak, demanding and brusque. Bjarne responded on a deep rolling note. Then he bent over her as Thomas had done. Propping her up, he held a bowl to her lips. She sipped, then gulped down the curdled milk. After that she slept.

She woke to hear Thomas declare himself to be an Orcadian and Lik-Lodin reply that in that case he must of course be one of the lost thralls the Icelander, Thorstein, had described to him. She sat up. "Thorstein?" she heard herself exclaim. This time she couldn't ignore the reference to the Icelander, though it was hard to connect Lik-Lodin with the gentle seafarer she had known in the time when the hilt and blade were separated. If Thorstein was alive now, that would mean she was in his time again.

"Thorstein is the man who gave Lik-Lodin the knife handle you and Thomas have seen. He also gave him a sheath to match. Lik-Lodin, show these two your sheath."

Lik-Lodin pulled out the sheath, which was cream-colored like the knife hilt, but scratched with a design of spirals and tendrils that just showed in the dimness. In one glance Claudia could tell that, as with the knife handle and sword hilt, this sheath copied the shape and decoration of the scabbard that belonged to the sword of Culann. All at once everything that Thorstein had told her came back to her: how the people of his Vinland settlement had been struck down by disease; how they had believed the ancient scabbard with its blade to be the cause of that disaster; how they had left it with their dead when Thorstein, himself sick and helpless, could do nothing about it.

"Why?" she demanded. "Why did Thorstein give these to . . . him?"

"Because he knew Lik-Lodin's work. For four years now Lik-Lodin has searched out and carried back the bones and bodies left by the tides in rocky crevices and in the ice fields of the summer hunting grounds. And Thorstein knew where many lay in a Vinland settlement far to the west. It was a chance to recover those long-abandoned dead."

"Yes," Lik-Lodin added, "and don't forget the crow and how, if it lives long enough, it may show me the way to the cave where those dead and some of their belongings lie buried. Thorstein gave me the crow. Tell her that too."

"Then I must also tell her what you said about it. That the Icelander was reluctant to part with the crow, since it might yet find his lost thrall children." Bjarne turned to Claudia. "And though you and your brother are children no longer, I suppose your master continued to think of you that way. He had dreamed of his death. Otherwise he would not have given up the crow. But he beseeched Lik-Lodin to look well with it. That's right, Lik-Lodin, isn't it?"

Lik-Lodin nodded. "Tell her."

Claudia waited, her mind grappling with all of this.

"Explain," Lik-Lodin urged Bjarne. "Go on. She gets me mixed up."

Bjarne smiled. "You had better get used to her if the crow must show you the Vinland grave. It does not seem willing to be parted from her."

Lik-Lodin shook his head. "Anyway, I may not even attempt to find it."

"You mean that you will refuse Thorstein's dying wish? After he gave you the means of finding that one settlement of Vinlanders? And charged you with his errand?"

"But no one wants me to fetch the bodies away from there," Lik-Lodin exclaimed. "Last night I spoke to people at Gardar who had been in Thorstein's settle-

106

ment, on that same island he described, when the sickness took their people and the forest folk turned on them. From what I heard at Gardar, Leif Eirikson of Brattahlid and his settlers had only a taste of the fury of the Vinland skralings. It was much more terrible for those who settled farther to the west and south."

"Then what is to become of the hilt and sheath that Thorstein had made so that the blade scabbard placed with the dead in that cave could be recognized and returned to the true hilt?"

"I don't know. Bjarne, I tell you no one wants me to bring anything back. I tried. I tried to find a crew. One old man in a boat on Einersfjord recalled how those dead were packed away under the cliff like codfish stacked in a storehouse for winter. One was his own daughter. And he, not yet strong in the Christian faith, left her dower chest there with her when the tide was low, and a spindle in her hand. He regrets that heathen burial now, but even so would not have me recover anything from there, though the chest was finely made and filled with costly goods. He said that if I brought anything from that place I would bring the curse of Thorstein's blade and scabbard. 'Touch it not,' he told me. 'Bring it not to Greenland.' Even when I told him I had been charged with returning it to some monks in the Orcades, it made no difference. He only said that if I took it I would never return alive. And then who would bring my body back here?"

After a long silence, Claudia said, "Is he dead then?" The words didn't sound real to her; it wasn't real yet because she hadn't named him. She swallowed; her mouth felt stiff. "Is Thorstein dead?"

"Likely," Lik-Lodin mumbled. "He had settled all his debts. Only you thralls were still on his mind, he told me, you and the blade and scabbard in Vinland. Even though his mind wandered, that much was plain. He explained how he had had to leave you for the sake of the wounded in his care; he looked for you afterward, for he believed that someone had found you and taken you away. Looked, only never this far, never in Greenland. He spoke much about you when he gave me the crow. I think he meant me to be your master if the crow ever found you."

"Lik-Lodin," Bjarne intervened, "you mentioned nothing about being given these two. And if you abandon your promise—"

"Intention, Bjarne, not promise. I promised nothing. Thorstein was on the verge of death. I was his last hope. I said I would have to see, I would need a boat—"

"For which he gave you silver."

"Well, that can be returned to his family."

Bjarne shook his head. "You came here full of plans, of purpose. I was to set aside the scythes, the mending of chains, the forging of nails. When you lost the crow, you said I must put the knife blade before any other thing because now it was all you had to help you find that grave. You told me Thorstein believed that the real hilt could lead a man through unknown waters and beyond known bounds and that maybe the one fashioned to its shape would do that too. You said that to me, Lik-Lodin, and asked me to keep the clothing since time was short and it was already late to begin so long a voyage. All of that you said to me not three days ago."

Lik-Lodin nodded. "Perhaps it is an omen that the crow was found just now when I have been so discouraged and warned against this errand." He paused. "I'll have to take the maid then, won't I?"

"Not without me," Thomas informed him. "We belong with each other."

Lik-Lodin studied Thomas for a moment. "No, not you," he said. "You look a troublemaker."

"Still," put in Bjarne, "you'll need a crew, and if word spreads from those who fear your errand, that may be difficult to gather."

Thomas and Lik-Lodin eyed each other.

"If word spreads," said Lik-Lodin, "I'll get no boat, never mind the crew." He was sunk in gloom.

Bjarne held out his hand to Claudia. "Can you stand yet?" She got to her feet. Steadying her, he led her to the door, then turned back. "Would there be a head scarf in all that clothing?"

Lik-Lodin looked up. "What? Oh, she'll need a proper shift and apron if I'm to take her across the fjord. And a comb." He got up too and moved close to Claudia. He picked up the ends of her hair.

Thomas flung himself at Lik-Lodin who, caught unaware, crashed over a stool and against the wall. He groped his way back toward Thomas. Bjarne stepped between them. "Wait now." He swept Thomas backward while he addressed Lik-Lodin. "This youth works well. If you have no liking for him, don't spoil him for me."

"He's trouble," Lik-Lodin growled. "He needs—"

"He's only looking after his sister," Bjarne pointed out. "Now, Lik-Lodin, I think you should seek some

109

other counsel on this matter, for I have work to be done and little time for arguments and scuffling."

"You think I should go to the woman under the ice field?"

"I suppose you could. Though Grima makes folk pay dearly for her seeing and telling." He led Claudia outside and beckoned Thomas to follow. "We'll let Lik-Lodin work out his plan. He is a slow thinker, but not bad. Like so many who can brave the hunger and cold of the north, it is those things he cannot see or feel that weaken him."

It was hard for Claudia to understand Thorstein's reliance on a youth like Lik-Lodin, but then Thorstein must have been desperate. Anyhow, Claudia reflected, he had always tended to be too trusting. The trouble was that she knew as well as Thorstein that hilt and blade and scabbard were meant to be joined; she didn't want to know that much, to be the only one left who cared. She wanted to take the crow and get away from Thomas and these people groping blindly toward the blade and scabbard.

But she did care, and she didn't trust Lik-Lodin. She found herself musing out loud. "If Lik-Lodin takes what he finds, probably—"

Bjarne cut her off. "When he finds the scabbard of Thorstein with the blade locked inside it, he will not keep it for himself." He ducked into the shed.

Thomas spoke in an undertone. "You stay clear of that Lik-Lodin."

Claudia wheeled on him. "Don't you think about anything else? Look where we are. Look at these two men. All the strange—"

"Strange and not strange," he flared back. "Like you.

110

Why shouldn't I think most of you when anything . . . .
Here we are where anything could happen. At least I
know . . . know. . . . You're all . . . all I can be sure of."

"Oh, Thomas," she whispered. She was overwhelmed
by what he couldn't know. He was more dependent on
her than he could possibly realize. He would never get
home without her, without the bronze man. "We'll stay
together," she promised, thinking too that if she could
only make him care about the crow, he would help to
keep it from Lik-Lodin. "But as for Lik-Lodin," she
tried to explain, "I can't really avoid him, you know.
He's after the crow, and the crow sticks so close."

"The crow," Thomas burst out. "How can you find
fault with me for thinking only of you when all you
think of is that bird? If it's going to keep Lik-Lodin
at your side, then I'll kill it."

"You're out of your mind," she shot back at him,
then clapped her hand to her mouth. Her face burned
with anger at him and at her own temper. Shame silenced her.

Bjarne rejoined them, a white square of cloth in his
hand. "What's this about killing the crow?"

"To keep Lik-Lodin from taking her," Thomas retorted.

"If you hold your temper," Bjarne said to him, "he
might be glad to have you along as well."

"She's not to go with him at all," Thomas declared.
"He's to keep away from her."

Claudia wondered whether Bjarne was growing angry with Thomas, but to her surprise he only nodded
quietly. "We'll see how things go," was all he said.

At that moment Lik-Lodin emerged from the house.
"I have thought hard," he announced.

Bjarne had the hint of a smile. "That is remarkable for so short a time."

Lik-Lodin blinked at him. "I will go at once to Grima and ask her for her sight, so that I may be certain of my next move. If I am to leave for Vinland, I shall begin at once. If not . . . ." He faltered.

"If not?" prompted the smith in his deep easy way.

"Why then," said Lik-Lodin, floundering in thoughts he couldn't quite grasp, "why then I will . . . do . . . take . . . ." He looked at Claudia.

Thomas stepped forward.

"Fine," Bjarne remarked expansively, seizing Thomas by the shoulder and turning him around. "You go to Grima for your great decision, and we'll get on with our work."

SIXTEEN

THE day stretched on. The sun's glare seemed to be softening. Claudia rested between each trip from the shore to the field. The cow suddenly appeared in the yard lowing for her calf. Claudia went around to the back and waited while Bjarne finished shaping an enormous hook. Thomas held a shackle with long-handled tongs while Bjarne bent the hook to it. When he plunged the hot iron sizzling into the cask of water, the steam shot up, engulfing them. Through the vapor they greeted her with smiles.

The cow had brought a sort of order to the day. It was time for Bjarne to milk her before letting her in with the calf. Meanwhile Thomas could drag some lumps from the bog iron heap to renew the supply for the forge; Bjarne showed him the flat sledge that could be dragged over the ground. And Claudia could build up the fire; presently Bjarne would bring her a strip of fresh seal for the evening meal.

The sky was still bright, though there was a sharpness to the air now. It was hard to get used to the dimness inside. Claudia was kneeling over the hearth when everything was plunged into darkness. She heard quick panting. Then Lik-Lodin came through the narrow doorway and the house lightened.

"Get the crow. I have to take it to her. To Grima."

"What for?" She looked through him to the bright rectangle of light. She was not like Thorstein. She would never let Lik-Lodin take it.

"She wants the crow."

Still crouching, Claudia mumbled, "Get it yourself."

Lik-Lodin came closer. His skin pants reeked. She shrank away from him, but was checked by the hot embers she had been fanning.

"If it's your crow," she declared with more boldness than she felt, "don't bother me about it."

Lik-Lodin grabbed a handful of her hair and jerked her head back. "You're nothing but a thrall maid. Wherever you have been since Thorstein lost you doesn't matter anymore. Doesn't matter that he spoke of two thralls, then of three, and wandered with his talk of you. Now that his crow has found you, you are mine for the selling or the using."

"Bjarne said—"

113

"I am telling you what is. Because Thorstein said he could not pay me enough for the service I would perform if I fetched back the scabbard and blade with those bodies. That is the reason for it."

Claudia said, "I'm going to call Bjarne." The smith would show this lout that he could claim nothing if he gave up the Vinland quest.

Lik-Lodin released her. He seemed to droop with dejection. Suddenly she felt perfectly equal to this young man. She had been cowed because of her own revulsion.

"Why did you go to Iceland in the first place?" she asked him.

He seemed surprised by her shift from hostility to neutrality. "A ship was sailing. I'd collected many things. Furs and ivory and fine wadmal cloth like the thing you're wearing. So I went to help with the voyage and to sell my goods. When Thorstein heard I was there, he sent for me. He is . . . was important, a lawmaker, and with many horses . . . ." Lik-Lodin's words trailed off. "I never saw such a man. It wasn't only the silver he gave me. I believed . . . . He made me believe that I must go to Vinland for him." Lik-Lodin's voice was constricted with the effort of conveying all this. "Had I not found those folk frozen on the ice and stopped to bring them back, I would be on my way now. It wasn't until I mentioned my errand to those in Gardar who had been with Thorstein in Vinland . . . ." He shook his head in bewilderment.

"So now you're going to let this woman, Grima, decide for you?"

He nodded. "She wants the crow. I told her about it,

114

about what it meant to Thorstein, and the white feather in its breast, and that it is larger than ordinary crows, more like a raven. She says it must come to her alive. If you would bring it to me, I'd put it in a sack."

"But what if she keeps it?" Claudia demanded. "Or kills it. You need it to show you the way." The light was blocked again. Bjarne and Thomas stood inside the doorway. She told them what Lik-Lodin proposed. She let Bjarne take over with his calm, fair-sounding consideration.

When Bjarne had delivered his cautious judgment, Lik-Lodin protested that Grima wouldn't complete her prophecy without the crow. "Besides," he argued, turning to Claudia, "I have the knife, and its hilt may have power from its shape, like the one that leads people across known bounds—"

"I thought you just said Thorstein's mind was wandering," Claudia pursued. If she had to discredit Thorstein to save the crow, she would. Besides, if she could sway Lik-Lodin that way, she could probably convince him that this Grima was simply taking advantage of his confusion to get something she wanted or thought she wanted.

"What I think," declared Bjarne, "is that the crow is a sad, decrepit creature that may barely survive an ocean crossing, though it has shown great power in finding the lost thralls. Would you give up such a weak but powerful creature when it has already proved itself, or would you cosset and nurture it?"

Lik-Lodin mulled this. "Don't forget," he pronounced slowly, "that Thorstein also described the island to me, its deep water, its bare islet, and its great thick wood. Why should I not find it? And there are still folk at Gardar who were there. They too might—" He stopped. "No, I suppose there is not one among them who would go near that island again. Bjarne, what am I to do? Grima has already cut out the heart of her own rooster. She awaits the crow."

Bjarne rubbed his huge hands over his knees, peeling off bits of blackened dirt and dropping them into the fire. "Is this crow surely Thorstein's, the one he called Memory?" His eyes sought Claudia's.

She looked away. "I don't see how anyone can be sure. I . . . I don't remember the feather, but it was much plumper and sleeker. Now the feathers are all loose and patchy." She stopped.

"I am certain," Lik-Lodin retorted. "Though at one moment Thorstein said something about the thralls having a crow too. Only, yes, it must . . . of course it's his."

Bjarne nodded. "Then we will all attend Grima. We will hear her and help you, Lik-Lodin, in your hard decision."

Lik-Lodin sighed. "We'll have to hurry. Grima is impatient."

Bjarne laughed. "I know."

"Perhaps I should go ahead with the crow in a sack. You could follow."

"If you put it in a sack," said Bjarne, "it may beat itself to death."

"Then I'll take the maid. It will stay with her."

"Well thought," said Bjarne. "We are fortunate that I have just killed a seal. It will not take long for me to make these thralls some shoes."

116

"Shoes," exclaimed Lik-Lodin. "Don't you understand? Grima has already begun her spell. At this moment she may already have visions to impart. I can't—"

"You are right again," Bjarne agreed. "You must hasten to her and assure her that we will shortly follow with the crow. Neither thrall has foot covering; they can't make their way across the stones and ice without. I'll cut them shoes in no time. And then we will join you at Grima's house. With the crow."

Lik-Lodin was torn between indecision and urgency. "You give me your word, Bjarne, that you will bring the crow?"

Bjarne said, "I am glad that you still set store by a man's word. Since you did give your word to a man facing death."

"I only promised that I would . . . try," shouted Lik-Lodin. "And I am doing that. I told you."

"Now you are wasting precious time," Bjarne told him gently. "I know that in your way you are trying to do what is best. Go on to Grima, and I give you my word that in a while these two and the crow and I will meet you there."

Lik-Lodin hesitated. Then he said he had nearly forgotten that Grima also required the new knife with the man-shaped hilt. Not to keep, but for the taking of the crow's heart.

Claudia gasped, but at a signal from Bjarne managed to keep still. He sent Thomas to fetch the knife. Claudia didn't move. Thomas returned, the knife lying flat on his hand. He held it, and as Lik-Lodin reached out, it slid to the floor. Lik-Lodin dropped to his knees, scrambling for the knife as though he expected it to be snatched away from him, stumbled to his feet, and ran out the door.

Before either Claudia or Thomas could speak, Bjarne told them firmly that he would need them for fitting the shoes. It was clear from his manner and tone that he would allow no further discussion about the crow and Lik-Lodin. They followed him to the walled yard.

"She can wear no seal," Thomas declared as Bjarne flopped over the soaking skin.

Bjarne took his foot and set in on the skin. "If you mean to carry her," he commented as he cut through the wet hair to the elastic skin, "I suppose we could dress her feet in gull skin." He reached for Claudia's mud-caked ankle, making quick sure cuts with his curved knife. "You must get the salt out of this before you tie it on."

Thomas changed his tack. "If it's not a gray seal, I suppose—"

"This is from a bladder seal, which hauls out earlier than the others." He cut a fine edge around and around one piece, pulled the narrow strip off, and scraped at the hair. "There is your lacing." He pulled it back and forth across a stone, then trimmed another. A few more cuts, holes pierced, and he declared the shoes ready for rinsing.

"You mean," Claudia asked, as Bjarne left them, "that I'm supposed to put them on all slimy like this?"

Thomas was already squeezing the water out of one. He nodded. "It's just the way some of the old people at home make the rivlins. They fit wet to your foot." He dunked the other shoe in the cask of water.

Claudia did her best to copy Thomas. She saw how

he pulled the sides around his ankle and drew the skin tight with the lacing. He paused. "It is like the old folk," he mused. "And your frock, though at home the wadmal is usually all black." He peered down at the fjord. The water was paler now; haze surrounded each pinnacle of ice. "And the houses like those with walls of turf, with the stones between . . . ." He saw Claudia trying to wiggle her toes inside the slippery skin. "Don't lace too tight at first," he advised, and then went on with his thoughts. "But if this is the Greenland I have heard about, where the whalers and sealers go . . . ." He rubbed his eyes. "Eskimos live in Greenland, and wear clothes of skin like . . . . Only Lik-Lodin is not an Eskimo, is he? Sibbie told me that the stranger who brought my knife from Greenland said that my father had it from an Eskimo. And others who have been to the whaling have seen the Eskimos in skins and . . . other things different." He faced Claudia. "Then what place is this? They call it Greenland, but— Where are we?"

Claudia said, "Are you afraid?"

"I don't know what I feel," he answered impatiently.

"Well, you aren't afraid of Bjarne," she offered, though she knew that credulity, not fear, was his enemy.

"And I'm not afraid of Lik-Lodin either," he declared as Bjarne called to them from the path above the steading. "But I don't like him."

"Well," said Claudia, starting up toward Bjarne, "if it makes any difference to you, I'm not afraid of him either." She tried to sound unconcerned, but she knew her voice was a little shaky.

Bjarne led them up through tough willow scrub. Then they followed a path between two mountains into a deep gorge beside a narrow winding river. The clear water teemed with fish. They followed long stretches of silt and sand, with yellow poppies and dense clumps of lavender surprising in the desertlike ground. Clouds of midges swarmed around them. Bjarne picked the leaves of a low plant with reddish blossoms. Claudia and Thomas followed his example, crushing the delicate leaves and wiping them over their faces and necks. The insects still hovered, but at a distance. Claudia began to unclench her toes. The shoes were becoming a part of her.

They started to leave the valley. There were shrubs along the path; tiny birds sprang up and fluttered tamely about until the crow came flapping up with noisy greeting. There was something eerie about the brightness, cold and spectral. In under the mountain's cliff, snow stood deep and smooth. Streams, silver-black, trickled down to the river. Beside them, under hoods of luminescent ice, lay mats of soft pink blooms and upright blossoms of yellow and purple. Yet in the upper reaches there was no color at all. Dark shapes, ravens or crows, circled black against the shadowed snow of the highest crags.

When they came within sight of the small steading nestled in under the bare rock, Bjarne halted. Where the river seemed to begin, an enormous white tongue, thick and scarred, lolled out of the mouth of the mountain. Bjarne waited for Claudia to catch up. He pointed to a high round spur, like a knuckle, protruding from the rock face. "If you must hide," he told them, "you won't be seen behind that outcropping. If you flee there, I'll suggest that you may have headed for a cave across the river bed. Then when they seek you there, you will come down quickly and return as we have come, following the river, then the fjord."

"And then?" asked Thomas.

"I don't know," said Bjarne. "Back where you have come from. Or not." He thought a moment. "You may take any food from my house. Take nothing that is Lik-Lodin's."

"When—"

"You may not need to flee at all," Bjarne continued. "It will depend, I think, on how strong Lik-Lodin is once Grima works her will on him. Only listen carefully. Don't try to go on, to escape across the mountain, for this is the end of all the living land. From here there is only ice. Do you understand?"

Claudia, determined to hold them to the direct, palpable danger, said, "We'll run as soon as anyone tries to kill the crow."

Thomas objected. "If the crow is killed, Lik-Lodin will have to give up going to look for the . . . that thing."

Claudia whipped around. "How can you say that? That's a terrible—"

"Enough," Bjarne ordered. "You two cannot guess the power of the woman Grima. It is the old power. It existed long before the new faith and still rules many lives. The image of Thor is carved on Grima's chair; she can call on Odin. Though she may seem shabby and poor, she possesses rare treasures, silk and gold and the wood of the ash tree. She has ale too and other brews

121

for her seeing and healing. So leave your quarrels behind you and keep your eyes upon her. Forget Lik-Lodin now. He is like the prey; Grima is the carrion crow who devours the remains."

Silenced, they followed Bjarne. The crow, beginning to grow weary again, perched now on Claudia's head. But when she reached up to stroke it reassuringly, it grabbed her fingers in its beak. She trudged on, her head bowed under it. She mulled Bjarne's warning, his note of awe. Would she be able to count on him?

The first sign that they had arrived came with the sharp unmistakable odor of burning feathers. Claudia was struck with sudden dread. The crow uttered a guttural croak and flapped skyward. It came to rest among the hens on the thatch. The hens exploded in a flurry of feathers; two eggs rolled and plopped to the stone path. A cow standing on the far side of the house nibbling green shoots from the low roof gazed moodily at the black intruder and rubbed its chin on the thatching.

Lik-Lodin, in the doorway, beckoned with frenzy. Then he staggered toward them, falling on Claudia and dragging her down with him.

Bjarne restrained Thomas while Claudia extricated herself from Lik-Lodin's helpless limbs and wavering stare and sickening breath. After she thrust him off, he lay on his back, his face soaked in sweat, his tangled hair matted and stuck with egg, declaring that Grima had spun the world like a top and now was tipping it over so far that at any moment they would all be tossed right off it.

Bjarne stepped over him. Claudia and Thomas fol-

lowed. At the doorway they caught a glimpse of a
woman seated before a fire. The smell from the steep-
ing pot combined with that of singed feathers, both
sweet and bitter. Claudia felt breathless; her eyes swam
with tears. Bjarne drew back. "I thought it was the
unfamiliar ale," he murmured, glancing down at Lik-
Lodin. "But we may all soon be rolling our eyes."

Lik-Lodin lay blinking up at them. "Where is the
crow?" he whispered. "Quick. I must—" He broke off,
rolled over, and began to vomit.

SEVENTEEN

THE woman who came to the door was so bent that
she seemed almost round, but her face looked ageless.
The heavy brooches at her shoulders clasped the straps
of an apron that was finely trimmed though its threads
were frayed. The chain between the brooches carried a
bird's talon, the shriveled nose of a seal, the tip of a
tusk inscribed with runes, amber beads, the shrunken
head of a white owl. There was even a silver cross with
the hammer of Thor gouged out of its center. As she
gazed down impassively on the miserable Lik-Lodin,
all these relics dangled grotesquely.

"I'll get you another drink to bring you round," she
offered, turning into the house again. Her voice was
small and wispy, that of a child.

"Don't drink any more," Bjarne advised. "It's brewed from the bog berry and from certain valley plants that will put you in Grima's power."

Claudia started to protest, then realized that would only provoke him. She couldn't imagine what made this huge man fearful of that ridiculous little woman. Couldn't he see that she was absurd, masquerading in all that finery and bedecked with those ludicrous charms? Couldn't he see that Lik-Lodin was hopelessly drunk?

Lik-Lodin managed to sit up. He held his head. "I must know all, and then be away from this place."

"You'll go to Vinland then?"

"Never," he groaned. "No, never to Vinland."

"What has she shown you that is so terrible?"

Lik-Lodin groaned again. "She won't say. Not till she has the crow and has eaten its feather at its dying, and then its heart. But she says this much: Death. A wall of water. A wall collapsing inward like the walls of a burning house."

Grima stepped out carrying a bowl and a flat, round loaf, which she proffered to Claudia. Uneasy, but determined to show them there was nothing to fear, Claudia reached out for the drink. She hoped she was right about Grima. She had to be. This woman with the voice and face of an old child might be half-crazy, but how could anyone take her seriously?

Bjarne could and did. He pushed past Claudia to fend off the brew. Then he bent to help Lik-Lodin to his feet. As soon as he turned, Claudia took the bowl and gulped down some of the warm, pungent liquid. Bjarne cried out. Quickly, to prove her point, Claudia ate from the loaf, which tasted of the earth, of moss and roots. There, she thought, she had shown Bjarne and she had called the woman's bluff.

"Will you drink some more?" asked Grima in her small plaintive voice.

"She will not," Bjarne answered for Claudia.

Grima held the bowl out to Lik-Lodin, who gulped and then, choking, stopped to demand the crow.

"It is there," said Bjarne, pointing to the roof. "And a poor ragged thing it is."

"Poor, yes; ragged, yes," said Grima in her child's voice. "But it is of the ancient race of birds that carry their wisdom with them into death. See how like the raven it is, only diminished like the mountain of ice that melts each spring since the world began. Usually that one white feather is hidden deep in the plumage. Anyone who can seize such a bird at the moment of its dying and pluck its white feather of wisdom will possess all the knowledge of the wild, all the vision of the future, all the memory of the ages." She smiled gleefully. "And these will be mine."

"Has it ever been done before?" asked Bjarne.

"Till now the birds have always managed to swallow the white feather when death was upon them. This one will not."

"You may be disappointed," Bjarne told her. "It is such a dismal creature."

"Do not concern yourself with my disappointment, Bjarne. This crow has the white feather of the ancient race. Soon its wisdom—"

"I don't believe you." Claudia staggered toward her. "You're just saying all that about a wall of water so that Lik-Lodin will leave the crow to you. You're making it up."

"So you are not a believer," declared the woman, her voice still thin, but menacing.

"Not in you, I'm not." Claudia's own voice sounded huge and hollow to her ears. "And if you touch my crow—"

The woman disappeared inside and returned in a moment carrying a glowing turf in a pair of tongs. "Stay back from me, or you will be like the rooster. And the crow." She dashed at Claudia and brandished the burning turf over Claudia's head.

Claudia felt her hair stand up and sizzle; she could smell her scorched hair. "You're a liar," she shouted. "A liar and a bully. Poor Lik-Lodin is just a fool, and you know it. How dare you go around making poor people like him break their word and be scared and everything." She was suddenly queasy; she could barely make out the tiny woman she was screaming at. "You can't see the future," she blurted, "but I can. And I don't have to carve up somebody's crow to do it. I know what's going to happen. I know what's happened. And things you'll never know because you'll be dead by then, and nothing left of you, nothing. Not even bones for Lik-Lodin to gather up and . . . ." Through the blur of her senses she could feel a change in Bjarne, a guardedness. And Thomas was gaping. Had she gone too far? She felt exhausted. It was as though the day had stretched on in an endless connection of days without any relief between, without night.

The little round woman waved her firebrand, but the gesture seemed aimless. "I want the crow; all my life I have striven for that power."

She seemed ludicrous to Claudia, a bundled woman laden with the emblems of her profession, wheedling now for the final trophy. Claudia felt weak and groggy; she felt like giggling at the preposterous woman. And then suddenly she wanted to comfort her instead, to reassure her. She could hardly remember where she was. "Why does Lik-Lodin get so upset over that wall of water?" she wondered out loud. She turned a look of inquiry to Bjarne, who bent to her.

"Prepare to leave," he directed, his voice low.

That confused her. She had expected him to answer, to explain. Vaguely she was aware that Grima had gone. Another question to put to him: Where was Grima? She leaned against him. She had a terrible thirst; she could hardly keep her eyes open. Weren't the others thirsty too? she meant to ask him. She was like a sleepy child at bedtime, slipping from the waking world. Small questions broke off from the day's events and sur-faced as she sank.

Thomas's voice, urgent and harsh, broke through her peace.

"Thomas is too noisy," she complained.

She heard Bjarne speak; probably he was telling Thomas not to disturb her. Then she was splashed full in the face. "That's right," she heard as she gasped and spluttered. "Do it again." She closed her eyes be-fore the water hit her; it dripped down her face and front.

Opening her eyes, she saw Grima with another bowl. Automatically she opened her mouth, but Thomas blocked her, keeping her from the drink she yearned for. Someone slapped the bowl out of Grima's hands, and the bitter-sweet ale steeped with herbs that clogged her senses splashed up. Claudia leaned toward Grima, preparing to wipe her wet little face for her, but

Thomas yanked her back. Then she couldn't see Grima anymore, only Bjarne's back. It occurred to her that Bjarne, who had been supporting her, was now taking care of Grima. "It's not fair," she cried.

She heard something harsh. It wasn't Thomas, who was using all his breath to haul her after him. It was the crow squawking at her. "Why don't you just go to sleep?" she told it. "Why doesn't everybody go to sleep?" she complained, feeling her legs being stretched almost beyond endurance. She kept stumbling on loose sand and being dragged up again, made to climb against her will. Once she fell on the bronze man and yelped with sudden pain. She didn't know where her feet were. She crawled through pale green succulents with their desert heads of yellow and orange, and then she was scrambling over bare rock; she scraped at the colors, but they were lichens now and could not be plucked free.

After a long time they stopped. She thought, Now they'll let me sleep. She curled up at once into a tight ball; she was very cold. But Thomas wouldn't let her alone. He pulled her arms from her face and rubbed handfuls of snow into it. She squealed, cried, fought him. She heard sobbing and couldn't imagine why, since she felt a breathless hilarity rising in her. Thomas was still shaking her and rubbing her with snow, which melted and trickled down her back. She listened to him calling to her as if she wasn't right there and wondered what on earth was wrong with him. Laughter started and was overcome by sheer exhaustion. She closed her eyes.

But only for a moment. She had collapsed with her head on her knees; no one could possibly sleep that way for long. She raised her head, feeling strangely composed. It was all she had needed, she thought, a brief, deep sleep. Thomas sat back on his heels watching her. She said, "Hello. I had a nap."

He made a sound that was awful; it was the sobbing she had heard.

"What's the matter?" She saw the crow hunched on the rock; it eyed her. "Did something happen?"

He pointed past the boulder. She looked down across a range of rocky peaks and plunging valleys. In some of these steep valleys, small, still lakes reflected the black mountains, the blue sky. Where the peaks gradually descended she saw the land of ice stretching away into the pale distance, silent and empty.

Claudia covered her eyes. The glare hurt them. They hurt anyway. She had a funny thought. "Thomas, was I drunk?"

"I don't know what it was," he answered. "Your voice was different. Like a . . . baby's. You were . . . well, without any . . . sense. I thought we'd lose the crow and you as well. Bjarne thought so too."

Claudia shivered.

"We should start back now. Can you manage? I'm a bit weary from the hauling. And keeping track of your bird."

Claudia stretched. Her head felt light. She wasn't sure of her balance. She realized that Thomas believed she had been under some kind of spell. More likely the spell of fatigue and sunstroke, along with aromatic fumes and the stuff Grima had prepared with some kind of dope in it. Claudia felt like telling him this, but she just nodded, and forced herself to stand.

During the descent there were sudden slides on loose

silt. It took concentration to keep dizziness at bay. Her skirt kept catching her up, and twice she lost her balance entirely, landing in a heap at Thomas's heels, with the crow scuttling out of the way.

They passed close to the steading. The cow was still there, the roosting hens, but neither Grima nor Lik-Lodin nor Bjarne in sight.

"How long will they take hunting in the cave?" asked Claudia, longing to rest.

Thomas couldn't tell, but he let her stop at the river for a drink. When they started up again, he set a faster pace. Claudia slowed and grumbled; Thomas said they must take advantage of being on fairly level ground. She was sweaty; she was cold. Her feet hurt; her feet were numb. Thomas wouldn't let her sit down.

Claudia was close to collapse by the time they reached Bjarne's steading. She looked on bleakly as Thomas shoved the boat into the water. He nodded her into place in the stern.

Settling the crow down between her legs, she looked across the fjord at Brattahlid and saw no people about. Was it night? The light was hazy, but still bright. Midges and mosquitoes swarmed in moiling black clouds. To escape them, Thomas allowed her to help him row away from the shore. Weary and numb, they sat side by side, passing icebergs, passing mountains with gray shadows softening the crumbling scree. When they came to the place where the fjord branched, they turned in toward the pack ice, for the only known alternatives were the steading where they had slept or farther out, straight out toward the open sea.

They sat close together for warmth. The sky looked

duller, but the surrounding ice gave off a kind of light which was translucent whiteness. Claudia glanced at her feet braced for rowing; the shoes looked rigid, as if frozen, but her feet were only wet, not icy.

Rowing between floes, around bergs, they grew careless, and barely maneuvered in time to avoid the menacing shadow of an underwater ice block. Spinning them around, Thomas sat tall for an instant, drew in his breath, then urged Claudia quickly on.

"What is it?" She looked down, expecting further danger from under the water.

"Lik-Lodin, I think. Keep rowing."

"It can't be. We came all the way down the fjord without seeing—"

"The shore was dark." And they had left the shore to escape the insects. "Harder," he pressed.

Suddenly Claudia stopped. "I can't. Nor can you. Look, if they or he has followed us this far, there's nowhere we can get away."

"All right, we'll rest a minute there." Thomas pointed to the high arch of an iceberg.

"Why don't we go right in? Maybe they'll pass us."

"And if it rolls? Like the one this morning."

Claudia considered this. They were just under the start of the arch. This morning, he had said. If this was the same day, they might still get through, back to her time or his. The icy gloom emitted its own close breath. Claudia pulled in her oar; she was so near she could touch the inside surface. "It isn't the way it looks," she whispered. The ice amplified her words and sent them echoing to its low curved ceiling. The opening turned, narrowed, then widened again into a circle of blue-green light. "I think we can get all the way through," she whispered. "Thomas," she pleaded, willing him to understand more than she could tell him. "Thomas, we may be able to get all the way through." She felt the bronze man secure under her woolen dress.

They pulled themselves along until the channel under the ice grew so narrow that they were blocked. On one side the ice leveled to a kind of platform. They clambered out, losing their footing on the granular surface. "Perfect for dragging," Thomas whispered. "We can slide the boat." The sides curved up so abruptly to the ceiling that there wasn't any standing room, so they worked on their hands and knees, slithering on hard ice balls, gasping, gulping in the frozen white breath.

In the darkest, closest part of the tunnel the boat dipped sideways and was wedged, partly suspended over the narrow lead. Claudia didn't care anymore about Grima or Lik-Lodin; she wanted to grab the crow and get out. But Thomas reminded her that she wouldn't last a minute in the water. Steadily he pressed and shimmied one end of the boat. The other end was lifted a little and held. He spoke softly, tension clamped around his directions. At his word, she was to jump in. Timing was crucial. All the time he spoke he was pushing, swiveling, rocking. Then in a burst that filled the cavern of ice, he shouted, "In."

Suddenly released from the grip of the ice, the boat shot forward. Thomas and Claudia fell face down. The boat surged through the gray hole and out into whiteness. Clear. Water sloshed over them, drenching and freezing them. The crow was the first to gain a thwart.

"Quick," shouted Thomas, "the oars."

Claudia groped blindly and felt the boat hit hard through the soft white haze. She couldn't even see what it was they had collided with. Then they bumped again. It was the bottom. They were beached.

A wave carried them off, then slapped them back, shoving the boat broadside onto the shingle. Claudia was thrown sideways, whacking her head hard. Dazed, she peered out over the gunwale as Thomas leaped out and hauled the boat back from the sea.

She sat on the wet shingle, slowly absorbing the dim, familiar outlines of the shore. There was the long rock where Thomas had been standing when she first saw him. It wasn't far to the stone sheep pens from here. "But where are the oars?" she asked Thomas as he turned the boat to drain it.

Thomas set it down. He started to pull off his shirt. "I'll have to go in after them, or Davie'll be at me to pay and I don't know what."

Claudia grabbed him. "We've had enough. Stay out of the water. Besides, I don't think they're out there. Can you see them anywhere?"

They stared over the water. Thomas went to stand on the rock so that he could peer down into the trough of the waves. "They're not there," he pronounced finally. "We must have left them in the ice." Slowly, thoughtfully, he brought out his knife.

Claudia turned away. She reached under her soaking skirt to untie the bronze man. Then she held it up for him to see.

Thomas frowned, half in puzzlement, half in denial. "Davie'll be after me about those oars," he declared, fending off what he couldn't or wouldn't grasp. But she kept the bronze man there before him till he nodded. It was all the acknowledgment he could muster. In the next instant he was shaking his head in grave dismay. "To be sure," he muttered once again, "Davie'll be after me."

PART THREE

eighteen

THOMAS, grappling with the appearance of time not spent, kept looking across to the smoldering turf on Rousay's high hill. The May Day smoke heralded a new season; yet time had not stood still either. Ewes in and out of pens pawed and circled in restless preparation; already there was an abandoned lamb, born during the night. Claudia and Thomas were caught up in the work, confining the errant ewe, forcing recognition and mothering, turning from this task to the next, and the next.

Thomas refused to discuss their passage through time. Only the crow intruded into the resumption of their old ways. Thomas considered it a nuisance, begrudging it both freedom to feed on its own and food from their own diminished supplies. Claudia picked greens from the foreshore and the marsh, till Thomas put a stop to that because she was taking the shepherd's clock whose flower would close at the approach of bad weather. Exasperated, Claudia gave in and learned to wind grass twine with him. The crow set out to peck the tether to shreds.

"I don't know what you want with it anyway," he grumbled. "Crows are bad luck. And it's already brought us trouble . . . there."

136

"If I hadn't been looking for it, I wouldn't be here," she retorted. "If that's what you mean by trouble." She stirred the meal into the fresh sheep's milk; a faintly rancid odor rose from the tinnie. Something that didn't belong there appeared on the frothy surface and she fished it out with her finger. "I mean of course it's the bronze man I follow, but—"

"But you didn't have the bronze man when you came to Eynhallow. It was here in the ground."

Startled, she glanced up at him, his face dark with dirt and weather and his shaggy head of hair, his eyes wide and pale. Quickly she lowered her head over the tinnie.

"What you're saying . . . ," he began, and faltered. "All right, it led us then, just the way the Icelander told Lik-Lodin it could, through unknown . . . through the unknown. We were . . . were backward?" Now that he was finally coming to grips with meanings he'd avoided, he couldn't stop. "It's like those stories, isn't it?" He didn't seem to expect an answer; he had too much to say. "Not . . . like the Library of Romance and Adventure, where you get a new book each month if you've a sixpence for it. Not like that. We had a schoolmaster. For two years. He had books with whole long stories in them that would take days, weeks. . . . You could take one of those books and open the end of it and read it there. But if you turned to the middle or beginning, why then you would find things happening beforehand. Do you see? And you reading it, reading right there where something's happening, even though you know it may not tell what's really to come of it, because you've seen the ending. Because the end will

... did change ... everything. Only while you're reading that middle part, it's still happening, so it doesn't make any difference what you learned about what will happen in the end." He was breathless.

She wanted to calm him, to deflect his thoughts from her impulsive assertion about following the bronze man. She proffered the tinnie toward him, but he waved it aside.

"Sometimes, when Davie called me back to Evie, I'd miss out on the reading. I'd never find out. . . . I'd ask Nancy. She's Mansie's sister, and we started school together. But she went all the way through the fifth form, and I . . . . Only now . . . now I've been somewhere Nancy hasn't, nor Mansie, nor anyone on the hill." He held Claudia with his look. "I've been wondering," he said softly, "about that place."

Now it was coming, she thought. How could she handle his conclusions about the bronze man?

But Thomas was still struggling, groping. "Lik-Lodin was supposed to find the blade in its scabbard and take them . . . it . . . to an island with priests who had the hilt. So they could be together. Because they were supposed to be . . . joined. Those islands that had priests . . . . They had chapels. Like on the Brough of Birsay. Like Deerness. And right down here was a chapel that got turned into a house. And lived in so long that no one remembered what it had been." He took the tinnie from her and set it down between them.

Claudia reached for it, but he stopped her. She felt his grip on her arms; he was holding her away from him so that she was forced to look him in the eyes.

"Claudia, no one ever brought the priests the blade

and scabbard from across the ocean. The hilt was . . . is here alone. No one knows where the rest is, except the crow. Claudia, did you come looking for the crow because . . . because . . . ?"

"No, it wasn't anything like that. I don't even know if this is the right crow."

"But it knows you. And you know the Icelander."

"I never said—"

"I saw. I saw how you looked." He let her arms fall free. "You tell me the crow . . . brought you here. You tell me really it's the bronze man—" He paused, then plunged on. "Did you know it was buried here before I found it?"

She hadn't budged when he dropped her arms. "I had no idea." Speaking the simple truth freed her. She bent to fuss with the tinnie again. "And I've no idea why it was buried, or when, or anything." She wrinkled her nose at the cooling mash.

"Davie'll bring food soon," Thomas told her, adding wryly, "when he comes for the boat."

She heard the return of his ordinary anxiety about the oars and understood that he was relieved. "Listen, Thomas," she proposed, joining him in turning away from the incomprehensible, "just tell him he was lucky he didn't lose you as well. He knew how bad the fog was."

Thomas smiled thinly. "Lucky?" He made an effort to lighten his tone. "You're right. I'll tell him we nearly lost the boat too. That will make him appreciate what was saved."

She knew the prospect was bleak. "I wish I could explain for you."

139

Thomas burst out laughing. "That's what I need, isn't it? To have them find you chattering away like the gulls. You just see that you stay in the cave. Soon as any boat comes near. You and your crow. All I need is to have them find the crow tied down here. Let it off for a bit now," he added. "Give us a little peace with our supper."

But for Claudia the peace was an uneasy one until the crow came back to settle for the night. She knew how the blackbacks and skuas could sweep down over the island without warning. After the clamor, she would find the bodies of half-eaten chicks that had fallen into crevices deep inside the cliff. She soon learned that even the parent gulls might be transformed in the frenzy of defense. She had seen them change in mid-flight and dive in a murderous streak for their own young. And she had seen the larger birds attacking the weak and old as well.

She didn't want the meal and milk anyway. She wandered off toward the cliff, which reeked these days of smashed eggs and rotting chicks. The crow was drawn to the mangled bodies the larger birds could not reach. Claudia, trying not to notice what it fed on, cultivated a kind of blindness in the midst of her anxious vigil.

NINETEEN

WHEN the time came for Thomas to begin docking the tails of the farm Cheviots and castrating the ram lambs that would not be used for breeding, Claudia resisted. She refused to help at all until Thomas convinced her that she could speed the operation and lessen the pain if she held each lamb perfectly still for him. But she dreaded this work. Thomas was astounded at her vehemence; he seemed insensitive to the pain he inflicted. "If you saw the long-tailed ones with fly strike," he remarked as he wiped his knife on the grass, "you'd really be sick." He threw the tails to the gulls.

She resented his attitude. At least he could suffer for the helpless animals. But the closest he came to sympathy was when he watched a newly castrated lamb run bleating and stiff-legged after its mother. Thomas would always wait to make sure that the ewe didn't wander too far from her cut baby. "It's not anything I'd want done to me," he admitted. Claudia supposed this was some kind of attempt to see things as she did, but his clumsy empathy only made her cheeks burn. She couldn't even look at him. He waited a moment, shrugged, and started down to the lower grassland.

That was when he caught sight of the boat tacking in toward the beach. He shouted to Claudia and gestured her toward the north.

Sheep and rabbits scattered before her. She couldn't understand how the boat had come so close without their noticing. She trampled flowers, the yellow cowslip which had just begun to bloom, the lilac butterbur, the delicate pimpernel, Thomas's shepherd's clock, opening to the sun.

Getting down to the cave in her long dress wasn't easy. Her legs felt bound. When she needed to stretch or bend a knee, she found that she was trapped in the homespun. Finally she edged along the narrow rock to the entrance and picked her way in over the black and green slime.

She groped toward the needle of sunlight. She wondered how long she would have to wait. She could hear only the breakers on the outlying skerries and the backward wash of the ebb. Somewhere in that darkness water trickled down to a ledge and dripped onto the rock below.

When she heard Thomas calling her out, she was astonished. It was too soon. She made her way to the opening.

Thomas was lying over the grassy cliff edge to call down to her. The boat was gone, he told her. Stopped only to leave off food, pick up the rowboat, and leave Mr. Lindsay for the day. "And he's got a basket full of things to eat and he wants to see the hole and have a look at the bronze man. He talked to the other gentleman. And Davie is to take me off the island in a few days. To go over Hundland way for the peat cutting."

All the time he was babbling, Claudia was clambering along the cliff face until she could reach a foothold from which to boost herself up. Thomas was just above her. She held her hand out to him. Still bubbling over with news, he got to his feet, told her to hurry, and disappeared over the rim of the turf.

She screamed at him. "Thomas."

He was back. "We can't waste time now," he chided. "And, Claudia, you'll have to help me. I don't know what to do about the bronze man."

"Will you help me up?" she returned. Her rage was directed at so much more than this slight; she saw his indifference as part of the whole sweep of this island existence, of gulls devouring their young in a mindless reflex to consume, of Thomas wielding his knife with the spare, deft gesture used by generations of sheepherders without hesitation, without question. "Will you help me, you stupid idiot?" she screeched at him.

Thomas scowled his bewilderment at her. "You've not called me stupid before."

"Well, get me up," she ordered.

He regarded her steadily for a moment. "No," he told her. "Get yourself up." This time he disappeared for good.

Claudia had to slide back down and start over. She felt like ripping the dress to shreds. She fumed at Thomas for taking everything she said with equal weight. She could never even blow off steam without putting herself in the wrong. And why? she demanded as she gathered up her dripping skirt. Why on earth should she care what he thought? This whole situation was impossible. Now that she had the crow, or anyhow some crow, why couldn't she just go back where she belonged?

A brown camouflaged eider duck flapped off, dragging its wing, as she stomped down toward the bog. "Well, watch out," she muttered at it. If the dumb duck hadn't pretended to ignore her until she was practically on top of it, she would have detoured around the nest. "I don't even want your eggs," she told it. "I don't like any eggs. I'm tired of eggs."

"What's that?" said a voice. "Tired of eggs, are you?"

She turned. The man who had spoken was leaning against the stone cairn, well above her, taking some kind of sighting. He wasn't like the other gentleman. His open jacket was clearly made for the outdoors. A rucksack hung lopsided from one shoulder. He wore breeches and high laced boots. His sparse reddish-gray hair blew wild. His arms and legs, his entire body, seemed rubbery and capable of any amount of stretching and arranging. "Tired of eggs?" he demanded, slapping shut a kind of telescope instrument and plopping it into his rucksack. "Then you will have to sample my picnic. That is, if Thomas hasn't already made away with it."

She gawked at him.

"Hasn't Thomas told you about me?" He sprang down beside her. "I don't recall you. Says your name is Claudia. Well, but all you children grow. Suddenly you're people with names and not barefoot bairns playing about the stackyards."

"Thomas told you?"

He nodded. "I approve. He needed a companion. Though he's getting to an age where proprieties . . . . Well, but I suppose no one ever thinks of Thomas that way. So you're his cousin Claudia."

He seemed to be inviting comment, but Claudia

144

wasn't able to supply one. She followed him as he stepped nimbly over and around anything with feathers or petals, as though it was second nature for him to stroll through the ripening island bursting with its precarious new life.

Once he stopped, gazed intently at her, then announced that they would have their picnic first and then commence the digging. She supposed she looked like some kind of starving waif to him. It was an impression she had no intention of changing.

Mr. Lindsay's basket held an assortment of delicacies that were spread out on a cloth for them all to share. Thomas seemed shy in the face of Mr. Lindsay's generosity and couldn't bring himself to sit with them. But with not much pressing, he took a chicken leg, a buttered oatcake, and two jam buns. Didn't Thomas know him well enough by now? asked Mr. Lindsay. Thomas, sucking jam dribbles from between his fingers, only mumbled something about ewes to check and was off.

Claudia was glued to the picnic. How she craved the bread, the meat, the sugar. She couldn't help thinking of the way the other gentleman had accused Thomas of having been bribed by sweets. She gobbled everything Mr. Lindsay offered her and listened to him describe his meeting with Dr. Cameron, the other gentleman, in the Commercial Hotel in Stromness. They had been instantly embroiled in an argument about a completely different and, as far as Claudia could make out, unrelated archaeologist whose controversial work had recently been published. So inflamed was Dr. Cameron that he proceeded to warn Mr. Lindsay in front of perfect strangers, whom he called on as witnesses, not to attempt any highhanded business about the Eynhallow discovery and the misplaced object.

All of this Mr. Lindsay reported with good humor and no hint of having contested Cameron's claim to Thomas's find. The patter of his words fell about her; she barely felt them. Sheltered from the wind, the air sharp and bright, she methodically ate her way through Mr. Lindsay's food as though she had been incarcerated in that dark cave for days. Not until she had stuffed herself could she begin to absorb his intent. By then he was discussing Thomas, and how the lad was considered dull, though Mr. Lindsay thought otherwise.

"He has a way of hearing . . . hearing more than the other lads. I suppose that might be due to Sibella. Not an ordinary upbringing."

Claudia hugged her knees and gazed blissfully at the patchwork greens and browns of the fields across the channel.

"I suppose," Mr. Lindsay pursued, "that you had an ordinary upbringing." He paused. "Brothers and sisters. Parents."

"Yes."

"Sibella didn't tell me you were here."

Claudia said nothing.

"Did you see the thing Thomas found . . . and misplaced?"

She nodded.

"Do any of you youngsters believe the old legends about the little folk in the hill guarding treasures and hammering out old swords and so forth?"

Claudia said truthfully, "I don't know what I believe."

146

Mr. Lindsay eyed her appraisingly. Then he tried another approach. "Has Thomas told you about the . . . treasure?"

"A little."

To her relief Thomas jumped down from the turf bank. "The terns have come. I saw them over Sheepskerry before, and now they're gathering at Grory too." He rubbed his head and laughed. "They took a dislike of me."

"Strike you, did they? You should wear a cap." Mr. Lindsay stood up. "So your cousin knows about the treasure. That will make our task easier." He turned to Claudia. "Pack the basket, will you, my child?"

Thomas stood trapped in anticipation. "We'll be fishing before long. The kuithe always come with the terns."

Claudia, on her knees, was fitting parcels and jars back in the basket.

"But does the lass know about me, Thomas? That I'm not like the other gentlemen who come to take what they like from these islands. That I see more than those whose heads are filled with learning from books. Not an isolated stone or bone or piece of metal, but a whole picture."

Still on her knees, her eyes on the cloth she was folding, Claudia said, "The gentleman . . . Dr. Cameron . . . says what's found is for everyone. That's why it must go to a museum. So it can be shared."

Mr. Lindsay leaned over her. "Yes. Everyone but the people who plow the land and harvest the grain and cut the turf. What good are museums to the cottager from Birsay or Evie or Rousay?"

Claudia looked up at him. Their faces were very

close. Mr. Lindsay's skin, surprisingly smooth and pink, was damp, his eyes moist and dark. Mesmerized by his intensity, she murmured, "I know you've taught Thomas a lot."

He smiled down on her. "I'll teach you too if you've a mind to learn. And lass, never mock the notions of your old people. It is those things you will hear by the fire on the long winter nights that may be the clues to the puzzles that lie buried in the earth." Claudia had the feeling he was talking to himself now. Then his eyes found hers again. "But the scholars who are above sharing the brose and kale from the cottager's pot will never know what I've spent my life gathering."

Claudia got to her feet. His intensity was too much for her; she needed distance between them. Groping for a way out, she asked, "Do you often sit with Sibbie and others in the winter?"

Mr. Lindsay glanced at Thomas. "I sat with Sibella before you two were ever born."

Thomas turned a little. He hadn't even been listening. Claudia wondered if his remoteness was deliberate, if his excitement at the coming of the terns was feigned or exaggerated. He didn't know what to do about the bronze man. He was helpless before the claims and magnetism of Mr. Lindsay, who now announced that the time had come to examine the sheep's first grave.

But his approach was cautious and thorough. He walked about, siting the location in relation to other points on the island. He jotted things down in his notebook, which Thomas eyed with a look that fell somewhere between reverence and greed.

Next Mr. Lindsay strolled down to the houses and

poked around the chapel. Everywhere he stepped there were roosting gulls or oystercatchers. "You're taking eggs," he observed. "You mustn't touch the eiders', though. Do you hear, Thomas? The dunters won't replace their eggs." He nodded when Thomas assured him that they left the eiders' eggs.

They trudged back to Monkerness. Terns coasting over the Point of Grory swooped down with high, piercing cries. Mr. Lindsay waved his notebook over his head. Claudia ducked under the onslaught, alarmed by the thrusting beaks. She felt Thomas beside her. They ran.

Once they were at Monkerness, Mr. Lindsay began to talk as though he was musing out loud. "Could a priest be buried with grave goods?" he asked no one. Without directing his question at either of them, using the same speculative tone, he said, "What shape is the metal object?"

Thomas and Claudia were caught off guard. Thomas mumbled, "Do you want—" and to stop him Claudia declared that it was shaped like a man.

Now Mr. Lindsay addressed Thomas. "Do you recall your saga stories?"

Speechless, Thomas gave a small nod.

"Sweyn of Gairsay? How Earl Harald pursued Sweyn to a craggy island with a cave in the rock and the water right up to the cave at high tide so that the boat and all its occupants could hide there?" By now Mr. Lindsay was declaiming to the whole of Eynhallow, to the very sky. "A treasure was hidden as well. And when Sweyn left the island he departed in another boat, a boat belonging to the monks. Monks, Thomas. Does

149

that not suggest this island?" Mr. Lindsay fixed his burning eyes on Thomas. "And there's the other event which tells of Sweyn's son being stolen from Eyin Helga, the Holy Island, this island. What was Sweyn's son doing on Eyin Helga in the middle of the twelfth century? What else," concluded Mr. Lindsay in triumph, "but being educated in a monastery."

Mr. Lindsay let all of this sink in. Claudia could feel herself drawn to his vision. Thomas was enthralled. The three of them stood there, clouds banking down across the island, blotting out the greens, shifting browns, and grays. And under the swift dark clouds the strident terns flecked the sky with darts of white.

"I wonder," Mr. Lindsay mused aloud, "whether Sir Henry Dryden will see what we see when he comes to plot the chapel here. I wonder whether he will see more than the measurements he takes." He started to pace off the area between the sunken stones and the hole. He gestured, pointed toward the gray house, as though painting on the canvas of his mind a background of detail conjured up by his imagination. "The whole picture. And nothing is too trivial to compel my interest, nor too deeply buried—"

Turning mid-sentence, he dropped as though the earth had swallowed him. After the briefest silence, while Claudia and Thomas still stood thunderstruck, he resumed his speech. His arms waved, but at grass level. "Nor too deeply buried," he repeated, "though I fear I may have disrupted something here. What's this?" He tried to double over while standing in the hole. "Stone? Have we a cist here?"

Thomas hurried forward to help him, but Mr. Lind-

150

say hoisted himself up with surprising agility, scrambling and even rolling over as he emerged. He passed his hand over his head where bits of dirt and grass stuck to his pink skin. He said, "I suppose your cousin could fetch the metal object while you and I commence scraping."

"But Dr. Cameron said—"

"Thomas, I wouldn't place you in a position that might bring the wrath of those good antiquarians down upon you." His tone was grave, soothing. "However, I fear that through sheer accident I have already disturbed the arrangement of stones in this hole. I mean to do what I can to restore order for those who will come here to wrest, however blindly, what treasure lies buried." He whacked some rubble from his knees. "As for the metal thing shaped like a man, there is little, nay nothing, that I could do to alter its appearance if that were my object. I only thought you might benefit from instructive examination of it."

Thomas looked down. "The reason . . . the reason the gentleman didn't take it with him was . . . well . . . ."

"He told me. That it had been mislaid and there was no time to seek it out. Thomas, Thomas," Mr. Lindsay pursued, smiling and shaking his head in exaggerated disapproval. "I hadn't supposed you capable of dissimulation."

"I did it," Claudia blurted. "I didn't want . . . couldn't . . . ."

Mr. Lindsay eyed her thoughtfully. "Yes," he said softly, "it was not like Thomas. Yes." Then he spoke briskly. "Well, there's no problem now. Thomas wouldn't keep the thing from me, I know."

Claudia could guess that Thomas was sending her a look, probably imploring her to tell all and give all. She stalled, saying, "Dr. Cameron said it would belong to the society, that it would be in a museum where . . . where qualified . . . . He said," she burst out, "that you keep things."

"I do. For study. But I make no commerce with my possessions. I am no less dedicated than Dr. Cameron."

Claudia pushed on doggedly. "He said you aren't . . . careful. That something is . . . was missing from Maes Howe. That . . . ." She fell silent under Mr. Lindsay's burning gaze.

Then Mr. Lindsay turned to Thomas. "You stood by while he accused me?"

Thomas turned miserably from one to the other. He mumbled something about the sheep. He gave Claudia a glance full of reproach and entreaty.

Mr. Lindsay caught that look. Suddenly his manner became expansive, warm. "When we meet on the Mainland, Thomas, I'll take your cousin to Maes Howe and show her those runes that tell of a treasure away to the northwest. And all the others, including the runestone those learned gentlemen missed, the one that Mr. Farrer failed to include in his book. It only appeared in a later publication, you know. You see," he intoned, directing his words to Claudia now, "how absurd and groundless are the allegations of those whose own limitations cause them envy and resentment."

Claudia couldn't help feeling anxious to agree. She was almost ashamed at what she had said.

Mr. Lindsay seemed to gauge her discomfiture. "I feel no rancor toward Dr. Cameron," he assured her.

"I'm sure he believes himself motivated by the highest principles." He smiled. "I'm sure he made those principles amply known to you." He rubbed his hands together; his tone grew brisk. "Now, Thomas, we must set to work without further delay. I want to be able to leave everything in perfect order before the boat calls back for me."

Claudia took her time going for the bronze man. Thomas had been not so much persuaded as allowed to assent finally to what had been bound to happen all along. At least that was the way Claudia saw it. She supposed that whenever this man turned up he infused Thomas's existence with meaning and excitement. Just the way he spoke Thomas's name, with relish and expectation, was enough to command absolute loyalty. And why not? Claudia concluded, as she peeked into the sack that Thomas had deposited on the corner shelf. She picked a crumb from a fresh bannock; even though she was full, her mouth watered, but she gave the crumb to the crow, which sulked on its tether. She rubbed the bronze man against her skirt and held it to the light. Did she really care to make the figure presentable before she showed it to Mr. Lindsay? Why not? she told herself again. Why resist a man so full of earnest dedication and generosity?

TWENTY

BY the time Claudia got back to Monkerness, the burial hole was a shambles. Mr. Lindsay had scraped and then removed the broken slab that might have been a covering before he had fallen on it. Below the fragments there seemed only more rubble. Stretched out over it, Mr. Lindsay shook his head. "I suspect the weather has got to it already." His head and arms disappeared into the hole. "How long has this been exposed?"

"Dr. Cameron had me put back some of the turf," Thomas told him. "That was . . . the eve of May Day."

Mr. Lindsay sighed and pulled himself back. Then he caught sight of Claudia and reached for the bronze man. For a long time he sat amid the dirt and stone studying the face with its upstanding hair, its eyebrows meeting in a wild scowl. He turned it over and traced the faint cross incised on its back. He weighed it, shaded it, turned it again. "What would monks be doing with the hilt of a dagger?" he reflected, and then affirmed, "For it is a hilt; it must be. Yes, and ancient, I'd say." Suddenly he fixed Thomas with a look of pure resolve. "Do you know why you mustn't put this in the hands of those antiquarians?"

Thomas shook his head.

"Dr. Cameron and his colleagues scorn what they call unfounded speculation. Yet one and all they are ready to accept a hoard of silver relics found near the Bay of Skaill and now tucked away in Edinburgh as the treasure mentioned in the Maes Howe runes. Do you know why? No, of course you don't, but I tell you it is because those relics provide a neat answer to a disturbing question. Never mind that those are Viking relics, ring brooches, torcs, bracelets—even a penny coined in York at the beginning of the tenth century. How could those treasures have been plundered from an ancient burial chamber?" His voice dropped. "This hilt, I feel its antiquity." He held it out, balanced on the flat of his hand. "Your grandparents call such daggers trows' swords, and I think they have more understanding than those gentlemen of scientific bent who pursue the evidence of past civilizations without daring to make the kind of guesses that might bring them to true understanding."

"What if your guesses are wrong?" asked Claudia.

"What if they are?" he challenged. "Then they'll be disproved. But one must begin with boldness of vision. One's imagination must be open to revelation. What good is this or any discovery if it be piled onto all the others and set aside for future builders? It could lead us . . . lead to significant revelations. The most those gentlemen will ever build is a stack of stones and metals and bones. Like your peats stacked for winter fires. They are plodders." His penetrating gaze held Claudia. "I am an architect."

Claudia couldn't help remembering what Dr. Cameron had said about the way Mr. Lindsay had ransacked another excavation. She didn't know how to deal with this conflict, so she just replied, "Well, but anyhow it's theirs."

"But he's right," Thomas blurted. "He guessed about it being a hilt. And about it maybe leading—"

"What?" Mr. Lindsay cut in.

"Thomas is talking about how you thought it might be a clue leading to, you know, some treasure," Claudia supplied. "Maybe even the Maes Howe treasure."

"I see. Yes." He beamed at them, his pink face benign and cordial. "And I suppose it's not surprising that Thomas seems to have concluded on his own that this remarkably shaped object is a hilt. He has the wisdom of the old beliefs. And an uncluttered mind. Thomas," he declared, "you may yet find a way to make something of your gift of strangeness."

Claudia hastened to explain that Dr. Cameron had already offered Thomas the hope that he, with his powers of observation, might be useful at future diggings.

"I dare say," Mr. Lindsay remarked. "The hope of carting away the rubble." Suddenly he dropped the mask of affability. "I know how Thomas lives," he continued. "I know how he is viewed. And used."

"You used him too," Claudia retorted. She felt as though his sudden righteous anger had charged her with the same intensity. "When you made him stay in that mound. So people would think he was the hogboy of Maes Howe. You used Thomas."

Mr. Lindsay drew back. His expression became distant and sad. "How easily false accusations take root," he mused. "I don't blame you. I can see that my sharing with Thomas of all I learn, like his sharing with me what he has discovered, must fill you with anxiety. You're not accustomed to a man of my station speaking so openly. You haven't had the benefit of being raised by a woman as proud as Sibella." He turned to Thomas. "But this lad knows whom he can trust."

With a look of torment, Thomas ducked away from their struggle and made off for the sheep pens.

"I suppose I should have expected that," said Mr. Lindsay. "Well, but I mustn't let it set me back. Here." He handed over the bronze man to Claudia as if proffering her a spade. He sounded cheerful again, nearly jaunty. "I suppose I must set this hole to rights by myself now." He began to shovel in the dirt.

"Aren't you going to look underneath?"

"I doubt there's other treasure here but what Thomas already extracted. I can't help wondering whether there might be some connection between this bronze object and the bronze and iron bell of Celtic design we uncovered above the shore in Birsay." He rolled a number of large rocks to the edge and let them fall into the hole.

"But what about what's inside?" Claudia pursued. "I mean, wasn't there a sort of box?"

"A cist? Yes." He gave her a casual smile. "Unfortunately, more ruinous than the one in Birsay."

"But if it's where someone was—"

"I'm certain this was no human burial, but a hiding place for something precious. If it was also a grave, it might merely indicate that the treasure had to be hidden with haste." Grunts punctuated his argument as he heaved in the debris collected around the excavation. "A previously dug hole would have facilitated the

157

hiding. And also raise less suspicion." He marched in place to tamp down the filling. "Anyhow, it is not for me to explore or remove what Dr. Cameron has left for another day."

"Won't he have trouble finding it now?" Claudia ventured.

Mr. Lindsay offered her his earnest attention.

She started over. "I'm not sure Dr. Cameron wanted it that covered up."

"Ah, yes," he agreed cheerfully. "A good point. But you see, Dr. Cameron erred on the side of exposure. This hole was recently filled with rain. And water," he stressed, jumping heavily on the fill, "is a great spoiler, a wrecker. The difficulty is that every gale sweeping in from the north and east alters the fabric of this landscape. So it has always been. So it will always be." Panting, smiling, he began to cut out squares of turf with the spade.

Claudia wanted to argue that a gale wasn't exactly the same as rainwater filling a hole, but she only reminded him that there was also the fact that he had fallen into it.

"Quite right." He lifted one square and set it onto the depressed surface of the filled hole. "And I am making certain that no further harm can come to whatever remains." He took another square and fitted it next to the first. He brushed his hands off, considered his work, and sliced off part of another. "I am being careful," he elaborated, tucking in the roots at the edges of his turfs, "and thorough. Contrary to what Dr. Cameron may attest. At least," he finished, straightening and pressing the bulging grass cover with his muddy

158

boot, "no unsuspecting soul is now in danger of falling and possibly doing himself, as well as the buried material, any injury." He wiped his hands on the grass, then pulled out his watch and flipped the case open. "Do you think you could locate Thomas? I'd like him to help me carry my things down to the landing rock."

"I can carry something." She felt like thrusting herself between this man and Thomas.

"You may assist him then. After you send him." Mr. Lindsay's tone conveyed no harsh authority, only the expectation that she would not want to displease him.

She had no way out of this. Silently she started for the pens, then realized Thomas had gone on, and turned instead toward the houses. She saw the sailing boat reaching across the wind. She called Thomas and ducked into the chapel.

He was there watching a new lamb totter about on wet, rubbery legs. "Just wait here," he instructed when she told him how close the boat was. "Have you the bronze man?" Reluctantly she showed it to him, and when he took it, she almost yanked it away. He wouldn't meet her eyes, but he seemed to sense her impulse, her distrust. He just touched it for a moment, then set it down before going to help Mr. Lindsay.

She went to the door to peek around the wind wall. She saw the sail flapping and was glad that the boat wasn't landing at the beach below the houses where a standing stone had once been used to pull boats up. She recalled the wintry darkness there, the coffin boats setting off in the gray cold. That reminded her of the smoke and the burning feathers. Quickly she turned back, kneeling down to direct the lamb as it stabbed

159

blindly at its mother's legs and belly. She placed it squarely under the udder, forced its mouth open till she could feel it clamp onto the teat. She straightened and rubbed her slimy hands on the fringe that sprouted from a crumbled wall. The lamb's tail wagged; its wet sides heaved as it gulped. There was nothing for her to do but wait now.

Idly she reached for the bronze man where she thought Thomas had left it. It wasn't there. She went cold. For an instant she couldn't move, couldn't even look. Then she found it quite easily and felt stupid about her moment of panic. But she clutched it to her as if holding it could keep it safe. In a way it was like Eynhallow, beset by violent currents. Only it wasn't an island, wasn't rooted, and there could be no real safety for it on its course through time.

TWENTY-ONE

CLAUDIA wondered what Mr. Lindsay might say about her presence on the island, but Thomas wasn't concerned. He was filled with nervous energy at the prospect of leaving. He would take Claudia to Sibbie. He would see that Claudia had a proper skirt and shift. He didn't want to talk about Mr. Lindsay and Dr. Cameron. He didn't want to be nagged.

Fishing was an escape for him, since he did it after

supper, their usual time for talking. If the tide was right, he would head for a skerry, usually the Fint rock, picking his way out through the churning rip. Crouching near him, Claudia would crack the limpets for him to chew and then spit out onto the water. He seldom spoke as he plied his wand over the limpet patch of calm in all that turbulence. He would haul in a fish, crack its head on a rock, and cast his line once more. Claudia always felt relief when he turned, hoisted up the cubbie full of fish, and led the way back across the slippery rocks.

The island was different in the late evening. The low sun deepened its hollows and ridges; most of the birds were roosting by then. Thomas would gut the kuithe, sometimes sticking the livers back inside them before lying them on the fire. Fending off the crow, Claudia would set aside some of the roasted fish to be mashed and mixed with meal in the morning. The rest were strung up over the fire to smoke, making the barn smell so delicious they were forced to move the crow into the old kiln to get a night's sleep.

This busyness worked for Thomas until the wind came up fresh and hard and put an end to the fishing. Rain mixed with ocean spume gusted across the island. Claudia thought of the baby gulls on the shallow cliff edges. The terns had begun to nest too, their eggs utterly exposed. And there were still new lambs, though fewer coming now.

The constant battering got on her nerves. "Thomas, you can't simply move me in with Sibbie," she exclaimed abruptly.

Thomas had just found a dead lamb and brought it

home to skin. He would use the skin to graft a weak twin onto the ewe who had lost the baby. "We'll cook this if you like," he said, offering her the skinny carcass. Water dripped from his hair, down his sleeves and back.

"I wouldn't like. Take it away from here." It was incredible that he had forgotten all about that other lamb.

Thomas stepped out to toss it over the wall. "Let the crow go for it," he told her, returning for a moment. "Before the gulls." He stood in the doorway, waiting.

What did he expect? she wondered, glancing at him, meaning to convey the contempt she felt for his callousness. To her amazement she caught a look of pain in his eyes. "It's worse," he said, indicating the weather. "Like being ground between two quernstones." Then he bent under the wind and set off with the skin for the twin lamb that would wear it.

She was determined to make him face the reality of her position. When he returned, in high spirits because the adoption seemed to be working easily, she confronted him again. "You've got to understand." She was wringing out his drenched vest and hanging it up with the fish. "I'm going to have to leave here."

He shook his hair off his face and wiped away the wet. "You'll see Sibbie first."

She sat quiet for a moment. He had implied a measure of agreement. He didn't want to talk about it, that was all. She chewed on the vein of a lovage leaf; it tasted like celery. She wished she had a toothbrush. She wished she was back on Thrumcap Island with the crow and the bronze man and Mr. Colman taken care of.

"When they come for us," he said, "maybe you could pull some of the flowering squill for Sibbie."

She said, "Whatever you think I am is wrong. Where I come—"

"Sibbie will know." He looked at her. "She knows about all kinds of things, more than—"

"But, Thomas, there are other kinds of knowledge. Things to do with machinery and stars and how people . . . and languages . . . ."

Thomas nodded. "I've seen the machines they use making the bridges. And Mansie and I went down to the harbor when the screw steamer was new. Everyone went to see it. But Mr. Lindsay says anyone can learn to build a bridge or a steamer without a paddle. He says it's different with Sibbie. Because what she knows is a mystery to most men and cannot be learned in the schools." He let this sink in.

"Thomas," she began, "when I'm gone . . . ." She had to start over before his stubborn blankness cut him off from her entirely. "I mean, what Dr. Cameron wants done with the bronze man is right. It was meant to be . . . not meant for one person to keep."

Thomas scowled. "If you trusted me, you'd tell me more. . . . More about . . . yourself." He sat back on his heels and stirred the dirt of the floor. "And if I trusted you," he added without looking up, "I wouldn't keep the sealskin from you." He was drawing a design, avoiding her eyes. "But I will not give up the skin." Without another word he went to lie down in his stall.

Claudia, who had almost forgotten about the sealskin, supposed she'd never really understand how

163

Thomas put things together in his mind. Yet he seemed to be winning a contest she couldn't even begin to define.

By the time she woke in the morning, Thomas was already out on his island rounds. She felt changed somehow, prepared to meet Davie, to go to Sibbie's.

During the night the wind had subsided. The island was returned to its living creatures. She stood in the yard surveying the glistening world. A sudden flight of terns funneled up from the sea. They were eerily silent, as though tuned to the early-morning stillness. Only the waves still thundered, breaking up against the shingle.

Turning back to start the breakfast, she saw the picture Thomas had scratched into the dirt. It was the bronze man, only intact with its blade and scabbard. With uncanny accuracy he had shaped the scabbard to match the bone sheath he had seen in Lik-Lodin's hands. Recalling that sheath, she realized how crudely it represented the real bronze scabbard she had known so well in another time. But Thomas's drawing, rough and smudged, was more true to the bronze scabbard than Lik-Lodin's copy which had been made to ensure that the real one would be recognized.

Claudia was still staring at the picture when Thomas returned. In spite of the gorgeous weather, he seemed moody, impatient. Davie wouldn't attempt a landing till the sea had settled. Tomorrow maybe. Claudia must be ready. He broke off, aware of Claudia's preoccupation with the drawing. Had she gathered any eggs yet? he wanted to know.

She looked up at him. How could she phrase her

question and suppress the urgency she felt? How could she put the words so disarmingly that he would reveal something about the way he had come to this vision of the scabbard. "The eggs," she stammered, "yes. I mean no, not yet."

Deliberately, without a single wasted gesture, he ground his bare foot into the marked dirt. One twist of the ankle, and the image was gone from the earthen floor.

TWENTY-TWO

AFTER the storm, the crow stuffed itself with carrion. Black guillemots had been blown against the cliff; some of the puffin burrows had collapsed; inland, tern eggs had been swept from nests and eiderdown had been blown all over the island, leaving the duck eggs fully exposed. Thomas was pleased because the crow would be so gorged they could safely carry it in the caisie hidden under the fish.

The survivors and predators ignored one another. Only the terns fought back, once mobbing the crow so furiously that he left them to wander boldly among the gulls and skuas beating the lifeless bodies of hatchlings to a pulp to swallow them.

Claudia used her revulsion at the storm's aftermath as an excuse to stay close to the barn. During one of

Thomas's absences she retrieved her clothes and her bronze man and put everything on under her wadmal. When that was done, she had little more to do before she would be ready.

Looking down the slope and across the channel to the Evie coast of the Mainland, she wondered which gray steading might be Sibbie's. She pictured a cottage with white geese in back and flowers by the door. She went to pick the squill on the foreshore, then retreated, unable to stomach the offal. She passed the derelict houses on her way to the barn, and her image of Sibbie's cottage stood out in welcome contrast. She understood Thomas's impatience; she was ready to leave the crumbling walls, the incessant wind.

The boat came early the next morning. The day was fresh, dark-bright, with a cutting edge to the breeze. Ewes were grazing, the lambs heaped together in grassy hollows and against the old dike. Cowslip and primrose flecked the marsh like splashes of sunlight; sea pinks had begun to bloom at the edge of the rocks where no trace remained of yesterday's carnage. The island was picked clean, and they were leaving it.

Davie, incurious and taciturn, accepted Thomas's cryptic explanation that Claudia had been left on the island because she was to go to Sibbie. Few words were exchanged except those about the lambing, the lost oars. When they landed, Davie's only comment was that Thomas would have to leave Claudia with Sibbie and get right back down to the farm.

Thomas shouldered the caisie and the sack. Claudia carried the smaller cubbie and the squill. They passed a cluster of cottages. Each time people saw them and murmured something that might have passed for a greeting, Thomas would nod his head and stomp on. When Claudia said she had to rest, Thomas answered that he didn't want to anger Davie by keeping him waiting. "He's mad about the oars as it is." But he stood still for a moment and gave her a chance to catch up.

The coastal path seemed familiar to Claudia. Soon they would reach the high hill, its headland teeming with kittiwakes and razorbills. She caught sight of a corner wall overgrown with nettle. It was too close to the cliff to have been a house.

"It's called Colm's Kirk," Thomas told her. "Sibbie says my mother and father would meet there, the one from Evie, the other all the way from Kirbister Hill. It's all that's left of an old chapel, good for nothing but the stones of it." He hoisted the caisie onto his back. Deep inside it the crow stirred and muttered. "You stay quiet," he growled. "If I'm seen letting you about someone's house, I'll have more than the oars to answer for." He turned inland now, and the dirt road became a narrow track.

Claudia kept up with him until they crossed a stream and skirted the end of a small loch. Mud oozed around her ankles and weighted her skirt. She wished she could throw off the pretense of the dress and just wear her dungarees. Thomas was way ahead of her again. She concentrated on his back, and when he turned off the track she began jogging to catch up. He waited. When she reached him, she turned to catch her breath. Below her lay the loch, its water flat brown, a gentle hill, plump and neat, across from it. Did she know where she was? She pointed. "What's it called?"

"Claudia, we have to get on. It's the Loch of Hundland." He was already striding up the path through the heather.

She plodded after him as best she could. The wadmal scratched her arms and neck; she felt miserably overdressed.

She nearly fell over the caisie Thomas had been carrying. She looked up and around. Ahead, just off the path, was a small stone cottage. Its roof, part slate and part thatch, gave it a worn, mangey look. Uphill, where Thomas was heading, she could see a woman nearly doubled over and dragging something slowly over the ground.

Thomas returned and lifted the caisie onto Claudia's shoulder. "I'm off then," he told her. "Get the fish in where it's cool, but leave the crow."

"Does she know about it?"

He nodded. "I'll be back in a few days. For the turf cutting."

Claudia watched him descend the hill path at an easy run. She could see a good-sized farm across from the road, several smaller steadings. He passed the farm and disappeared at a curve.

She dragged herself and her burdens to the yard and found one of the grass tethers for the crow. She unrolled the straw mat, laid the fish on it, and extracted the crow, which immediately struggled to free itself. She stroked it, trying to calm it, then gave up and concentrated on the tether. Nervousness made her clumsy. The crow bit her warningly, then bit again harder. Flinching, she drew back and saw the woman standing over her. In her haste to separate herself from the crow,

Claudia scooped up the squill and held it out like an offering. The stems looked bruised; the pale blue star-like petals hung limp.

"You'd best attend the crow."

"It's been covered up for hours," Claudia said.

"Let it go then. But keep it away from here. Take the broom to it if it comes into the yard. I'll have no death-bird about this house." Sibbie took the squill without further comment and started toward the cottage.

Claudia set the crow free, dumped the mat with the fish back in the caisie, and followed, though her heart sank at what she saw. A few chickens and ducks scratched and picked through the remnants of grain stacks; a half-grown pig wallowed in the ditch that ran parallel to the house; brown water trickled, nearly dammed up by the manure. There were no white geese, no flowers. She tried to imagine living in this desolate place. The wind seemed to crawl through the heather like a wounded animal.

"Now," declared Sibbie, emerging from the house, "put the fish down and I'll have a look at you."

Claudia looked too. She recognized Sibbie from that winter vision, but there were changes, the face more severe, the hair gray and mostly covered by a white cloth bonnet that reached to her shoulders. Yet the hooded eyes still gave her the look of a bird of prey; they had not aged, and were all the more arresting for their contrast with the wrinkles, like surface cracks on a glaze.

Sibbie extended a spare, bony hand.

Mystified, Claudia placed hers inside the dry fin-

169

gers. Sibbie turned Claudia's palms just as Thomas had done. Instinctively Claudia started to pull back. Sibbie's fingers tightened and forced Claudia's hands over. Then, abruptly, Sibbie let go.

"Thomas is mistaken."

Claudia didn't stir.

"What have you to say?" The dark eyes were fastened on Claudia. "Don't try to mislead me. It will only make things worse."

Claudia flushed. "I don't know what you're talking about."

"Speak up," said Sibbie. "I'm growing feeble of ear. Though not of eye. Or wit." She gave a curt nod. "Who are you?"

"My name's Claudia. I came . . . looking for a crow. Found myself on Eynhallow." She was exhausted and hot and unnerved by this place. She wished Thomas hadn't left her. "I don't even know what Thomas thinks. Or why he looked at my hands the way you just did."

"Maybe you don't. He thinks you are one of the selkie folk. He thinks that as long as he keeps your caul, you'll be unable to return to the sea. What he doesn't know is that a selkie skin was brought to him the night he was born. I don't think it's your caul he's hidden from you, but the skin of a selkie killed many years ago. So you are not a selkie." She stared at Claudia. "You have not left him. Only not because he has the caul."

Baffled, Claudia looked at her hands.

"Folk used to believe that selkies could be caught when they were sunning without their skins. If a person took the caul, the selkie maid or man would have to remain. Such selkies were splendid, fair folk; they were said to make the best of husbands or wives." Sibbie spread her long calloused fingers. "But their children would be webbed here like them. I have seen such hands myself, all horny and knobbed and grown together. If the suggs are cut, they grow again. It is something I cannot cure."

"But you know I'm not . . . that."

"I know only what you are not."

Claudia felt unequal to any more puzzles. Haltingly she asked, "Is . . . is there anyone else here?"

"I have visitors from time to time. I hope no one will come before I find you proper clothes." She plucked at Claudia's sleeve. "I don't often see such cloth anymore. You will work better in a skirt and apron. You'll have to work well if I'm to keep you."

"But I won't be staying," Claudia quickly supplied as she followed Sibbie through the doorway.

"This is where I sleep," Sibbie told her, pointing to an opening in the stone wall faced by two thin upright slabs. "It is the only neuk bed, so you will have to share Thomas's place in the ben."

"I'd rather sleep by myself."

"Then," declared Sibbie, pointing through a small door at the end of the house, "you may sleep in the byre or the stable. After you've cleared out the winter's muck. There's only the calf left in."

Claudia looked through into the byre. Straw, ashes, and manure reached halfway up to the thatch. "I . . . I'll use Thomas's place for now," she amended, figuring it would take a month to clean out that much stuff. "We've just been sleeping in a barn," she explained.

"Not the house? The chapel?"

Light slanted in through the door and stopped just before the hearth wall in the center of the floor. Claudia could see a straw stool, a chair with a high rounded back. She saw a chest, a thing like a basin on a low stone slab; she saw a spinning wheel. Through the dimness she faced Sibbie. "Thomas stayed in the house, the chapel, before I came." A thin blue tendril of smoke wound up through bunches of dried weeds to the roof hole, which glistened black and swallowed the brightness of the sky. These walls, the roof, the darkness in them seemed to close all around her.

"And you came . . . looking for a crow."

"Yes. Not for me, but . . . ." She wanted to say she wasn't feeling well. She was hot and confused and breathless. "Could I . . . sit down?"

"There will be no laziness in this house. This spring I had to give up Thomas to his mother's people in return for extra corn. Times are poor. More and more the folk turn to the doctors in the towns. They'd sooner buy the Holloway's ointment or Godfrey's Extract of Elder Flowers than pay me to heal their itches and pains. And now that Thomas is old enough to return my care with a man's work, he's taken when I most need him. If you stay, as Thomas expects, you'll work, not sit. Yes, and even if you are to be the woman of this house some day, you'll not sit till the day's work is well done."

"I . . . I've never meant to stay," Claudia stammered.

Sibbie shrugged. "Stay or not, as you choose. I've the

172

harrowing up the hill yet. You may start cleaning the byre and stable, or else go down to the others and make your way as best you can."

"I don't even know what to do. I don't know how . . . where . . . ."

"The fork and spade are in the barn. Fill the caisie you brought and carry up the muck to the field yonder. Along each ridge. Like everything else here, it should have been done long since. I've had nothing of Thomas these two months past."

Claudia headed for the doorway to the byre.

"Not that way," Sibbie corrected. "Out and down past the stable. At the very end."

Claudia went outside. Ducks splashed in the ditch and spattered the snoring pig. The barn, an extension of the house-byre-stable, was at the lowest end, the kale yard next to it. In the light from two opposite doors, Claudia found a wooden hay fork, a heavy spade. Looking through the farther door, Claudia caught a glimpse of green and yellow. She saw Sibbie attaching herself to a kind of harness at the upper end of a small brown field. Then something caught Sibbie's attention; she seemed to be shouting, waving her arms. She looked like an animated scarecrow there on that hill. Scarecrow. Claudia rushed outside and called, and the crow came flapping to her.

It took a while for Claudia to find a safe place to tether the crow that was far enough from the cottage. She chose a stone and turf shelter built into the side of the hill. Quickly she removed her dungarees and sweater, wrapped them around the bronze man, and stuffed them under a rock in the darkest recess. The crow checked out its limits and settled down to peck at the bugs Claudia had dislodged and at the petrified sheep droppings.

She returned to the barn for the tools. Through the far door she could see that Sibbie had come to the end of a row and was turning, bent like a beast of burden, and trudging back again. The harrow jumped and lumbered over the clotted earth.

What a way to live, Claudia thought, rebelling at the meanness of that labor. Yet, within that hour, she herself was stooped under the weight of the caisie, with bits of rank, moldy straw and ashes clinging to her hair and dress. Before the day was over, she was counting the steps it took to reach the little field, counting her steps and looking no farther ahead than where she would next put down her foot.

TWENTY-THREE

IN the evening Sibbie went down to the Mucklehouse, the farm beside the road. She returned with clothing and directed Claudia to the stream for washing. When Claudia entered the cottage, Sibbie, stirring something in a black pot tipped beside the fire, nodded approvingly at the striped skirt and gray top. She beckoned Claudia to the fire. "Take my spoon, and I'll work the butter."

Claudia kneeled, leaning away from the heat, from the kernels popping out at her. Sibbie plunged the handle on a wooden kirn, stopping only to show Claudia how to empty the bere and throw fresh handfuls into the pot. Claudia couldn't help wondering about the fish. Her mouth kept filling with saliva. When the second batch of bere had burst in the pot, she dumped it in with the first. It had to be chopped, stirred, and winnowed. Claudia followed this process with fatalistic desperation. She would have done anything that would have speeded them toward their meal, but after the stirring there was nothing Sibbie trusted her to do until it was time to grind the "burstin."

Sibbie noted her hungry gaze. "Be glad for this. We had many weeks without. Nothing but kale soup and a few potatoes from Candlemas on, till Thomas went down to Evie for the plowing."

Claudia swallowed. "On Eynhallow we had meal and bannocks and—"

"That he had from Davie. This too." She gestured at the bere. "I've made bread from the roots of the meadowsweet, but I had none put by this year."

"They let Thomas help with the plowing?" Claudia asked. "Even though he mustn't plant the seeds?" Her skin felt prickly under Sibbie's scrutiny. Hunger seemed to make her careless.

Finally Sibbie answered, "Yes, though they have both ox and horse. I had a garron once. It's his collar I wear now when I pull the harrow."

"Then how did you get your plowing done?"

Sibbie answered with a low laugh. "I'll be fortunate to get my turnips and potatoes in."

"Still, they give you food."

175

Sibbie snorted. "Give? They took Thomas, didn't they? It's nothing more than what they owe. They take him when they will, and give me enough bere or oats to keep going. But never do I get along with the season, for everything is always late on this side of the hill. There's standing water long after the Mucklehouse fields are ready for turning. I didn't even get seaware this year, though it was piled on the shore, my share of it. I owed the farm two pounds. For lack of two pounds," she muttered, "they had my seaware." She resumed her churning with a vengeance.

It took a moment for Claudia to realize that she was supposed to take over the grinding. She grabbed the handle of the upper stone to rotate it the way Sibbie had shown her. It didn't budge. She stole a glance at Sibbie, intent on the butter-making. Didn't Sibbie know that nothing was being ground? Claudia waited; she heard the fire sputter, the milk slosh inside the kirn. "There's no point learning all this," she announced, her voice sounding sullen and childish to her own ear. "I told you already I'm not staying."

"I half expected you to disappear when you could," Sibbie replied.

Claudia spun around. "When was that?" Had she missed an opportunity to get away?

"When you were at the burn to wash, and the light fading. I thought you'd take off in the grimlings. I only hoped you'd leave the skirt and petticoat behind." She noted Claudia's astonishment. "Why do you think I left you on the hill alone? I was careful not to look. Now grind that burstin if you hope to sup. Then set it on the bink." She pointed to a stone shelf.

Claudia pulled the stake harder and the stone commenced to turn. She used both hands. She found that the faster it went, the easier it was.

"Slow," Sibbie directed. "If you grind like that, you'll make coarse meal." She placed two of the fish on the fire.

Claudia sighed.

Sibbie sent her a sharp look, then took over at the quern. Round and round, slow and smooth, the stone ground the cracked grains. The meal emerged at the rim of the netherstone, and Sibbie fed more bere through the hole.

Claudia couldn't contain herself. "Why not do it all at once? It'll take forever."

Sibbie eyed her. "Forever is a long time. The burstin can't be hurried. You cannot burn the bere nor force the grinding with overloading. No more can you hasten the butter. You must have given Thomas a run for his worth with your impatience."

"I helped him," Claudia retorted.

Sibbie grunted. "And led him a chase with that manshape as well."

Claudia gasped. It was the last thing she had expected to hear mentioned. She moved aside as Sibbie reached for a round flat sifter made of skin pierced with holes and stretched on a stave. The fine meal piled up on the bink. Sibbie spooned out the thick topping from a pail of sour-smelling milk and plopped it into a wooden dish with a handle. She dumped in a few handfuls of meal and gave it to Claudia to stir.

"What about the rest?" asked Claudia greedily.

Sibbie turned the fish. "That's for bannocks. Have

177

you a large appetite?" Before Claudia could reply, Sibbie went on. "You must earn the food you take from here. Now bring that bummie. We'll eat. And mind you take your time."

They had the fish first. Then Sibbie supplied two shallow horn spoons. They sat with the bowl between them. Sibbie ate methodically, sucking the thick kirn milk and burstin, making no attempt to speak, though she watched Claudia with hawklike sharpness. Claudia gulped the first few spoonfuls, but the lumps of dry meal choked her and she had to slow down.

"Yes," Sibbie resumed, "I half expected you to take off in the grimlings, though I thought you might not leave without the man."

"It's not mine. It's going to be in a museum. Didn't Thomas tell you how he found it? About Dr. Cameron?"

"Mr. Lindsay was here," Sibbie returned.

"Oh." So Sibbie was expecting Thomas's "cousin." "Then why did you think I might not go without it?"

"It's a hilt, isn't it?" Sibbie got up from her chair and went to the neuk bed in the wall. She returned with the bronze man in her hand.

It had never occurred to Claudia that Thomas would bring it to Sibbie. Quickly she said, "It belongs to Dr. Cameron."

Sibbie ignored this assertion. "It's too small for one of the old-time swords," she remarked. "I've seen the old swords they've dug up out of graves. Even crumbled to nothing, you can tell they're mighty things. And with handles fit for a man to grab." She held the bronze man out to Claudia. "This is not like any of them. It's a trow's sword, surely."

Claudia's spoon clattered to the hearth. She went diving for it.

"Don't try to turn me from what I know. You and your crow and this . . . this man-hilt the likes of which we've never seen before. And Thomas. Thomas who was forespoken and taken by the trows." Sibbie leaned toward her. "Have you come for Thomas now? Or to give him back?"

Claudia could only shake her head. She had never felt more cut off from all that was familiar and reasonable, not even when she had first found herself with the sword of Culann, with its enchantment of oghams on its bronze blade. Here in the darkness of stone and the thickness of smoke she could hardly recall her errand for old Mr. Colman. She was too distant and at the same time too close; any word or gesture might reveal her origin to Sibbie or to one of those antiquarians with their nearly modern way of looking at things. She couldn't predict what their responses might be. Would they regard her as harmless or consider her dangerous and deal with her accordingly? The only thing she could be sure of was that she could never rely on their feeling for her as she could with Thomas.

"When will Thomas be back?" she asked weakly. She could feel the tears begin to slide down her cheeks.

Sibbie seemed to be sizing up this show of misery. After a moment she declared, "When the peat's cut in Evie." She wiped her finger around the bowl and sucked at it noisily.

Claudia watched. She wondered whether Sibbie would have to pay for the clothes she had brought from the Mucklehouse. She said, "What do you own here? I mean, besides this house and the cow and things."

179

Sibbie laughed. "Own? I'm a tenant-at-will. I can be turned out of this cottage at any time. I pay for the use of this land, poor as it is, and for this house where my father and his father were born. Even the calf must go down the hill before long. Mr. Lindsay says there will be a change one day. One day," she repeated. "But if I be turned out of this croft before that day, what will become of Thomas?" Her dark eyes met Claudia's. "And when I'm here no longer, who will help him? You? Mr. Lindsay? Mr. Lindsay said he'd give most anything for the man-shaped hilt." She paused. "I thought of a garron to carry the turf and pull the plow."

"Mr. Lindsay gives you things?"

"I give him stories and spells for his notebook, elf arrows and other things found in the turf. Sometimes he brings me a bit of cloth, a sack of sugar once. That man-shaped hilt seems very dear." Her voice faded. "I thought of what it would mean, a garron in the stable again, on the hill. . . ."

Claudia wanted to remind her that the hilt belonged to Dr. Cameron, but she found herself saying, "Yes, but even if you had a horse, even if Thomas could manage . . . . I mean, no one will look at him but you."

"And you."

"I don't know why I'm here," Claudia whispered.

"Nor do I," murmured Sibbie reflectively. "Yet. But Thomas believes you are here for him, and though he may be mistaken as to what you are, I'm not ready to doubt that he is right in some way about the reason you have come."

Claudia raised her head. "Reason?"

"To wed him," Sibbie declared. "That at least."

"No, no," Claudia protested. "I'm not old enough, and besides—"

"No more is Thomas," Sibbie retorted. "And a good thing. For you have much to learn before you will make him a wife."

Claudia shook her head. "You can't let him think that I'll still be here when . . . ." Claudia's words trailed off. What could she let him think? From the moment he was born, his future had been set by whatever cruel accidents and omens this woman and the others believed in. Now that Claudia had come with the bronze man, was it possible that he might break away from his forespoken fate? "It's not fair to mislead him," she finished.

All at once she realized she was speaking for herself too. Was it also possible that the more she tried to help him here, the more she would end up hurting him? She had to back away from that thought. It was terrible to consider that she might be using him, using his need, even if she truly believed it was for his sake. How could she be justified when she knew she would have to leave him? Turning from confusion and guilt, she reasserted the clear-cut injustice. "It's not fair." She had no trouble summoning indignation. "Everyone forces him . . . ." But she fell silent under Sibbie's gaze.

"And so you have come to save him. Just as I said."

Claudia groaned. She could never explain without explaining too much. Feeling defeated, she said, "I'll stay for a while. Because I have to. And because . . . because of Thomas." But she didn't know whether she meant because of what he expected of her or because of what she hoped she might be able to do for him.

That night she lay in the stuffy bed closet at the end

of the cottage and thought about Thomas. How could the bronze man lead him, not as it had already done when they were together, but toward a new life? Would Mr. Lindsay really make an effort for him, or was the suggestion of hope offered like a bribe? Well, but the bronze man belonged to Dr. Cameron. Even Mr. Lindsay acknowledged that. It was hard to imagine Dr. Cameron attempting to free Thomas from a superstitious spell. Claudia tried to imagine Thomas in Sibbie's place, hauling the harrow, planting the kale and potatoes and bere and oats, and always alone, since no one would dare to join him in those tasks.

She stretched and yawned. The straw under her rustled. She was too tired to figure anything out tonight. Then suddenly she was alert to the sound of rustling around beyond the hearth. Was Sibbie pondering similar questions in the darkness of her stone-encased bed?

TWENTY-FOUR

In the morning Claudia was so stiff that she could hardly straighten her legs. She wondered how she could dig another caisie load of manure and bedding, let alone carry it. When she heard Sibbie at the bink, she rolled over with a groan, only to discover that her period had started.

Sibbie received this news impassively. She showed Claudia where to gather absorbent moss from the bog and gave her enough squares of cloth to keep herself clean. Gradually it dawned on Claudia that Sibbie didn't expect her to work in the byre that day. Instead she was sent to gather unripe blaeberries for the scouring calf.

The day was fine. Claudia let the crow follow her onto the moor. It fastened itself to the dense red hill dike, gorging on the dying crowberry flowers and on the coppery shoots of blaeberry. The hard, unripe fruits hidden in the leathery foliage could have fed a flock of hungry birds; the crow seemed to gobble everything that was tender and succulent.

From the crown of the hill Claudia could see lochs on either side; she saw people, farm animals, carts bumping along a road. But she felt apart as she had on Eynhallow. After feeding, the crow sauntered beside her, lazy in the bright sun. Rabbits went springing crazily in all directions, startling the scattered sheep. Grateful for this day, Claudia decided to apply herself to whatever job Sibbie assigned her.

But that very night when she changed the direction of the grinding to give her aching shoulders a rest, she found herself grabbed and hauled from the cottage. She faced an outraged Sibbie.

"None of that behind my back," Sibbie shouted. "I'm no fool, and I'm on to your trowie ways. There'll be no grain ground against the sun in this house."

Aghast, Claudia began to understand that she was bound on all sides by rules and rituals that would demand her constant vigilance. She could take nothing for granted.

Sibbie remained edgy and curt for the rest of the evening, but by the next day she was sharing secrets about the flowers that bordered the fields and followed the tracks and throve in lush profusion along the banks of the hill burn. She showed Claudia how to part the springy heather and find the perfect yellow head of the tormentil; its roots would dye the wool bright red. Claudia recognized it as the plant Thomas had brought for tanning the lambskin. She turned from the memory to gathering leaves of the coltsfoot, long past blooming, so that Sibbie could brew a kind of tea with them for curing coughs.

In the evening a girl, shy and breathless, came to the door and whispered a hurried message to Sibbie. She gathered up herbs and packets, told Claudia to keep the fire alive, and was gone all night. At first Claudia waited. Then she did her best to milk the cow and feed the calf left hungry in the stench of its dark, wet manger. She imagined the cow waiting through other nights in dumb misery, its udder hot and hard, unable to lie down.

Sibbie returned mid-morning, satisfied with her night's work. She had brought a baby boy and twin bull calves into the world in a single visit to Kirbister Hill. She acknowledged Claudia's half-pail of milk and dozed for an hour beside the smoldering embers.

The life of the croft resumed. Claudia, provided with a sheepskin cover to protect her back, carried load after load of manure up the hill. When the stalls were scraped clean, she pleaded with Sibbie to be allowed to move the calf from the evil-smelling stable they also used for a toilet. Sibbie, amused and disdainful, argued that it was preferable to keep all the manure in one place, but then she shrugged. Either way, the calf wouldn't be there much longer.

For the first two days in its new, clean quarters the calf did nothing but stand blinking at the space provided it. It continued to lie in its own droppings. Claudia was appalled by its stunted expectations, which made her think of Thomas. From the moment of its birth the calf had been deprived of every natural comfort and hope. It had long since forgotten the sound of its mother's voice and never even raised its head when she approached.

The day they drove the calf down to the Mucklehouse, Claudia met some of the young people Thomas had mentioned. Mansie was the oldest son of the house and Andrew a little younger than Claudia. There were two sisters, Nancy, who was about fifteen, and nine-year-old Margaret, who took to Claudia right away and afterward made a point of coming on small errands and stopping to chat. They all showed up with Thomas early on the first day of the peat-cutting.

Other families gathered at Sibbie's too. The lonely croft was transformed. Everyone carried something— spades, tuskars, flaughters; cubbies and caisies, pails and jars. Dogs milled through the yard gobbling chicken droppings, running to the smaller children to lick at fingers, and dodging out of range as they were swatted aside. The young children were sent ahead with some of the women to spade the shallow turf along the burn. They set out on the peat road that crossed the ditch behind Sibbie's cottage, the children scrambling up the bank and scattering over the moor. Next the older boys and girls were directed to a fresh area to clear the yarpha peat from the surface. They had to go farther than the men, who started out at the deep trenches, swinging their tuskars in staggered rhythm, slicing the hard, brown sods and flipping them off into the pit of the earth.

The young people bantered among themselves while they worked. Mansie teased Nancy about a boy from a neighboring croft. The boy flung one of the shallow sods and hit Mansie in the back. But mostly it was words they flung as they dug and cut and set the yarpha. By mid-morning, when they stopped for breakfast, there were rows of wedge-shaped peats turned upon their heather tops like squat children standing on their heads.

Mansie hacked off a couple of tussocks and carried them over for Nancy and Claudia to sit on. That left a sallow-faced girl without a seat. Mansie glanced at Thomas. "You get one."

Thomas took his spade, wrested another tussock stool from the ground, and brought it over to Claudia. She held a bannock out to him. The pail of milk was between her knees.

"Give the stool to Betsy," Mansie told him.

Thomas stood waiting for Claudia to move to the one he had cut. The morning seemed to stand still. A lapwing wheeled, swerving low around them, and then took flight.

Claudia was tired. She wanted Thomas to take his bannock and leave her to enjoy her own. She wanted to drink some milk before one of the runny-nosed kids got to it.

Thomas used a voice she had never heard before. "You sit on this one." His tone was low, the words intended for her ears alone.

She flushed. "I'm fine, thanks." He had spoken as though he owned her. "Here." She proffered the bannock.

Thomas paled. He didn't move.

Some of the others snickered. Mansie started to laugh, but then seemed to want to help Thomas out of his predicament. "Thomas, we'll all of us wish we'd been sitting in a little while. Give Betsy her stool now and come and have a bit of breakfast while you can."

Claudia sent Mansie a grateful glance. Her cheeks were cooling. She was embarrassed for Thomas, that was all.

But Thomas still wouldn't budge. She guessed he'd stand there, refusing to move or eat, until it was time to go back to work. So she set his bannock down, took a swig of milk, and got up as though she had done so to pass the pail to Nancy. That left both tussocks free. She stretched in the pleasant sun, then ambled off.

In an instant Thomas was at her side. He yanked her around. "Sit down." His voice was still low, but his eyes were blazing.

"I won't. Let go." She waited until he had released her. "You're ridiculous," she hissed at him. "Why can't you act like everybody else?"

"I'm not like everybody else. Nor are you. And I'll not have Mansie cutting stools for you or . . . anything. It's I who brought you here. Found you and kept you. And now you'll show them." His voice was clotted with rage. "Show them."

"Show them what?" She hated his stupid intensity. "That you own me? Well, you don't. No one does."

"You're mine so long as I keep your caul." Suddenly more sure of himself, he sounded gentler. "I know you may wish to go. But, Claudia, I can't let you."

"Please," she begged, backing away from him, "please don't think . . . . I'm not what you think." She tried to soften her rejection. "If you acted differently, maybe they'd look at you differently."

Thomas's look held blunt pain. "You have to sit down." He glanced back toward the picnic, which had already broken up.

She didn't know how to deal with his stubbornness, his perpetuation of everything that was wrong. She could only flare up at him again. "If you think I'm going to sit down now on that tussock just to suit your pride, you're wrong. You haven't even eaten." Tears of shame and anger filled her eyes. "Why can't you just be . . . normal?" She stalked back and rummaged around looking for the bannock she'd set down. Nancy caught sight of her and called out that one of the dogs had made off with it.

Someone else shouted that if Thomas wanted to find Margaret he might be able to wheedle a crumb. Margaret always kept something for later, and they all knew how she favored Thomas. Betsy said it was a shame to have to work on an empty stomach.

Thomas ignored them, taunts and suggestions alike. He worked fiercely, tirelessly, never looking up. Soon he had left all of them, Mansie included, far behind.

In the late afternoon some of the women and the younger children went back to milk cows and prepare the supper. The rest of the peat-cutters stayed on the moss until evening. Going home, Claudia was too tired to think of Thomas. She plodded through the sudden chill of evening, checked only once by a flurry of golden plover. Vibrant as sun specks, the birds set up a nervous outcry, then sank like petals into the moor grass and heather.

At Sibbie's the men helped themselves from the pot, ate, then went out with their ale to lean against the cottage and talk. Children ran in and out, playing, taking the leavings and scrapings as they went. Mansie and one or two others spent a while with the older men to show that they could if they chose. Then they joined the rest of the young people in the kale yard and beyond.

Claudia listened in sleepy wonder to their jokes and games. In the last few hours of work, fatigue had wrung their conversation dry. But now they were at it again, all except Thomas, who stayed near them but didn't enter into their talk. She could feel him watching her. She didn't want to go through any more wrangling, so she made it a point to stand with her back to him.

Margaret found her in the last of the light. She slipped her hand into Claudia's, then leaned away, tugging happily, not bothering to say anything. Then she linked up with Thomas. Claudia, pulled a little too hard, caught one glimpse of him, and braced herself. She looked away quickly, looked up at the slate-colored streaks that banded the horizon. Even the darkest strands of cloud couldn't extinguish the distant light. She remembered the pale gleam of the Greenland night and found herself thinking of Thomas again, of the way he had weighed what was familiar there against what was strange. None of these others knew what he did. Listening to their silly chatter about gamfers, the ghosts they had seen or heard about, she wondered what they really believed.

"Have you ever seen one?" Mansie was speaking to her.

Claudia thought he was egging her on. She sensed a wariness in one or two of the girls. "I don't believe in them," she asserted. "And I don't believe any of you have seen any either."

"Only the old people see them," said Andrew.

Mansie laughed. "And would you go back on the hill now alone, Andrew?"

The others laughed too. They moved a little closer. Margaret squeezed Claudia's hand.

"No," Mansie concluded for him. "Nor would any of us. But Thomas."

190

"I've heard," said little George Bews, "from my grandmother on Gairsay, that folk who died in the old faith of Odin will come back at certain times."

"A time like this? Is this such a time?"

"Ask Thomas," said Effie Brown, a big laughing girl with wild red hair. "Thomas would know."

"No," George declared solemnly, "it's not just any of the trowie folk from the mounds, Grandmother says. It's real people that lived long ago and can only come back for a night. At Johnsmas."

They were attentive now. Claudia felt Margaret try to tug her closer. Some of the women beside the cottage called to their youngsters. Tomorrow they'd all be at the peat digging again. They would be at it for days until enough had been cut to see each family supplied for the year.

"I saw a thing once," said one of the youths. "With my father. The light was on the slope like a sheet of water all stirred up. We saw something moving in it."

"Was it a person?" asked Nancy. "Our granny says there's a felyo used to live in the district. You know, like Sibbie. Only she could do more . . . more harm than good." Nancy's voice dropped. "My granny says she's seen her. Says she looked some like Sibbie."

"Maybe it was Sibbie," Mansie pursued. "Maybe she was out there talking to the hill folk, giving them a report on Thomas. Telling how bad he'd been over the winter, how lazy."

The high, serious voice of their informant began to protest that what had appeared in the teebro was nothing like Sibbie, but more like the standing stone that is said to walk to the loch each New Year's Eve. But his father had dragged him away, for everyone knows

191

how a stone walking is like a giant that will crush any man in its path, never mind a peerie boy.

Margaret drew Claudia and Thomas closer to her. The others started to leave. When Margaret broke away to join her family, Claudia was left standing beside Thomas. Without looking at him, she felt the heat of his unspoken rebuke claim and surround her. She couldn't bring herself to leave him until she heard Sibbie calling her.

When the cleaning up was finished and Claudia was finally allowed to go to bed, she listened for Thomas, determined to go to him with an apology. She tried to stay awake, but Thomas didn't come in. Toward morning she started awake at the sound of the door creaking open. But it wasn't Thomas after all. It was the pig, which shuffled over to the hearth and stretched itself out with a long, drowsy groan of contentment. Sibbie spoke to her out of the darkness. "You'd better sleep while you can. There's another long day coming, and one after that as well."

Annoyed at being caught out, Claudia made a point of going through to the stable. On her way back she saw Thomas in the byre lying in the middle cow stall. It was the arrangement they had had in the barn at Eynhallow.

She left him sleeping there and returned to her bed closet. She passed to the other side of the fire wall, deliberately in front of the stone neuk where Sibbie slept as lightly as a hungry hawk.

TWENTY-FIVE

Even though Mansie was easily distracted by Effie Brown and her boisterous sense of fun, he was curious about Claudia. More and more often he would confront her with a pointed question. Could it be that she was a Shetlander? Maybe she was from across the Firth, from Caithness. Anyway, what sort of name was Claudia? It had an uncommon ring, like the queen's own name.

Even when Thomas was some distance off, Claudia could sense his attentiveness. She was careful to be non-committal, until finally Thomas, engrossed in sharpening his spade, rose to the bait. She was not from here, she had told Mansie with a smile. She didn't know how long she would stay.

"She'll stay," Thomas declared.

Claudia felt her cheeks grow warm.

"Maybe Thomas means . . . he hopes."

"She has to stay," Thomas responded. "That's the way of it."

It was Nancy who broke through Mansie's careful inquiry. "Is she here for you then? Or for Sibbie?"

Claudia started to get up. They were all together along the deep trenches now, and the adults had already started back to work.

Thomas also got up. "I'm the one that found her. She might be . . . is . . . ."

Claudia felt their stares. She said quickly, "It's true. He did find me," and hurried off. She didn't have a long-handled flaughter for flaying, but soon she was on her knees, slicing off the surface layer of turf from each peat that Sibbie cast up onto the bank. She knew that she had to convince Thomas that he was wrong, before he forced her to contradict him in front of all the others.

That night the peat-cutters left the hill early. Heavy clouds blotted the evening light; there was a bitter cast to the wind. Thomas settled onto a bed Sibbie had arranged for him beside the fire, and Claudia took this as a sign that he felt she had made amends by admitting he had found her. When Thomas had gone through to the stable, she said to Sibbie, "I'm going to tell him. I have to."

Sibbie was banking the fire for the morning. She said nothing.

"It's not fair to let him think . . . ."

Sibbie moved stiffly. "You will take away his hope."

Claudia spoke in a hushed voice. "I'll be gone soon, no matter what you tell Thomas or what he thinks. It'll only be worse for him then. They'll never let him forget that he made a fool—" She stopped.

Thomas stooped to come through the byre door. For the first time she realized how much taller he was than Sibbie. She had been seeing Sibbie with her memory as well as her perception.

"Thomas." The note of command brought him up short. "Claudia wants you to understand that she is not a selkie. She will not tell us what she is. She comes from somewhere we have never been. She will return there."

Thomas set his eyes on Claudia, but he spoke to Sibbie. "I found her off the rocks. Swimming and sunning without her caul. I saw her. Only I. Saw her, and she looked at me as if she would know me."

Sibbie said, "She might be unable to stay, even if she wants to. Folk who come through the mists and the half-light of the grimlings will vanish if we turn our eyes from them for a single instant. Even when they are caught for a time, as some be caught in the sun, they'll not remain. For they belong in another place."

"But . . . ." Thomas's voice cracked. "I saw her. She was real. Is."

Claudia spoke very softly. "I didn't want you to say something they could use later to . . . tease . . . ." Her voice trailed away.

"It is because she cares what happens to you," Sibbie said for her.

"If she cares," Thomas blurted, "she'll stay. She'll let me tell . . . everyone. Even Mr. Lindsay. Wouldn't Mr. Lindsay like that, a selkie come true?" He laughed. "He'd write it in his notebook and then years from now some other gentleman would read his writing and come. To see our children. For proof. To find those suggs between their fingers to show all of Evie and Birsay—"

"Stop it," Claudia shouted. "When you talk like that, people call you dimwitted and trowie. You don't have to be so stupid. I'm telling you I'm not something out of an old legend. I'm real. And Sibbie's right. I do care what happens to you. I don't want to fool you and I don't want you to fool yourself. Everything I've told you is the truth. I came looking for a crow. I chased it, and then found myself on Eynhallow. Only the crow wasn't there. I mean, I didn't even find it until we . . . ."

195

She was about to mention Greenland. Instead she finished by saying, "Until after you found the bronze man."

Sibbie walked to the corner bink, scooped something into her hands, then dumped whatever it was into a bucket. Her gestures were quick and spare. Claudia and Thomas watched her in silence. When they looked at each other again, the pressure was down.

"Is it the bronze man you want then?" He said this with a slight air of detachment.

"No." She wished Sibbie weren't there so she could tell him she had the same bronze man from another time. "No, I want something for it, but not it for myself."

"What is that?"

"I want it to be put safely into the hands of people who will . . . can . . . understand."

"You don't want it joined with its blade and scabbard?"

"You know I do." She was aware of Sibbie's sharp look. She wanted to warn him to be careful; he would give too much away. "We can't . . . you and I can't . . . ." Her eyes pleaded with him

"You don't think Mr. Lindsay could understand?"

"Maybe. But it wouldn't do any good."

"Why wouldn't it?" demanded Sibbie. "Why not Mr. Lindsay?"

"Because they don't respect him. What good is his intuition if he's so sloppy and secret that no one pays any attention to him?" She saw their obstinate rejection of this characterization. "He might just keep it and never tell." She pictured him stamping down the turf over the hole. "He won't share what he has. And if he can't have something, he's perfectly capable of wrecking it so that no one else can—"

"They won't even pay Thomas for that thing," Sibbie charged. "How many times have I found things . . . oh, things more than elf arrows, let me tell you, things in the mounds where the gray folk hammer their shapes and—"

"It wasn't shaped that way. It was cast. That man is bronze. With bronze you melt—" She stopped. They were staring at her, Sibbie's deep-set eyes like black coals, Thomas's reflecting the flickering haze of the lamp. Claudia sighed. "I just happen to know about bronze," she said lamely. Groping for something forceful to say, she added, "Anyhow, what's strange isn't that I know that. What's strange is that you both trust Mr. Lindsay. Dr. Cameron actually invited Thomas, you know, maybe to work. . . ." She spun around to face Thomas. "Don't you see? He'd never do what Mr. Lindsay did at Maes Howe, using you to get something."

"Dr. Cameron intends to get the bronze man."

"Not for himself. Dr. Cameron doesn't get things that way. I know he seems less . . . friendly. He probably isn't used to . . . other kinds of people. He didn't offer you much. I know that. But I don't think he'd make promises he couldn't keep. Mr. Lindsay is so full of interest, so—"

Sibbie said, "You don't have to warn me about Mr. Lindsay. There is nothing you can tell me about him." Her voice sounded lifeless.

Claudia felt like a child caught in a blunder. Looking away from Sibbie, she said to Thomas, "We'll talk about this, though. We have to. Will you listen to what I have to say?"

"I always listen," he muttered, making for his bed beside the fire back. "It has never helped," he added. "I listen anyway."

Sibbie reminded Claudia that tomorrow would bring another long day on the hill. Claudia nodded. Sibbie had already loosed her hair; when she turned, it fell like a gray cloud, brushing against Claudia and spreading an aura like a cloud's cool shadow.

"Anyway," Claudia resumed, "I won't have to be afraid of tomorrow. I mean of what the others might think." Maybe now that the illusion was shattered, Thomas would feel easier about her with all of them. Maybe through her a new understanding and respect would emerge. She would back Thomas up from now on; she would show the others that he was neither to be feared nor ridiculed.

She fell asleep with her mind full of bold resolve. But in her dreaming she trembled and broke out in a sweat, because Thomas was being pursued by a kind of giant bronze man, while she stood helpless, clutching a tiny version of the hilt that had led her all the way to the place where Thomas had found her.

TWENTY-SIX

ONCE the peats were cut and raised, only the Mucklehouse folk continued to mingle with Sibbie's household. Mansie returned from a day in Stromness where the ship *Windward* was in port to complete its crew for the whaling; he was full of talk about it, how he wished he were free to sign on. But here it was rooing time, and the turnips not yet planted. Another year he might, though, when Andrew could take on more at home.

The Mucklehouse dogs rounded up the sheep, driving the wily ewes and the shrill lambs first to Sibbie's and then on down the hill. Sibbie pressed through the ragged sheep, grabbing each ewe whose ear bore her notch. She did all the rooing herself, plucking the wool with strong, deft fingers. The ewes, looking more moth-eaten than naked, were baffled at their own lambs' confusion. The hill resounded with the thin frantic wails of lambs who could not recognize their mothers.

Sibbie and Thomas didn't pay much attention to all this commotion, but Claudia raced around to head the lambs toward the bawling ewes. The crow accompanied her, soaring low and mocking the shrill bleats with its grating laugh. By the next day most of the animals were settled and quiet. Claudia went out to count them just to make sure. The ewes were grazing along the dry burn where the heavy scent of meadowsweet merged with the ground mist and wrapped her in the stillness, the timelessness of the hill.

On her way down to the cottage, she heard a shout. She saw Thomas come around from the kale yard, slow but watchful. Then she saw the crow diving where the chickens were scratching. That was all she could see till she passed the end of the barn. Sibbie stood glaring at Claudia, charging laziness, threatening to keep her from the outing on Eynhallow. The crow flapped away to the safety of its shelter. Thomas, silent but with the hint of a smile, resumed his solitary work.

But there was no question that she would go with the others to the island rooing. Thomas went ahead to help Davie with boats and barges. Claudia thought about wearing her clothes and bringing the hilt and the crow, but decided that was too cumbersome. She ended up with her bronze man tied around her waist.

Sibbie sent her down to the Mucklehouse at dawn. Three dry cows had been sold to the Westness farmer on Rousay and were to be taken across to Eynhallow for the summer. Mansie was tense over his responsibility for them, but Margaret paid no attention to the preparations. She skipped up to Claudia, full of chatter. They were going to gather eggs on Eynhallow. They would let Thomas down on the ropes because he was so good at it and nothing ever scared him. Had she ever seen Thomas on the cliff like that? Mansie snapped that if she was old enough to come, she was old enough to carry a cubbie and hold her tongue.

The three cows started off in every direction but the right one. The two black and white collies kept bringing them back to the yard. Then the old grandfather appeared with a magical croon and lurched off down the path with the cows hurtling after him. Claudia was afraid he'd be run down, but as soon as the cows had momentum, he managed to stagger off to the side, and was on his way back by the time she and Margaret and Nancy were following downhill.

"What did he sing to the cows?" Claudia wanted to know. The strange drawling croon had seemed to cast an instant spell.

The girls shrugged. It was something they had heard all their lives; it was nothing.

The cows led them on in mad plunges interspersed with wayward explorations. When they reached the jetty they were breathless and dusty and limp. The first person Claudia recognized was Mr. Lindsay, who was jotting things down on his lined paper. Beside the jetty men and boys, and women too, pushed and pulled at roped cows to force them out where they could board the barges without grounding. There were screams and splashes, caisies upturned, children scrambling to retrieve the dinners.

Thomas was holding back one of the cows, his face streaked with grime, his shirt torn.

"Mr. Lindsay's here. Did you know that?"

He nodded. "Told Davie he wanted to come across for the rooing. Take the other rope, Claudia. No, around the front. This one kicks."

"So he's coming?" The cow was cross-tied between them.

Thomas shook his head. "I think he changed his mind when I told him I left the bronze man at Sibbie's. He thought it was still on Eynhallow." Thomas shook his hair from his forehead and rubbed his face against his sleeve. Someone shouted to him, then grabbed Claudia's rope and shoved her aside.

"Wait," Claudia called as the cow was nudged and kicked into the water. "Is he going to Sibbie's then? What does he want?"

"Wants to have another look," Thomas shouted to her.

She moved back out of the way and heard Mr. Lindsay's voice beside her. "Thomas's cousin. Going too? As far as I can estimate, only five families own sheep over there, and most of the Border Cheviots belong to the farm. Yet there must be at least thirty souls preparing to share a rather questionable crossing with a number of unquiet cows. I'll be well out of it, though I should have enjoyed observing the doings."

Looking up at him, Claudia felt like asking him bluntly why he was trying to give the impression that it was the crowding that prompted him to change his mind. She saw in his hand a sketch he had just penned; it showed the various ways some of the men had wound straw or grass around their legs. She could see at a glance that he had an eye for detail, accurate detail. She felt her mistrust petering away. Maybe it was Sibbie who ought to be mistrusted. What would happen if Mr. Lindsay went up to her today? Claudia drew in a breath. She offered him a confiding smile and volunteered that she was glad she hadn't forgot, as Thomas had, to bring the metal man along. To leave it for Dr. Cameron.

Mr. Lindsay's response was direct, beyond reproach. "How fortunate for me. You see, I did want another look at it. In fact, that was one reason for coming

202

today. Now that I've decided not to, I can see it here and—"

Claudia glanced around and tried to look scandalized. "I'm afraid I can't really show it to you now." She saw that Thomas was on board Davie's boat. If he got off soon, she'd at least have time to consider what she might have to explain about the hilt if Mr. Lindsay forced her to make its presence known. "You see," she whispered, "no one else knows about it. Thomas thought that would be safer."

Mr. Lindsay nodded. "Quite right. Thomas is a sensible lad. We'll just stroll up the bank a little way, and then—"

"I couldn't." Claudia spoke earnestly. She even managed to blush. "You see, it's here." She patted at her waist.

For a split second Mr. Lindsay's affability faltered. "I thought you had it in your basket."

She could feel herself blur under his look. She wanted to run, but knew she mustn't show her sudden aversion. She smiled at him. "Thomas didn't want anyone to know about it. Because some people might, you know, think they could . . . sell it."

Mr. Lindsay leaned down to her. "What a pity if you lost it overboard. In those crowded boats it would certainly be in danger if you were thrust to the side. Of course," he added, "I don't know how you are holding it." His hand came down as though it had no connection with his shiny face and vague eyes.

Claudia felt it on her thigh, felt the bronze man press against her. She jumped back, her hand flying to her side.

"Perhaps I'll come after all," he told her. "Then when you divest yourself of the object, I'll have a chance to study it once more before it's lost to the Society for good." He forced his eyes to focus on her face, her caisie, her bare feet, anywhere but on her hand still covering the shape of the bronze man under her skirt.

She only had time to nod before Margaret pulled her away. She was surrounded with calls to stragglers, squeals of dismay at tilting pails and sliding jugs, children yanked from spattered cow droppings. She hardly noticed anything. No matter how clever she was at dodging and delaying, she knew that if Mr. Lindsay made it to one of the boats, she would have to present him with the bronze man, her bronze man. Not only that. She would have to tell Thomas that it wasn't the one he had left at Sibbie's. And then what? Then what would she tell him, so that her own bronze man would be left to ensure her return to Thrumcap Island?

TWENTY-SEVEN

THE landing was an invasion, Eynhallow overrun. The cows headed for the heart of the island. Twisting and kicking their heels, they stampeded through the low mist of bog cotton. Children, set loose and wild, chased the cattle through the marsh to see them buck. In their wake, eiders squawked, terns swooped and wailed above trampled nests.

Everyone rounded up the sheep. It was part of the sport of the outing. Teams of rooers and shearers started to work before the last of the sheep were caught. The dogs, sent after stragglers, stopped to gulp down tails just cut from late lambs, and left the newly hatched eiders to the gulls and skuas. Shears snapped through wool; the ewes, turned on their sides or doubled over, could hardly be distinguished from the bundled fleeces. Usually two bonneted women worked together, one pulling wool from the neck, the other clipping the back. The men finished the castrating, tossing the baby rams aside like peats when they were done.

Claudia carried away a few of the hurting lambs to reunite them with their mothers. One small one was too weak for its mother to hear its feeble bleat above the din. Claudia paused at the stones of Monkerness, casting about for an anxious ewe. She hated the idea of walking inland where mutilated nestlings with gaping beaks flopped about in the grass. But even while she stood still, a blackback swept down, uttering a low, curt bark; almost at her feet, it snatched a baby tern from a clump of sea pinks and flew off to consume it.

"There you are. Have you the bronze hilt still?" Mr. Lindsay reached out one finger to scrub under the lamb's chin.

"Yes. No. I've been too busy. I'll have to get away by myself."

He looked around. "It's like a painting here. The color, the movement . . . ." He turned to Claudia. "And you, too, holding this little fellow."

"I'm looking for its mother," she mumbled.

"When will you have the—"

"Soon." She hugged the lamb. "I . . . I'll go down to the cave. After I find the ewe." She moved away from him, heading north. She kept to the foreshore. It was a relief to see all the eiders out beyond the skerries. As the coast curved and she followed it to the west, she heard the hoarse call of a sheep. The lamb tensed and thrashed. Quickly Claudia turned inland. There was a ewe nosing the turf around the cairn. When the ewe seemed ready to bolt, Claudia set the lamb down and backed away. The ewe called. The lamb, its hindquarters stiff, its legs splayed, stepped toward its shorn mother. When the ewe dropped her muzzle to sniff and claim it, Claudia went on past the cairn toward Ramna Geo and its cave.

Lost in thought, wondering how soon she would have to tell Thomas about the hilt, she didn't notice Mr.

206

Lindsay until he jumped down onto the square rock in front of her.

He held out his hand. "Do you have it?"

"I haven't had a chance. I told you."

"You're not teasing me?" He reached out as he had to caress the lamb.

She saw that his hand was groping toward the place where he had felt the hilt before. Instinctively she swerved aside. She could feel herself blurring again. She slipped, stumbled.

Mr. Lindsay lurched forward to grab her before she fell. He was steadying her when she saw his expression shift to astonishment and then to sheepish confusion.

She only realized he was looking past her at Thomas when she heard Thomas ask, "Did Claudia tell you to come here?"

Mr. Lindsay recovered his balance. He looked from Thomas to Claudia. "Have I inadvertently come between . . . interrupted a meeting? I had no intention—"

Thomas shoved past Claudia. "Like the other," he pronounced. "Like Lik-Lodin."

"Lik-Lodin?" exclaimed Mr. Lindsay, taking a careful step backward.

Claudia spoke rapidly. "Thomas, he just wanted to see the hilt. You see, I brought it. I didn't have a chance— You said he wanted to see it, so I told him."

"You brought the hilt?" Thomas gave Claudia a puzzled look.

"Because I thought you might have meant to leave it here for Dr. Cameron." She blushed. She had meant to tell him the truth.

Mr. Lindsay said hurriedly, "I'll go along now. I mean to watch the shearing, and I want another look at the Monkerness site." Twisting around and grabbing hold of the blackened outcropping beside him, he swung himself up onto the turf above.

As soon as he was gone, Thomas spoke in soft anger. "You took him . . . to the cave?"

"Of course not. I didn't know he'd followed me. Anyway, he already knew about the cave. Don't you remember when he told us?"

Thomas muttered, "It's not what I was thinking."

They sat for a while watching the wary eiders. Rafts of ducklings were led and guarded inside the Fint rock where Thomas had fished.

Claudia said softly, "It's awful on the island like this. It's worse, worse than the gale. Nests, eggs, chicks . . . . And the lambs, the way they're grabbed—"

"They have to be done, though. Some things must be."

She drew a breath. "Like me going."

He answered with silence, with a bewildered scowl.

"Having to," she pressed. Now was the time to tell him, but she couldn't bear his look, didn't know how to start. Finally she said, "Do you remember what the Icelander told Lik-Lodin about the sword? That it leads . . . some people?"

Thomas nodded. "I thought at first it was the knife, with its steel, but—"

"Yes, Thomas, and before then it led me too. Before we were together. The same bronze man."

Slowly Thomas met her eyes. "Led you," he said stumblingly, "before . . . ." He groped for something

208

intelligible, concrete. "Mr. Lindsay thinks it might lead to treasure. Maybe the Maes Howe treasure."

"Mr. Lindsay makes lots of guesses."

"He was right . . . right about it being a hilt."

"And wrong thinking it's connected with a treasure."

"But it is, Claudia."

She decided not to argue. In the back of her mind was the thought that Thomas might discover he could prevent her leaving. So she let his assertion stand for the moment and said instead, "Mr. Lindsay doesn't believe in swords with special powers. He thinks he has the power. The hilt is simply a clue for him. A way of finding out what he doesn't yet know."

"Let me see it," Thomas demanded.

Claudia leaned sideways and fished the hilt out from under her dress. "This is the one that brought me," she told him. "Before."

"It's the same," he pronounced after a long look. "How . . . how can it . . . ?"

Claudia shook her head. "I don't know. Except that it does lead. Only not just anyone." She was both terrified and relieved at telling so much to him. "And it has to be given," she rushed on. "If it's stolen, taken, it won't . . . ." She wanted to reveal everything now, to speak the words inscribed on the blade: *Gift and giver am I. Wield me who would follow. Fear me who would follow me not.*

He was holding out the hilt with the knife beside it. She couldn't imagine what he was up to. Finally with an effort she nodded, speaking as she would have to Margaret. "Yes, the one was made to be like the other."

"It was given to me," Thomas said. He was declaring

his right to possession of the hilt in all its power.

She stared at him. She thought how Mr. Lindsay craved the thing. She recalled that Dr. Cameron expected it. That Sibbie wanted a horse, oh, at least a horse. And Thomas wanted her. She turned away. "I don't know," she lied. "I can't be sure of that."

They heard voices calling Thomas. He remained unmoving, knife and hilt in his hand, offering them to Claudia's understanding. At last he said, "Does this . . . all of this mean that you come from . . . ." He was at a loss for words. Suddenly he exclaimed, "The Icelander. You really did know him."

Reluctantly she nodded.

"But he . . . that was . . . ." His hand was on her arm. He was giving her the bronze man. "Do you come from . . . long ago?"

She took the hilt from him. "It brought me to him once. I mean, to where he was. To when he was." Her fingers closed over the metal.

"Would it take me? Do you think it would lead me too?"

Nancy called, "Thomas, where are you? We want you to go down the cliff."

"It might," Claudia answered. "But you can't decide . . . . You can't know where."

"And if I give it to Mr. Lindsay? Would it lead him to the treasure? To something that would make his picture whole?"

"But he doesn't believe," Claudia cried. She didn't continue, though. She wasn't sure whether belief mattered, wasn't sure whether Mr. Lindsay might not after all be one of those capable of being led. "The important thing," she said, "is for the hilt and blade and scabbard to be joined."

"Is that you down there? Thomas, answer me. There he is. They're down there. Thomas, we're all waiting for you."

Claudia waved. "He's coming. He'll be right along." She lowered her voice. "When Dr. Cameron gets it, it'll be safe. Whenever the blade and scabbard are discovered, the hilt will be there. Not hidden. Not hidden, Thomas."

"I have to go," he said.

"Thomas, wait. I wish you'd keep the hilt till we're back." She felt a kind of panic. She didn't want to have to show it to Mr. Lindsay. But Thomas couldn't; if it came loose when he was let over the cliff, it would be gone for good.

Later, when she did show it to Mr. Lindsay, she made a point of letting him know that she'd been mistaken in bringing it and that she was taking it back for Dr. Cameron. But she had the feeling that this precaution was unnecessary. He was standing among the fowlers, who had just returned with their loaded caisies, and he was thoroughly absorbed in their talk. It was hard to imagine him sneaking off to hunt for the hilt in the chapel or barn. Still, she preferred not to be accused of teasing again.

After his perfunctory examination of it, Margaret sidled up to her. "Did you see Thomas hanging down off the rocks?"

Claudia, the bronze man wrapped in a fold of her skirt, shook her head.

"He's brave, is Thomas. We're going to the Brough

211

of Birsay next week. Where the cliffs are much higher. And where the birds—"

"Not brave," Mansie interjected. "He doesn't know enough to be afraid."

"Anyhow," Margaret retorted, "he does it better than anyone else."

"You'd best take care," muttered Davie, as he flipped over a limp tystie and tossed it back onto the heap of dead seafowl. "A lad collecting eggs fell off the rocks at Eday last week and was killed."

Thomas arrived, lugging two bags of wool. He halted beside Claudia so that she could take the caisie from his back. "There's a small cave down on that cliff," he told her. "I never saw it from above. I thought . . . thought I saw a crow in it."

Andrew overheard and said, "Everyone knows there's caves there."

"Are we really going for eggs next week?" asked Nancy.

"Yes," Andrew told her. "And fowling too."

Others confirmed the plan. They would meet at the Brough in a week to gather the guillemot eggs. After sunset, in case some early young were ready to make their way from the steep ledges to the sea. Mr. Lindsay remarked that he hadn't known that people went fowling in the old way anymore. He'd been shooting with Davie and had seen the men set a net at the mouth of a bird cave where they trapped hundreds at a time.

Davie muttered that it was too early for the plump fledglings and that anyhow hardly anyone could handle the old fowling fleyg but himself and Thomas; he regarded the plan as reckless sport. "Thomas will have to

212

work hard for me these next few days to be free to go fowling or egg-hunting in a week's time."

The others fell silent. Without Thomas there would be no point to the outing.

Davie repeated his account of the accident to the egg-hunting lad. When no one responded, he said, "Well, just take care then. Make certain of your ropes before he goes over. You hear that, Thomas?"

Thomas picked up the wool bags and hoisted them over his shoulders. Without a backward glance, he pushed past them, Mr. Lindsay included, and made for the boat pulled up to the long rock.

TWENTY - EIGHT

CLAUDIA found Sibbie aloof and wary. Wariness became a part of the atmosphere of the cottage, along with silence, the absence of Thomas, the waiting.

It wasn't until Claudia indicated that she'd prefer to stay on the hill than go with the others for the eggs that Sibbie began to pelt her with questions. Why did Claudia resist doing what everyone else enjoyed? What was she trying to avoid? Claudia mumbled something about the harmless birds, how she had seen them make their nests.

Sibbie seemed to digest this for a while. Then she muttered that it was the razorbills' feathers that were best for fishing, the fat young tammie-norries that had the tenderest meat. Claudia couldn't begin to defend herself. She didn't want to help kill the birds, that was all. Or watch the others kill them.

"Where are you from?" Sibbie's question cracked like a whip.

Claudia, on her way to the crow with a few morsels, whirled around.

"When did you come?" Sibbie's eyes glinted in the light from the low sun.

Claudia stammered, "I don't . . . . I'm not sure."

"Why did you come?"

"I told you. I told Thomas. I was . . . looking for my . . . a crow."

"That bird you keep is more raven than crow."

Claudia couldn't imagine what Sibbie was trying to get at.

"It's not an ordinary crow."

"Well, it may not even be the one I thought I saw in the . . . in the first place." She wouldn't mention the cave. She felt cornered.

"And when was the first place? Where?"

"When I—" Claudia faltered. "Why do you want to know?" She closed her eyes to shut out Sibbie's look. She saw the cave on Thrumcap's islet, the ledge across the chasm. And the black bird. She had followed it out. No, she had started to, but the winter wind and waves had been so fierce she'd been driven back inside. "I sort of . . . I'm afraid I chased it."

"When?"

How could she be certain when she had crossed into the Other Place in the half-light of the cave. Was it winter? Was it spring? She had backed away from the storm; she had waited; she had dozed. And in that twilight between she could have dozed a century. "It was . . . . The weather was awful. It was," she concluded with sudden certainty, "the beginning of February." She opened her eyes to see Sibbie still facing her, facing the doorway light.

Sibbie nodded thoughtfully. "And then," she murmured, "then you were day-bound." Her eyes no longer held Claudia, who seized the opportunity to get out.

She could never tell when the crow was genuinely hungry. Even when it had just been feeding on the hill, it had an infinite capacity for tidbits. She stroked its plumage. Its neck shone like the sea at night, green-black with purple tints. Had it once been lusterless and scraggy? Bjarne had agreed with Thomas that it was so old and worn that it must be on the verge of death. She tried to remember the black bird she had seen at the mouth of the cave, but all she could recall was the outline, black against the winter gray. A young shag. Yet Thomas had glimpsed something on the Eynhallow cliff just days ago. Another shag? A crow?

She looked down at the bird feeding from her hand. Maybe it didn't matter what this crow was so long as it stuck with her and could be presented to Mr. Colman. On a sudden impulse, she reached to touch the bronze man, back in its crevice with her clothes. She needed to get home, not only for Mr. Colman's sake, but for her own. She was becoming too much a part of this life here, too attached. Then, on reflection, she left the hilt in its hiding place. It wasn't time yet to follow it.

As Claudia clambered over the low wall of the kale yard, Sibbie, leaning against the side of the cottage, watched her from half-closed eyes. "You went chasing the crow?" She spoke in an undertone, without moving.

Confused, Claudia glanced back nervously toward the crow's shelter. For the first time she felt uneasy about keeping her things there.

"On some islands girls will go chasing the first crow they see on Candlemas morning. Wherever it leads them, that is where they will find their future husbands."

"No," Claudia blurted, just realizing that Sibbie wasn't referring to her going to the crow now, but before. "I mean, you see, I didn't . . . . That is, Thomas . . . ." Had she come through that February dawn, only to retreat and sleep and wake to the April light? "It was April when I met Thomas."

"You chased the crow in February. It brought you to the place where Thomas first saw you." Sibbie pulled herself away from the wall. "Are you from one of those islands? You and the crow?" Without waiting for a reply, Sibbie turned into the cottage. She said no more about what she was thinking, but showed Claudia the caisies that she must take down to the Brough so that there would be eggs enough for the cottage, and seafowl as well.

The following day broke dark and cold, with gale winds and lashing rain. Claudia considered the storm a reprieve, but by midday the wind had moderated. The sky was suffused with angry purple clouds, and the air stayed chill, but when the time came for her and the Mucklehouse young people to go down to meet Thomas, there was no way to get out of it.

They took their time until they reached the coast, where Thomas was supposed to meet them. Then when the terns came at them, they started to run, arms flailing. There was a vehemence to the attack that might have been stimulated by the storm. Margaret shrieked under the seething violence and flung herself to the ground. Claudia stopped to pull her to her feet. She thrust a caisie at her. "Use this. Come on. Run." But Margaret was ready to burrow into the hill rather than continue.

"There'll be nothing left of you if you stay," Thomas jibed.

Claudia, trying to haul Margaret up, turned with relief and gladness at the sound of his voice.

Margaret cried, "Thomas, you've come." She lifted her arms to him. "Save me."

"You just wear the caisie," Thomas told her. "And be off. Save yourself."

"Oh, please," she wailed, "let me stay with you."

"Between us then. Claudia, you put the other over your head." He shouted to make himself heard above the clamor of the terns. He wanted to know if she had brought the bronze man.

Nancy came racing back toward them. She yanked Margaret after her, dislodging the caisie.

"She's all right," Claudia shouted. "Leave her with us."

But Nancy shook her head. "She might fall there." She pointed to the geo, a sheer drop where the sea churned in through a slit in the cliff. "Come on now. We've a long way to go yet. What are you crying for?" Nancy tore after the others, dragging the screaming Margaret.

Claudia slowed. The terns were dispersing. Those that still darted and plunged were less determined now. Here razorbills stood like penguin sentinels on the upper ledges where some of the kittiwakes had begun to roost; more kept winging in from the sea. Claudia looked east toward the great height of Costa Hill. She remembered it from that other time when Nessa used to hide with the seals in caves along this coast. She dropped down at the edge, wet with spume, and peered into the chasm below.

Thomas stretched out beside her. "What are you looking for?"

She didn't know. Solitude, she supposed, and the quiet they could still so easily share. Waves crashing over rocks rushed to the edge of the land. Birds crisscrossed everywhere, high and low, linking sea and land and sky with the invisible lines of their flight. Here, where everything merged, Claudia and Thomas were part of a kind of stillness they had known before. For a moment there were no differences, no separateness.

Then Claudia raised her head. Off to the northwest she could just make out the rounded shape of the Brough.

Thomas was the first to speak. "If you don't have the hilt with you today, that means you'll not be going, not now." He took a short breath. "I kept thinking you might leave."

"You can only come or go at certain times, you know."

"Times?"

"Like Beltane. Like May Day."

"When would be the next time then?"

She didn't answer.

"When, Claudia?"

"I don't . . . can't be sure."

"Yes, you can. You know."

She faced him. "You know too."

218

That brought him up short. He considered, his eyes on her, unblinking. "Midsummer," he whispered, "Johnsmas." When she made no reply, he said, "That's so soon." He turned away. "If something happened . . . if you didn't have the man and you tried anyway, would . . . ? What would happen?"

"I don't know. I might just . . . be lost."

"But where? In the hill? Under the earth?"

"I'm not sure. But it would be awful." She grabbed at him to make him look at her. "Do you understand that?"

"When you asked me to take the hilt for you, I thought if . . . that I wouldn't give it back." He brought his face close to hers. "I wondered if you were afraid afterward that I might do that."

She stared right into his eyes. "I was . . . am afraid that you'll do the wrong thing with it, with the one you have."

He frowned and rolled away from her. "Anyway, we're safe for today. You don't have the man. And it's not the time for . . . going."

Claudia wondered whether Sibbie would tell him about the crow-chasing and then find out that the crow had come to them in Greenland in an earlier age. Did that matter? Could it make any difference to Sibbie, or to Thomas, for that matter, if in the final instance it had brought them together?

TWENTY-NINE

THEY followed the coastal track to the west, skirting geos, keeping clear of the cliff where the turf was eroded and dangerous.

When they finally rounded the Point of Buckquoy and scrambled down the embankment, they had to slither and splash from one rock to another to reach the Brough of Birsay. It was like picking a way to Thrumcap's islet when the tide wasn't quite low enough. Claudia thought of the paved causeway, wide enough for wagons, that had spanned the little channel when the Orcadian earl had lived there. She couldn't imagine any wagon or cart loaded with barley clattering across now or climbing the steep foreshore. It looked as though centuries of storms had carried off not only walls, but the edge of the land as well.

Thomas, already ahead, turned impatiently. Gazing at the jumbles of stone, the partial foundation of a building, she had lagged behind.

"There won't be many fowl to take," he called to her. "Let's get to it now. They're all waiting."

She wished she could just speak her thoughts. She would say: This is where I first saw Thorstein, the Icelander. Long ago the same bronze man brought him here, to this very spot.

"Claudia, I'm going."

She thought of Thomas puzzling over what had seemed familiar to him in Greenland: houses and byres, the sealskin shoes, even the woven wool of her dress. Yet so much else had been beyond him. She looked up now and saw him turn toward Mansie and the others. They all seemed embroiled in some argument. She started to climb the slope, and when she drew near, heard the subdued urgency of their tones. They didn't want to alarm the roosting seafowl; already the oyster-catchers, their long red beaks parted in shrill protest, were spinning around them. "But what if it's true after all, what the old folk tell us?" demanded one of the youths. "What if it is unlucky to take the birds in the waning of the moon?" The others hushed him, but no one offered an answer.

The issue was finally settled by the almost casual withdrawal of those who had boasted of their prowess on the cliffs. Only Thomas was left.

Claudia found all this maneuvering silly. Last night the sun had barely dipped below the horizon. Now that the sky had cleared, it wouldn't be much different to-night, whatever the phase of the moon. She saw how they avoided one another's eyes. She didn't believe they felt menaced by the moon's waning, but that they were thinking of Davie's warning, of the lad that had fallen to his death, wedged between the jagged rocks.

Mansie concentrated on the ropes, checking the rein-forcement of pig hair for chafing against the sharp rocks. Far below, waves sloshed. Muted growls vibrated in the eerie calm as the whole bird colony muttered in its various sleeping voices.

Thomas, a caisie on his back, was let down over the cliff just past a small geo. Leaning as far as she dared,

Claudia saw how Thomas used his pole and his legs to keep himself from hitting the jutting rocks. Suddenly a piece of the cliff edge crumbled under the strain of the rope. Stones clattered. Mansie and the others fell forward. Some lay sprawling as the rope snaked down. A girl shrieked and was slapped silent. The rope was caught and snubbed around a body held by others.

Claudia had shut her eyes. Now she dared to look. She saw Thomas twirling over the sea rocks. Slowly he was raised till he was abreast of a narrow ledge. He tugged on the rope, signaling. She watched him swing and touch and swing and then grab hold. He landed on that tiny shelf of the cliff.

The rope was slackened. The handlers sighed, then set to work to secure a new hold. The girl who had shrieked cried out that it was a warning, the moon waning. The others tried to bluff her out of her foolishness, but they looked uneasy until the rope was tugged again, another caisie lowered, and the first load of eggs was hauled up.

"No fowl?"

"He's got some tied round him."

"Tell him to send them up."

"Tell him yourself. If you can't wait, dig some tammie-norries out of these holes."

They lay on their stomachs to watch Thomas. The boy who had wanted the birds sent up appeared with a nestling in his hand. He showed them the fuzzy creature, a lump of gray down, an outsized beak, dark round eyes. "They're all like this, too small," he said. When he flattened his fingers, the baby puffin pulled itself upright and spread its feet as if it meant to waddle back into its burrow. "Put it back," Mansie told him. "Let it grow then." The hand tilted, the fingers opened. The nestling's tiny wings beat the air as it toppled. It lay on its side where it had fallen; Claudia could see the pulsing of its heart. Then someone picked it up and tossed it out to the gulls that rode the massive swell beyond the rocks.

Without a sound, Claudia backed away from the cliff. The sole intruder in the oystercatchers' domain, she tried to keep a lookout for nests, but her eyes were filled with tears. The anxious pleep, pleep of the parent birds made her want to run. She hated the birds, hated their defenselessness. They were like Thomas, all of them. Only the terns would fight back. She hated Thomas for acquiescing. She hated herself most of all, because she had wanted to scream, had felt like murdering the boy who had murdered a bird that would probably not have survived the blackbacks anyway. But all she had done was drift away from the others, caring only about getting far enough off so that she wouldn't have to see or hear them anymore.

"Crying? Has there been an accident? Is Thomas. . . ?"

She stopped in her tracks at the sound of Mr. Lindsay's voice.

"You are crying."

"No. Yes. Only because of the birds." Choking, she stopped.

"Oh, yes." He nodded. "I imagine you eat them, though."

She glared at him. What was he up to here?

"I'm surprised to find you here at such an hour. Do you know why I've come?" He sounded as though he

223

meant to distract her from her grief. "Do you see these stones?"

Grudgingly, suspiciously, she looked.

"This was once a church. Probably grander than the one on Eynhallow. Sir Henry Dryden will be here to plot it next month. I am here to make a different kind of measurement. I've come to see it in the dim hours when my imagination can make free with not only what can be observed, but also surmised. And over there," he went on, pointing across the exposed sea bed, "is the beach where I first had the privilege of assisting Mr. Farrer, who has so distinguished himself with his excavation at Maes Howe. Mr. Farrer is due in Orkney very soon. He will be an ally. He has never suspected me of despoiling the monument of Maes Howe."

Claudia listened, but she didn't trust him. Why did he try to pretend that he hadn't known they would all be here tonight? Involuntarily her hand touched her side where she had, the week before, concealed the bronze man. She saw his look flicker; he had caught the gesture.

He stepped into the midst of the stones. "Come and look," he invited.

She shook her head.

"I know," he offered. "I'll take you to Maes Howe. Would you like that? And then you'll understand what Thomas knows about the secrets covered by those stones. And you'll forget your sorrow over the birds."

Starting to shake her head again, she reconsidered. Why not go with him? Since she didn't have the hilt, no harm could come of it. She wanted to see the tomb

224

Thomas had described. "I'll just tell them," she said.

"No need," he assured her. "I've a gig hired. The horse will get us there and back in no time."

The horse was tied to one of the standing stones at the head of the beach just across the channel from the Brough. Mr. Lindsay, more nimble than Claudia, led the way over the rocks. The two-wheeled cart was nothing like the heavy farm wagon at Mucklehouse. When the horse trotted off, pulling them toward the ruined walls of the old earl's palace, Claudia couldn't help feeling that they could travel anywhere this way. Mr. Lindsay told her about the history of the palace. Then they had passed it, and he lapsed into silence.

Claudia drew her arms to her sides. "I don't want Thomas worrying," she said.

"Would he worry?" Mr. Lindsay asked quickly. Then he said, "Yes, I suppose he might. He was certainly worried on Eynhallow, I should say. Worried and agitated." He was gazing straight ahead as the road climbed a low hill. "When he was agitated, he spoke of Lik-Lodin. That's the name of a person from one of the Norse writings." Suddenly he faced her. "Do you know what Thomas was talking about?"

"I don't always understand him," she answered.

Mr. Lindsay drew in the reins to check the horse on the downhill slope. "I think he was comparing me, not flatteringly, with the corpse carrier, Corpse-Lodin. Someone must have read to him from the medieval accounts of Greenland. And this must have lodged in his strange mind. Because of my practice of digging up old burials. Now that I've been thinking about it, I imagine I . . . all of us may be offending people with

225

our digging and prying and removal of old bones." He seemed to be musing aloud now. "Long ago Sibella warned me. She said it was asking for trouble to open up the mounds."

They were heading south on a straight road now, passing cottages, farms, sleeping fields spread under the vast incandescent sky.

"Thomas interests me," Mr. Lindsay resumed after a long silence. Water, gleaming black like wet slate, spread away from the roadside, seeming to fill the lowland. "The qualities that his people deride may be the signs of a special gift."

Claudia stared at stone pillars that stood above the loch. The slabs, enormous as the space they marked, rose from within a dark, encircling ditch. "He'll always be different," she responded. "Apart."

He smiled at her fascination with the stone circle. "I suppose you believe like everyone else that those slabs were raised by giants."

"Is that wrong?" she murmured.

"Wouldn't it be more impressive if ordinary men had set those great stones there, not giants? Men from long ago, in the dawn of civilization?"

In spite of her uneasiness, she felt herself succumbing to his intensity. She was able to believe in his eagerness to share the heritage of this land with the least of its inhabitants.

"Like that," he said as the huge mound appeared. "Maes Howe. Giants, they think, the hogboy, the Mound of the Maidens. But consider the vision that brought man to construct in the earth a stone palace for his noble dead. This is a grave of kings."

"How can you know?"

226

"My child, we may never know." He drew the horse up and alighted. Claudia jumped down. "But that it was a residence of the dead is unmistakable. Think of the gold therein before the treasure was plundered." He pulled out a key, unlocked a gate, and, stooping low, ushered her in through a long black tunnel. At the inner opening she reached out uncertainly and stumbled. Loose stones cut her feet, and she sucked in air. "Steady," Mr. Lindsay called. "I'll light the lamp. Did you hurt yourself?"

She was standing in a chamber with high walls canting in to an opening at the top. At each corner there was a tall, smooth upright stone. She felt the weight and magnificence of the space, the deadness of its core. "Thomas spent a night here?" she whispered.

Mr. Lindsay's voice broke through the hushed darkness. "Almost. He didn't mind." He was standing at the entrance to another cell. Ahead of him, where his lantern lit the wall, she saw designs incised on the stone, an animal like a seal, a fantastic lion. Mr. Lindsay raised his hand. Everywhere in the yellow glow, she saw lines of markings. "And here," said Mr. Lindsay, "are the runes that speak of treasure. Here, and again here." His voice seemed high, almost shrill. "Now, because a hole was dug for a dead sheep, we may have a clue to that treasure. Just think. If Dr. Cameron had taken it that day, mankind might have had to wait for years, perhaps centuries, maybe even forever, to fit those pieces of the picture into a whole."

"What if your picture is wrong?"

Mr. Lindsay stared at her. The light shook.

"I mean, if you're incorrect. After all, it's just a guess, isn't it?"

"Brilliant guesses have brought us some of our greatest advances in knowledge. Not everyone is willing to stride boldly onto the unfinished map of history. Now." He smiled at her. He cleared his throat. "How would you like to help me in a little experiment?"

"If it doesn't take long. I should be getting back."

"I'm going to the top of the mound. Then I'll call down to you through the opening left from the excavation. I want you to tell me what you can hear. And whether you can see my light at all."

"What for?" She wished she could back out now without appearing ungrateful or untrusting.

He sighed. "The nice thing about Thomas is that he's thoughtful, but not talkative. He always did what he was asked."

"He was younger then." She refrained from a more pointed retort. She watched him crouch at the low passage. "It's getting late," she cried. She hadn't meant to sound alarmed, but she did. The chamber darkened. "Can't you leave the lamp with me?" She heard the gate clatter. She stood in utter stillness. She stared up to the partial opening in the roof. Mr. Lindsay's voice came to her from there. It sounded diminished, muffled.

"Claudia?"

"What are you doing?" she demanded. "You shut the gate. You didn't have to do that."

"Calm yourself," the small voice chided. "It's the hilt that is in jeopardy, not you. Do you hear me? Dr. Cameron arrived today. I saw him in Stromness. When I mentioned the object, he was incensed that I had seen it. He won't wait for Dryden now. To confound me."

"I don't have it," she called up to him.

"You don't? What a feeble story. I saw you—"

"It's the truth," she shouted. "If you don't let me out right now, I'll tell Thomas and . . . Sibbie."

"Tell Thomas." There was a pause. "What a good idea. You don't want him anxious about you."

"How can you?" she gasped.

"Now don't fret. You're quite safe here. I'll only be gone for a little while. I'm not going to do anything terrible. We're just going to play a little joke on Thomas, aren't we?"

Claudia refused to answer. He called down, pleading with her to understand. She hoped he would be concerned enough to return, but he only cajoled and reassured her. Then he left.

To her surprise, she wasn't scared at all. She was too furious at him and incredulous at herself for having thought him almost appealing when he was speaking of the ancient stones. She thought of Thomas out on the cliff. How long would it take Mr. Lindsay to reach him? If she got out somehow, she would go straight to Sibbie's to intercept Mr. Lindsay. She thought about time. She tried to imagine the hour. Where was Thomas? Where was Mr. Lindsay?

She felt her way to the entrance into the smaller cell and climbed onto its raised floor. It wasn't so grubby there. She pulled back till she felt the wall, drew up her knees, and closed her eyes.

She woke up at some change she could only sense. She listened. "Mr. Lindsay?" she shouted. "Mr. Lindsay?" Nothing happened. Now for the first time she felt a small bubble of panic rising inside her. She clambered back into the main chamber and stared up. She was still staring when the gate rattled. She held her

229

breath. She hoped Mr. Lindsay would get at least a moment's fright from her silence.

But it wasn't Mr. Lindsay. It was a farmer who grazed his cattle in the field. His son had been out walking and had seen a light coming from Maes Howe. Of course he didn't believe in the hogboy. He believed in mischief-makers, though. What was Claudia about there?

Unable to collect her thoughts, afraid of exposing Thomas to any kind of trouble, Claudia burst into tears. Once she'd begun, it was easy enough to keep on crying, while at the same time conveying that she had been tricked, trapped.

The farmer relented and led her off to his house, where she was seated beside the fire and given a mug of powerful home brew. His wife started up the fire, heard her incoherent plea to be allowed to go home, and finally took her down the road to wait for a ride. The woman stopped a van, spoke to the driver, who intended going only as far as Dounby, and arranged for Claudia to be carried all the way to Birsay village. Claudia, perched on top of a heap of sacks, waved to the farmer's wife, gazed at the steep mound under which some Norseman had written a cryptic message about stolen treasure, and looked back with relief as the great circle of standing stones shrank into the distance.

She was let down beside the crumbling walls of the earl's palace just where the road turned inland. No one was about. The early morning air was moist and still. She tried to thank the driver, but he only grumbled about time lost, turned the cumbersome van, and pulled away.

230

Thirty

CLAUDIA took the coastal track just in case Thomas had lingered or else returned to look for her. She remembered her resolve to get to Sibbie's as quickly as possible, but she wasn't capable of quickness. She could never catch up with Mr. Lindsay in that gig. She didn't want to anymore, didn't want to have anything to do with him.

She stopped once to look back at the Brough, now separated from the Mainland by a sheet of dull gray water. The tide looked nearly full. She calculated from last night's arrival time that it might be about seven o'clock. The cliff teemed with bird life now.

Rounding a point, she froze in her tracks. There ahead of her was a horse and cart. She had to skirt one of the smaller geos, its chasm bright with darting kittiwakes. When she finally arrived at the next geo and found the empty gig, she stood looking at it, stupefied, until she heard a sound at the edge of the cliff. She wheeled about. Thomas, reaching for a firm hold to pull himself up, squirmed there on the bird-limed edge like a fish on a hook. It was only when he flailed his arms as if he might fall back that she crossed to him and stooped down. He grabbed her, and at once she was soaked. Beside her finally, one hand still clutching around her waist, he pointed with the other. Pointed down under the cliff.

"Mr. Lindsay," he gasped. "Mr. Lindsay."

Claudia could only hold his drenched, freezing body against her and wait for his trembling to subside. She listened to his raw, strangled breathing. The birds shrilled; the horse stomped and shook its head; the harness creaked and clinked.

Thomas whispered, "Mr. Lindsay is down there."

"Down there," she repeated, and saw again the fuzzy puffin chick hurtling over the cliff of the Brough. Had Thomas pushed him?

"A cave."

"Down there?" It seemed to be the only phrase she could pronounce.

Thomas nodded. "He was sorry. Sorry. I—" Thomas choked. "I didn't care what he thought. I told him about this cave where there could be something hidden. I just wanted to kill him. Kill us both."

"But why, Thomas? Why?"

Slowly the fragmented account took form. Mr. Lindsay had never carried out his trick. He had worried all the way to Birsay and then had doubled back because he couldn't bring himself to keep Claudia against her will. But when he got there, she was gone. He had searched, called, and then, in panic, beat the poor horse into a lather to reach Thomas, who was just quitting the Brough before the incoming tide. Mr. Lindsay had harbored some sort of hope that he would find Claudia safe with Thomas. When he didn't, when he found instead an uneasy, suspicious Thomas, he had blurted out everything and begged for help.

"At first I couldn't . . . didn't believe," Thomas stammered. "Then he said something . . . something about Lik-Lodin."

Claudia could see how Thomas, inflamed, had suddenly taken it all in: Mr. Lindsay had stolen Claudia, had locked her into the mound, and without the bronze man she was lost.

"Mr. Lindsay said we'd look together. He thought . . . it was possible to find you. And I thought of the cave, of what you said about the cave you came from. I knew about this one. I thought I would lose myself there too. Or drown. And I wanted Mr. Lindsay to be killed."

"But how did you get him to go there? It's so dangerous."

"I told him how we'd used the cave on Eynhallow. I said this one was like it. I said some folk believed caves like that had treasures. . . ." Thomas fell silent.

"Then what happened?"

"He came with me. He was . . . ." Thomas covered his face with his hands. "Brave." His voice was muffled.

She leaned to him. "Tell me."

"The tide was coming fast. It was just up to the floor of the cave. I had one of the ropes. We used that. But couldn't get close enough. We had to swim."

"Did he get to the cave too?"

Thomas nodded. "And I almost changed my mind. You know, because he was so . . . so willing. But then he asked—" Thomas drew a breath; his voice hardened. "He asked where I thought something might be hidden, if there was a treasure. Not about you. Not where you were. But his . . . treasure." Thomas expelled a long, harsh sigh. "So I said, 'Way back. Around back.' I knew

233

that if he went deep enough he wouldn't see how fast the water was rising."

Claudia reached for his hands; they were like ice.

"He told me not to worry about you. He told me we'd find you. All in good time." Thomas laughed. "All in good time, I thought, we'd be trapped."

"But you weren't. You're here. Thomas, can't Mr. Lindsay get out too?"

Thomas shook his head. "The water was rising. Sliding in at the entrance. I . . . . Suddenly I thought of the bronze man and how if you were lost and I was lost too, then no one would ever . . . . And I didn't want to die under the cliff. I didn't want to. So I called him. I yelled. Told him the tide was coming fast. I said, never mind about the treasure, because by then I think I believed there might be something buried way in where he was. He wouldn't come. The water was all around me. I dove into it. Against it. Swam for my life." Slowly his fists opened. He pulled his hands to his knees, then turned the palms up, empty.

"Then you came up here," she finished for him.

He shook his head. "I tried to get back to him. Twice. Maybe if I'd had help. The rope, you know, or . . . ." His voice died away. Finally he looked at Claudia and said, "I can't remember . . . don't know how I could have wanted to kill him. Now that you aren't lost, it seems so . . . ."

"He didn't hurt me," she told him. "Only made me mad."

Thomas nodded. "Yet I've killed him."

"What happened when you tried to get back to him?"

He shrugged. "I got down to the opening once, but then . . . I was afraid."

"Listen, Thomas, do you think you could try again? Would he still be alive?"

Thomas stared bleakly at her. He didn't see how he could make it out of the cave, even if he managed to get in, even with a rope. Besides, the cave opening would be deeper now. But Claudia pressed him. What if there was still time? What if Mr. Lindsay was still clinging in the deepest recess, half submerged? Thomas just stared. He was past thinking.

So Claudia had to think for him. It would be important to get Thomas there without expending too much energy. He'd need it all for the underwater work and for bringing Mr. Lindsay out. She crept along the precipitous cliff edge till she found a rocky outcropping. She had seen one like this severed by the sawing rope and Thomas's weight. "Can you get that loose?" she asked him. Thomas cracked it with a small rock. Just as it split, he leaned forward, caught it, and tipped it back toward her.

Thomas secured the rope to the loose rock with a slip knot. Its weight would help him descend through the water, and once submerged would keep the rope end level with the cave mouth. What he couldn't tell was whether the rope would be long enough to let him all the way in. If it wasn't, he might have to leave the rock tied to the rope and drag Mr. Lindsay to it. Would he find breathing space there? If not, it would all be impossible.

"But at least we'll try," Claudia declared. She wound the slack of the rope around another outcropping so that she could let Thomas down in easy stages. The bitter end was still secured as Thomas had left it.

It seemed a long way. The rope gave a little at a

time. Thomas hung with his knees drawn up. She shivered.

"And don't take that dive without giving me warning," she reminded him, her bossiness masking her terror. She dreaded the double tug on the rope that would signal his readiness.

He made no reply, but swung down in awful silence, till his feet grazed the slop of the flood. She felt the tugs. She knew he was taking in all the air he could hold. Quickly she wrenched the remaining length of the rope free.

She watched it flip and jerk and spin itself wire-tight. Then, in slow motion, the rope slackened and moved as though drawn with the incoming tide. She knew that Thomas must have slipped it from the stone. She waited. Her eyes were fastened on the patch of water impaled by the angled rope. A kittiwake fished beside it, then fluttered as an arctic skua swooped down. The skua made two more passes and the kittiwake dropped its catch, which was snapped up by the menacing bird. The kittiwake flew up and merged with hundreds of its kind suspended over the deep chasm.

Thomas surfaced some distance from the rope. He gesticulated, and for a moment Claudia thought he was shooing off the skua. Then she realized his urgency. She pulled on the rope. She took a turn around the outcropping, then another, just as they had planned. At first the rope came easily. She wrapped another length; midway, it held fast. Thomas dove. He came up beside the rope, propping up Mr. Lindsay's head.

"Hold on," she shouted. "Hold the rope." This wasn't part of their plan. She was sure she wasn't strong enough to pull both of them.

236

Thomas seized the rope and raised Mr. Lindsay farther out of the water. Mr. Lindsay looked dead. Then Claudia realized that Thomas had some new scheme; he wanted her to slack off. She let go one turn, then one more. Thomas was able to make it to the cliff. Again she pulled. The water was now almost level with a narrow ledge. This was where Thomas dragged Mr. Lindsay. Thomas hung him face downward over the side and slapped and slapped him while water and vomit gushed out.

It took another few minutes for Thomas to pull himself up by the rope he had tied to Mr. Lindsay. Finally, white-faced, shivering, he reached the upper end and began, with Claudia, to haul the inert man.

Sweat and sea water mingled as they strained. Thomas had to clamber down a little way as they drew Mr. Lindsay closer. And then, shortening the rope, the last bit of hauling was done directly, grabbing at limp, slippery hands, at legs that seemed to weigh a ton, and at a head that might snap at the neck if it wasn't supported. Finally they had him, and he was bubbling and hideous looking, but not dead.

With their last reserves of strength they dragged him up into the gig. He couldn't help them at all. He didn't seem to know where he was, though for one ghastly moment his eyelids slid up, revealing unfocused eyeballs and veins like bloodied webs.

Claudia shuddered. "Where can we go? Where's a doctor?"

But Thomas, too spent for words, set the horse toward Hundland Hill.

thirty - one

Sibbie, unaccustomed to having carts arrive at her door, was there to greet them. She showed no surprise, however; she asked no questions. As soon as Mr. Lindsay was dragged inside and stretched out on Claudia's closet bed, Sibbie sent Thomas to unhitch the horse and water it at the burn.

Thomas moved stiffly, as if in a trance. While Claudia recounted what had happened, Sibbie's sharp eye took in Thomas's state; she snapped orders at him to keep him going, to get him away from the spectacle of the man he had meant to kill. Thomas would have to stay with the horse and give it a chance to graze the lush grass of the ditch.

"Will he die?" whispered Claudia, supporting Mr. Lindsay's head as Sibbie directed.

Sibbie was massaging his chest and back. She grunted evasively.

"If he dies, will Thomas . . . . Will it be his fault?"

"The man was a fool," Sibbie muttered. "Now go and stir up the fire. Set the pot on."

"But if he dies—"

"Thomas tried to make him come out, didn't he?"

"He wanted him to die. He can't hide that. You saw how he is."

Sibbie hauled Mr. Lindsay over onto his side. "Didn't

you say that Thomas tried to save him before you got there?"

Claudia said, "Yes, but he couldn't go through with it. He was—" She broke off. She stood up. "Sibbie," she shouted.

"Hush."

"Sibbie, Thomas was afraid."

Sibbie went still for a moment. Claudia couldn't see her face, for she was bent over the man in the dark bed closet. Then Sibbie resumed her ministering. She was brisk, absorbed in her work. She took tiny sacks of leaves and roots hanging under the thatch and, rolling a stone on the bink, she ground a fine powder from them.

"What does it mean?" Claudia finally ventured. "About Thomas."

Sibbie dribbled a little bit of one of her infusions into Mr. Lindsay's mouth. Mr. Lindsay uttered a kind of exclamation, but he didn't choke.

"That he is . . . himself," Sibbie replied. "He may have his true name. Colm." She pronounced it in two syllables: Collum.

"I thought the man said Callum," Claudia blurted.

Sibbie turned, the horn spoon suspended over Mr. Lindsay's face. There was a pause, during which Claudia digested what she had just revealed. "So." Sibbie gave her a curt nod. "So you came with his name too."

There was nothing Claudia could say. The atmosphere in the dim cottage was charged.

"The name is Colm, or Collum," Sibbie continued in a flat voice. "For the old kirk where Thomas's parents used to meet in secret."

The pig ambled to the doorway and rubbed lazily

239

against the jamb. Sibbie proffered another spoonful toward Mr. Lindsay. The pig rubbed harder, lurching forward and back, and emitted a long groan of satisfaction.

Mr. Lindsay stirred, then thrust himself forward. Sibbie pushed him back. "Oh," he moaned, an exaggerated echo of the pig. He subsided. He slept.

Sibbie told Claudia to spread Mr. Lindsay's clothes out to dry on the stackyard wall. "Set stones on them. We'll never hear the end of it if he doesn't get everything back."

Claudia heaved a sigh. Sibbie was proclaiming that Mr. Lindsay would not die.

When she came back in, Mr. Lindsay was awake. As soon as he saw her he became excited and tried to rise again. Sibbie beckoned her away. "Found?" he gasped.

Sibbie murmured to him. She was trying to get him to drink directly from a bummie, but he turned his head from it. "I thought it was a judgment. For my prank. Thomas so distraught. So certain she was lost. How could she be?" he babbled. "But I . . . I felt it was a judgment." He closed his eyes. Sibbie allowed him to rest a moment, then pressed the bummie to his lips again. He sipped from it and made a face. "Poisonous." He swung his head to the side. "Take care, Sibella. A woman was jailed in Wick only a fortnight ago for selling cures."

Sibbie didn't bother to respond. Patiently, firmly, she made him take the mixture.

"But you must get me to a doctor."

She nodded. "In time. When you are out of danger."

Mr. Lindsay actually managed a kind of laugh. "Only for you would I swallow such vile stuff. You must be

240

trying to finish what the sea began." He drank some more. "Do you know," he confided in a high, breathless voice, "I think I'm seeing double." He sank back. Again he slept.

The next time he awoke he seemed stronger, but he was confused. "Did I really see the lass? Is she here?"

At Sibbie's gesture, Claudia came closer, though she couldn't bring herself to go right up to him.

Mr. Lindsay rubbed his eyes. "Then . . . then . . . . How did I get out of there?" he mumbled. "I don't remember. I mean, yes, I tried once, but it threw me back. Like a wave. It hurled me. . . . I just clung. Where the air was. So little." He reached out and grabbed the bummie.

Sibbie took it from him. "No more of that now." She told Claudia to set it on the bink. "Do you know where the eyebright grows down by Greengates? I want some leaves. But only from flowering plants."

Claudia was glad to escape the closeness of the cottage. The liquid in the bummie had an unpleasant odor that seemed to fill the house with an oppressive sweetness. It made her joints feel wobbly, and it interfered with her concentration. She had a vague feeling that those sensations were familiar, but she didn't want to think about that. She wanted to get out and fill her lungs with fresh clear air.

She ran all the way to the ditch. There Thomas sat, pinched and white, holding the horse on a tether. "Mr. Lindsay's all right," she shouted. "He's talking and . . . and even complaining." She couldn't blame Mr. Lindsay for objecting to Sibbie's brew. "Thomas, he's not going to die," she insisted.

Thomas's nod reflected neither relief nor gladness.

She wanted to make him talk, but Sibbie was waiting for the eyebright, so she ran on along the peat road to the wetland. Dropping down, she wriggled snakelike, her face at grass level. Yellow eyes seemed to stare back at her out of milky faces tinged with the palest violet. Taking care not to crush the bronze-green leaves, she plucked the slender stalks.

When she came abreast of Thomas again, she slowed. "Whose horse is it, do you suppose? Where must it be taken?"

But even this neutral inquiry couldn't rouse him from his languor. Davie would know, he muttered; it didn't matter.

She felt a gust of irritation. She didn't blame him for being exhausted, but why was he incapable of feeling triumph, or else just plain relief? There he sat, plunged in misery, not even bothering to dry out properly.

She started on, and then halted at the sight of a gray figure approaching from the road. She stared. It was a gentleman, not a farmer. It was Dr. Cameron.

She raced to meet him before he reached the cottage. He regarded her with a faint air of disapproval which made her look down at her filthy feet, her soiled skirt and blouse, the plucked flowers in her fist, their wilted petals hanging limply across the dead yellow eyes.

"I'm looking for Sibbie's. They told me in Evie that the herd boy—"

"Yes, he's here. That is, not just at the moment." Claudia suppressed an urge to glance back toward the ditch.

Dr. Cameron remembered her. "I met Mr. Lindsay

yesterday. Something he said led me to believe the object . . . . You remember the object you weren't able to locate? I had the impression that Mr. Lindsay was . . . ah . . . anxious to procure it for himself, and as I'm here to complete arrangements for Sir Henry Dryden, I thought it would be well to check, in case the herd boy had brought the article from Eynhallow." He paused.

Claudia lifted her eyes from her squalid self. She supposed she might as well appear struck dumb.

"Well," demanded the gentleman, "and has the lad seen Mr. Lindsay then? Have you?"

"Yes," she replied boldly. "He gave me a ride yesterday."

"Here? Was he here?"

"He gave me a ride over Birsay way."

Dr. Cameron drew a sharp breath. "And the object? Is it here?"

Claudia's thoughts raced. She would give him whatever answer would make him go away.

"I trust he didn't give it to Lindsay. Yesterday that rogue suggested— Look here, did the lad bring it back or leave it on the island for us?"

Claudia swallowed. "Mr. Lindsay just wanted a look."

Dr. Cameron leaned toward her. "So he told me. But the man is irresponsible. It wasn't yours or Lindsay's to do with." He wagged his finger at her. "It belongs to the Crown. Do you understand that?"

Claudia shrank away from him. How long before Sibbie would come to the door to call her in?

Dr. Cameron seemed to realize he was too overbearing. He stepped back, lowered his voice. "It probably

243

belongs to the Crown," he amended. "Eynhallow's proprietor has already taken a vigorous stand in opposing claims by the queen and the lord treasurer's remembrancer to finds of all articles of antiquity. But Crown or proprietor, the lad will be compensated. As finder, he'll be paid its full value, and that may be a tidy sum."

From behind her, she heard Thomas speak. "It isn't here. The thing is not here."

"Oh, there you are. Well, now, can you assure me of that?"

"I just said."

"No need to be surly. I was just telling your . . . this lass that you can expect to be paid for your finding it. For an enterprising lad, that could be the start of a new life."

Thomas's blank expression registered absolute disinterest.

"A new life," Dr. Cameron emphasized. "How would you like to sail off to a new life in Canada or Australia? There's an emigrant ship for New Zealand about to leave."

Thomas said nothing.

"But you must realize," Dr. Cameron pursued, "you will receive no payment at all if you have managed to lose or have taken—"

"I haven't managed anything," Thomas muttered. He stomped off to the stable.

"His manners have deteriorated," observed Dr. Cameron.

"He's, uh, not feeling well," Claudia put in hastily.

"Ill, is he? Best have a doctor for him."

"Oh, Sibbie will take care of him. Only we don't know what it is yet. Or if it's catching."

Dr. Cameron began to retreat toward the road. "He should be confined then till that has been ascertained."

"Oh, he is. We are. And please understand about his rudeness. He's feeling awful right now."

"Why is he all wet?"

"Maybe he tried to cool off in the burn."

"A fever, has he? Poor lad." Dr. Cameron was stepping more briskly now that he had reached the path. "If there's anything I can do. I'm returning to Stromness. Could have a doctor . . . ."

"You're very kind," Claudia assured him, walking him toward the road. "We certainly appreciate your kindness."

Thirty-two

THE smaller peat stacks were dismantled, the turfs once more laid, one upon the other, until they rose curving to a ridge from which the rain would fall away; they had a shape known to Claudia from long ago, like upturned boats. Broken peats, which could not be stacked, were set with the heather for Johnsmas Eve, for the young people of the hill combined this final stage of turf-drying with the preparation of their great Midsummer fire.

Margaret spoke of examinations; the inspector of schools would be coming in a month's time. Two older girls from school would be going off into service before they finished their schooling. Mansie and the older boys were looking forward to the herring fishing, which would begin soon after the peat mounds had been dismantled for the last time and carried home to the stackyards. George Bew's cousin from Gairsay had given up on the herring, as it had been so poor these last few years. George's cousin was away to Canada, where he had settled on an island with terrible fogs but plenty of fish. They spoke of matters closer to home, the temperance lecture some of them had attended, the rumor that the Christy Minstrels would be in Kirkwall in August for the Lammas Fair.

"Mansie will be going with Effie Brown," Margaret confided as she handed over an armful of heather for Claudia to fling high onto the growing heap. "Effie has a skirt of crinoline for the day. I suppose Thomas will be your Lammas brother."

"They're too young for that, the both of them," Andrew informed her. "Besides, they haven't real shoes, and that old dress of Nancy's is all I've ever seen Claudia wear."

"That doesn't matter." Margaret appealed to authority. "Does it matter, Mansie, about shoes?"

"You ought to wear shoes in Kirkwall town," Andrew insisted.

"They can stay at the fairground," Mansie answered. "They don't have to go into the town."

"You see," exclaimed Margaret, "you can go. And have sweets and listen to the fiddles and pipes and see

246

all the things for sale and maybe even get a look at a man with three hands."

Claudia didn't know what to say. She looked at Thomas, who had remained withdrawn since the day Mr. Lindsay was nearly killed.

He had barely even spoken to Mr. Lindsay when they had driven him down to Davie's to be taken to a doctor. Mr. Lindsay had had spurts of effusiveness between alarming fits of coughing, though he had only alluded once to the bronze man. He had been telling them that he intended to be recovered from this ordeal in time to meet Mr. Farrer when he landed next Saturday. Thomas's silence had driven Mr. Lindsay to stress the importance of this date. It was essential to get to Mr. Farrer ahead of Dr. Cameron, for Mr. Farrer was a man one could talk to. Mr. Lindsay must be there when the ship, the *Prince Consort,* docked.

"Dr. Cameron came for the bronze man," Thomas had stated in a lifeless tone.

That had caused Mr. Lindsay to fall silent. They had jogged along in the bright evening, past fields brown with bere, hay lying flat, green enclosures where cattle fed. A corncrake, unseen, had rent the silence with its rasping call. In the quiet that followed, Mr. Lindsay had lifted his head.

"When? He only arrived—"

"Today. While Sibbie tended you inside."

Mr. Lindsay had blinked, then managed a feeble smile. "I suppose it was bound to be. Well . . . well. . . ." He had looked up at Claudia, who was keeping his head from jarring, "How light it is," he had murmured. "We approach the summer solstice." He sighed. "I suppose your teeth will rot before long. It happens to them all." He had settled against her then, his eyes closed, his breathing harsh and labored. In the same tone and without opening his eyes, he had added, "And I suppose I was right there asleep when it was fetched for him. Right there."

Thomas had turned and looked down at the recumbent man. "I have it still," he had informed him.

Mr. Lindsay's eyelids had flickered. A smile had crossed his features, and then another spasm of coughing had seized him. When they had reached Davie's, his inflamed eyes had tried to convey something while arrangements were being made to get him to the hospital in Kirkwall, but Thomas had avoided his look. "A future," he had said in a strangled whisper as Claudia had raised him to a sitting position for a drink. "The lad has a future." And then Mr. Lindsay had slumped back and sighed. "Saved my life . . . . Deserving . . . ."

Thomas and Claudia had trudged home without speaking. Thomas had remained that way, not surly, not taciturn, but somehow locked away inside himself.

Now he barely seemed to hear Margaret enticing him to the Lammas Fair with Claudia. He dragged a bundle of heather tied with a rope made of the same plant.

"We'll have a fire as big as Costa's," someone boasted.

They looked at the surrounding hills, Costa toward the coast, with Skelday and Greenay inland, and the smaller Kirbister and Ravie to the west.

"We're not very high," Nancy admitted.

"Our fire will make up for that," Andrew retorted.

The morning of Johnsmas Eve was oppressive. On the hill the only relief from the sultry air was in the shade

248

of the peat stacks. Even the crow was content to poke for insects where the smaller peat clusters had stood.

Sibbie asked Claudia to see that the crow was well away from the cottage when it was time to carry the burning heather around the house and byre. Claudia took the opportunity to pull on her clothes and tie her sneakers with the bronze man under her skirt. She had a feeling that Thomas saw the revealing bulges or anyway guessed what she was up to. She appealed to him for help with the crow, and he suggested that they tie it to one of the peat stacks, bringing a slate to set into the peats. Neither of them could talk about the coming night and what it might bring.

But later, while they were completing the fire mound with a few of the best dried peats, he revealed that Sibbie had told him about his name.

Claudia overreacted, sounding more like Effie Brown than herself. Thomas didn't rise to her false-sounding gladness. "I'll keep my name," he told her.

"Why?"

"I'm no different."

"How do you know? Sibbie says—"

"Because I'd still go down the cliff for the seafowl."

"But Sibbie means something more than that."

Thomas shrugged. "If it's what my father wanted, then I'll give my son that name. If I have a son."

They eyed each other like antagonists. Claudia knew he was closing in on her, appealing, threatening, protesting the only way he could. "I'll keep my trowie self." He spoke slowly, deliberately, as if to make certain that she witnessed his avowal. "I'd not have you . . . no, nor the bronze man, if I'd been . . . ." He couldn't find the words to describe an ordinary state of being. "If I'd been like Andrew or Mansie. I will be Thomas. I'll stay Thomas."

She had to stall, to put him off. "I don't even know whether I'll be able to . . . go back."

He wouldn't dignify that evasiveness with his attention. Instead he told her that she could as easily go at Lammas time, and that would give them a little while more.

She said, "But I've promised. There's someone who needs me. Needs . . . ." She pointed at the crow, which was tugging something out of a clump of nettles.

"You weren't even sure that was the right one."

She threw up her hands. "Thomas, I can't help it."

"You can," he asserted. "If you want to, you can." He set off for the peat stack where they had decided to tether the crow.

She stalked after him. "I do want to. I wish," she shouted to his back, "I could stay long enough to make you see that you aren't . . . aren't what you've always thought. You can be anything you want. Even if Sibbie really believes you were forespoken, she says now you're found, Thomas, not lost."

"If you go, I'll be lost." He crouched in front of the stack. "Always."

"That's not fair. Not true."

"Except that I'll have the bronze man," he added reflectively as he dug into the stack. "As long as I have that, I suppose I may find you. And be found. There's that, anyway."

"You mean you're not going to give it . . . leave it for . . . ?"

"Why should I? Why should they have it? I already know more about it than they do. It might even lead me to the blade and scabbard. And other treasure. Yes, even across the ocean like Georgie's cousin."

Claudia groaned. "You don't know what you're saying. You can't . . . . The hilt leads you beyond known bounds."

He shrugged. "I've been there already."

"It would drive you, not just lead you."

"There would be a chance."

Claudia shook her head. "It goes back. To its time. It only goes back, and I . . . I'm from . . . . I won't be there."

He turned to her. "What do you want me to do with it?"

She thought. If he gave it to Mr. Lindsay, he would be handsomely rewarded. She suspected that Dr. Cameron's notion of payment would be scaled down by the time the deed was done. Still, Mr. Lindsay, if he recovered, wouldn't blame Thomas for having to give up the hilt to Dr. Cameron, and he would remain grateful for his life. Maybe not grateful enough for a horse for Sibbie, but enough for something to ease their lives, to help Thomas along. "It has to go to the people who will make it safe," she said finally. "Who will preserve it in a museum and study it so that . . . ." She couldn't bring herself to voice the cheerful confidence that through such men as Dr. Cameron it would one day be joined with its blade and scabbard.

"Then stay," he pronounced, "and I'll give it up to them."

She was speechless.

He sat back on his heels, nodding slightly, as if applauding his own tactic.

"Thomas." Her voice shook. "You can't do this. And you keep thinking there'll be a treasure, or me, or something . . . wonderful. You don't understand that you'll be caught. All your life you've been caught. Caught by a . . . an idea." She shook her head. "Oh, I don't care then. Call it a spell. Who cares what you call it? The point is it would be like that, only worse."

"Would you care, once you were gone?"

"How can I not?" she cried at him. "But, Thomas, don't try to keep me. Or it."

Thomas jammed the slate, the tether attached, into the deep hole he had made in the peat stack. He reached for the crow, which suddenly spooked and took to the air. He looked up as it circled and glided in a downward spiral; it wore an expression of astonishment as if it had truly believed itself land-bound in the terrible heat.

Thomas looked so helpless, the crow so surprised, Claudia couldn't help herself. The tension in her exploded; she burst into wild laughter. Thomas glowered. She saw his face working. Then he leaned back against the peats and laughed too.

Eyeing them with deep suspicion, the crow settled. Claudia found that she was sobbing with relief, because Thomas was restored, no longer an adversary, but the companion of Eynhallow in the time of discovery. He waited quietly till her crying had subsided. Then they sat for a while as the glare of the heat-stricken day softened around them. The color on the moor drew itself into a dusky red-brown. In the lowland the

252

bog cotton stirred in a feeble breeze, its soft whiteness hanging over the grasses like a ground mist.

The crow strutted back to them. It clambered over Thomas's torn trousers, shook its feathers, and hunched down between them. Claudia set her hand gently on its neck to soothe and reassure it before leaving it in a strange place. A question intruded: if she left it here, how would she know when it was time to take it with her? She felt Thomas's hand come down over hers; his fingers stroked the crow's scruffy head, the shiny neck, her own hand, and then closed over the wings.

thirty-three

CLAUDIA had expected flames leaping against a starry sky; she hadn't considered the lightness of the midsummer night. But the fire cast shimmering waves of heat that made the whole hillside tremble.

Only the youngest children kept running. They raced over the moor with their heather torches like burning streamers flung across the heavy air. Margaret stopped, breathless, to announce that her grandfather had set a bone inside the fire, and then she dashed off again. Thomas shrugged; it was an old custom that nobody really cared about anymore. Yet the image was arresting to Claudia; the old man who could croon the cows to the path would be circling the Mucklehouse with a massive burning torch. It reminded her that Sibbie had wanted the crow away so that she could do the same with her steading.

"Some of them must still believe . . . something," she remarked.

Nancy heard her. "It does no harm. Even if it can't help the harvest."

"It does no harm until they set fire to the new hay," Mansie responded with a laugh. He stood hand in hand with Effie Brown, who chortled and tugged at him, urging a quick check on the old grandfather. Together they set off for the Mucklehouse, with the others teasing and goading, declaring it was only an excuse for the two of them to be alone.

Claudia and Thomas wandered off, then headed home. Above the cottage they stopped to watch Sibbie, who moved deliberately from wall to path to field, always on a clockwise course, and casting her torch as though she were sprinkling its flames everywhere she trod. Claudia didn't see how the torch could last. "Why doesn't she hurry?" she wondered aloud. The question made Thomas smile. Then Claudia stooped down and pulled at a clump of heather. She turned and spotted another good clump, and then another. For a moment Thomas only gaped. Then he knelt down and began to bind a number of the roots. Within minutes Claudia had gathered enough for Thomas to tie together. He staggered the stems so that the handle would be long, then wrapped them tightly in their crude rope of roots.

He handed the bunch to Claudia, who hesitated. He gestured toward Sibbie. Claudia wondered if he believed himself to be a bad influence on the prosperity of the croft. She carried the heather downhill, past the turnips, past the bere, the standing hay, the kale yard and stable and byre and cottage. Sibbie, her eyes dark and staring, was just crossing back from the enclosure where the crow had been kept. Her torch was blunted and smoking.

Breathless, Claudia came to a halt in front of her. Sibbie seemed about to thrust past Claudia, as if she couldn't see anything but the invisible circle she was tracing with the Johnsmas fire. Claudia heard her own hair sizzle, but she stood her ground, holding out the fresh heather.

Slowly, trancelike, Sibbie lowered her own torch, drawing it away from Claudia's face. Claudia blinked. Her nostrils filled with the smell of her scorched hair and reminded her of the burning ember under the ice mountain. She stood rooted, willing herself not to recoil, her fresh torch proffered toward Sibbie.

Then, very gravely, Sibbie nodded. Their torches touched. Claudia's sputtered; it seemed to inhale the heat from Sibbie's dying fire. Suddenly blackness surged out of it; it was seething with smoke. It burst into flame.

Claudia never saw Sibbie's face, only felt her hand, bony hard, over her own, like Thomas's over hers and the crow. The hand was dry and hot. It pressed hers, took the torch, and Claudia was left, her eyes nearly blinded with smoke.

She stumbled back to Thomas, who was waiting for her higher on the hill. She kept rubbing her eyes to clear away the gray scum that seemed to coat everything she looked at. Gradually her eyes stopped burning; she realized that the grayness was everywhere around her. Hundland Loch itself had lost its margins; mist rose from it and merged with the lowland haze, then with the smoke higher up. It was close to midnight. Though the sun would not entirely disappear, the grayness had dimmed its presence on the hill.

Thomas led her back toward the fire, which seemed to have spread over the crown of the hill. They passed older people returning to their homes, but the younger ones were caught in the excitement of midnight. Some were already leaping the lower flames. Mansie rushed from among them, his hair wild, his clothes smoking. Shrieks of laughter and mock horror followed him, then Effie herself like a torch alight, her voice a flame cast onto his path, as if it were meant to burn him.

The fire kept tumbling. It writhed, expanded, then suddenly collapsed, shooting sparks into the brief gray night. The smoke and mist drenched that brilliant display. Like an ocean flooding the half-tide rocks, they seemed to wash away the claims of the earth.

Claudia felt herself dragged toward the heat. Yellow and orange waves splashed at her feet. She resisted, but Thomas yanked her, and it was either leap or be burned. She grabbed her skirt, terrified that she'd reveal her rolled-up dungarees. She felt rather than heard herself scream, was sure that she would land where there was no safe shore and would drown in the fire.

She was hauled so hard she thought her arms would be pulled off. Then she was clutched, dragged free and to her knees, Thomas still holding her, one hand around the hardness at her waist that he must have instantly recognized.

They were both frozen like that, while the challenges and shrieks rose all about them. Someone else landed, and they were knocked over. Only then did Thomas let go. She saw him examine his hand as if he expected to see the shape of the bronze man burned on it. Claudia looked and saw red welts, but they made no picture. Then Margaret's head pushed under Claudia's outstretched arm.

The child surfaced between them like a seal coming up close to a boat. "There's something down there," Margaret shouted. She tugged at Claudia, at Thomas.

They followed her to a group of children, all of them standing with smoking torches, with flames almost extinguished.

"It must be one of them," whispered a girl about Margaret's size. "After all, it's the grimlings."

"Probably just a tinker," said another. "An old tinker woman."

"George's grandmother from Gairsay says—"

"Go get George. He'll know."

"Get Mansie."

The children turned as Claudia and Thomas joined them. They pointed to Sibbie's peat stack, where the crow was tethered on the downhill side.

At first Claudia couldn't see anything at all. Then she made out a small, bent figure as it came around the end of the stack.

"If it is one of them," Margaret whispered into Claudia's ear, "it'll disappear soon, won't it? Won't it just go back into the ground before the night sets and it gets day-bound?"

"Ssh," said Claudia. "I think she's saying something. There's nothing to be afraid of. It's just an old woman. Listen to her, and you'll know what she's up to. She seems to be looking for something."

"We know she's talking," Margaret answered. "Betsy went close to hear, but it wasn't any words we know."

Claudia darted a look at Thomas, who was scowling and peering into the dimness. Did he see something else? Claudia couldn't imagine what made him stare so intently. Next to the others, whose skins were softened by the muted light of their torches, his face looked strangely pale.

Margaret said, "My grandfather says you're most apt to see them in the grimlings. On certain days. They come from the mounds, see, at Johnsmas and Hallowmas and the like. Maybe the fire made the earth too hot, and she had to get out for a time. Maybe when—"

Thomas slipped his hand over Margaret's mouth to silence her. "It's the crow she's after." He spoke so softly Claudia could barely catch his words. "There's feathers in her hand."

"But it's tied," Claudia wailed. "Caught."

"Ssh," he warned. "It must have got away from her." He freed Margaret, whispered something to her. She went off at a run.

"I'll go around one side," Claudia whispered. "You come the other."

Thomas frowned.

"We have to. Quickly." She pushed at him. This was no time for him to be slow and thoughtful—or vacant. "Thomas," she hissed.

He obeyed, but not quickly. It was almost as if he were acting a role, playing the dullard, the boy without his wits. She nearly screamed at him.

The woman was moving along, feeling her way up and down the stack as if she believed something to be

258

hidden in it. Claudia dashed away, making a wide sweep to the downhill side of the mound.

Thomas was not yet there. She looked for the crow, couldn't see it, and then ducked down as the woman's mutterings came to her from the end of the stack. Still crouched, Claudia swiveled to face the woman. Thomas was supposed to have come from the other end; she supposed he was still dragging his feet, pondering the wisdom of her plan, or else simply reluctant to approach.

The woman was not only bent; she was appallingly twisted. She shuffled on feet clad in wrinkled leather like the rivlins Bjarne had made for Claudia and Thomas in Greenland.

Claudia held her breath. She couldn't yet see the woman's face, which was nearly covered by a dark shawl wrapped over the head and around the stooped body. Then off to the side she heard a queer breath expelled, a kind of rusty squeak. She recoiled in horror, hitting against the peat stack where Thomas had removed the peats. Righting herself, she dislodged another peat, which unlocked a whole section, so that one after another they tumbled softly to the ground beside the crow.

She couldn't believe it was her crow. It uttered another almost soundless squawk. It staggered toward her, one wing dragging, its head held at an angle. It kept keeling over to the right.

The woman pounced and snatched it up. She sent Claudia a look of glee, and there under the coarse woven cloth was the ageless face of Grima, the skin wrinkled but baby soft and the eyes brighter than anything there around them. Only the tiny closed mouth

259

betrayed age and decay. While her eyes conveyed her triumph, her knobby hands closed around the crow's neck and began to twist. Claudia felt for the slate, still embedded in the turf mound, but only loosened more peats. She reached under her skirt, tugged violently at the bronze man, and then hurled it at that child's face of the old woman.

Grima clapped her hands to her forehead, and Claudia grabbed the crow. As she held it against her, she saw Grima recover from the blow and reach for the bronze man. "Thomas," Claudia cried. She lurched forward, seizing the hilt at the same instant as Grima. The crow fell to the ground and lay on its side thrashing its head. Claudia couldn't bear that. She let go of the bronze man to bend and cradle the crow. As soon as she supported it, its head arched as if vainly trying to preen. It was poking among its breast feathers the way it had poked in the grass of the peat beds. Grima waved the bronze man at Claudia's face, either as a distraction or a lure. Under the blur of the bronze pendulum, Claudia saw the crow extract something white. By the time Grima pounced again, the crow had consumed that single small feather.

It died very suddenly, its beak agape but without uttering another sound.

Claudia looked up slowly in a kind of amazement.

"The hilt," Thomas warned. He was behind Grima.

Claudia pointed to the crow. She didn't move. She could taste tears.

The old woman, the hilt clutched to her, was back against the peat stack and moving gradually closer to the huge, gaping hole.

Claudia wouldn't budge until Thomas acknowledged the death of the crow. Why wouldn't he look? Why did he keep staring at the old woman as if his life depended on it? "Look," she moaned, still pointing at the crumpled black bird.

"If I take my eyes from her," he answered, "she'll get away."

"Then let her. Let her go."

Thomas's gaze shifted. "You mean that?" His expression was full of terrified joy. "You know what you're saying?"

She was too dazed to see what he meant. She could only nod her head and repeat her demand that he look at the dead crow. She pointed. He looked. She leaned back, satisfied, as though something momentous had been acknowledged.

He touched the crow where it had plucked the feather of wisdom and said, "You see, it's safe too. Like you here, now that she has it."

"She doesn't though, Thomas. The crow swallowed—"

"I mean the hilt."

Squatting there, Claudia slowly absorbed this. She hadn't thought of the hilt when she had told Thomas to let Grima go. Now she understood his terrified joy. He had believed that Claudia had chosen this life, him; he had heard her abandon the hilt. She stumbled to her feet.

"No," shouted Thomas. "Don't look yet. Let her go. No, Claudia."

The woman had reached the crumbled cavity of the mound. Claudia flung herself onto the stooped figure, and they tumbled into the darkness of the turf.

261

She could see nothing but her own rage burning as hot as the sun itself, as all the fires of Johnsmas. But as soon as she had wrested the bronze man free, she knew that Grima was nothing but a shadow. It was the bronze man that was the object of her fury, because it had made her betray Thomas in order to save herself.

PART FOUR

ThiRty-FOUR

THE darkness stayed with Claudia. At first she felt trapped by it. Then it was her dress that held her, so she tugged at it and wriggled free. After that there was the cold, not ice-sharp, but deep as the earth through which she crawled. But she could lift her head now, rise to her knees, with only the bronze man, clutched in one hand, to encumber her.

The thought of Mr. Colman waiting alone drove her toward the gray opening. She began to see more. She was certain that the things lying across on the opposite ledge could not merely be the bones of birds and fish in a subterranean nesting place. The shapes were too abrupt and hard, too deliberately squared or curved. She supposed that the darkness of the night had prevented her noticing them before. No, it had been the bird sauntering out from that shelf that had fixed her attention. Crow or shag, she had seen nothing else in this cave. Now, peering through the dimness, she thought of an old wreck she had seen on a spring low tide, the hulk of a ship laid bare by the sea, a made thing unmade again but still somehow recognizable and unlike any natural formation of rock or shoal.

Craning, she imagined that she could detect the rounded belly of a pot. She braced herself and stretched across the narrow chasm. She propped one hand, with its bronze hilt, against the sharp edge; the fingers of her other hand could explore. The pot, if it was a pot, collapsed at her touch. Perhaps it was only a metal float swollen with rust. Flakes of something adhered to her fingers; they smelled of the dark cold, nothing more.

She drew herself up for one more attempt, this time aiming for a square object that looked like a box or a chest. She strained, but couldn't reach it. She decided it might be a holding box for lobsters. She wanted it to be such a box, stared at it to confirm this likelihood, only to see raised knobs like oversized nail heads outlining the front and curving down in a scroll to a dark center.

She gave up trying to get to it until she was sliding out, feet first, and seeking a foothold on the wet rocks below her. Then it occurred to her that she might at least be able to reach with her one free hand while she lay half inside the cave, even if she did block what little light there was. She stuck the bronze man into her belt so that her right hand could grip with all its might. Her left waved futilely for a while until it brushed against a queer fuzziness that made her gasp and recoil.

She turned on her side to look at her hand. At the point of contact her fingers bore tiny pieces of rust; the softness had been the raised and shed skin of iron.

Cautiously, easing herself off the bruising arms of the bronze man, she resumed her blind exploration. When her fingers found the face of the chest, she didn't flinch. Instead, she confirmed what her eyes had seen; the rounded heads of nails or rivets led to a latch of some sort. It dropped to the floor of the shelf. She fumbled, but couldn't find anything like it. Her fingers closed over something heavy and round with a hole, the size of a spindle whorl. She tried to drag it off the shelf, but it fell into the chasm.

Back went her hand, this time finding a different object, long and harder than rusted iron. She tried to lift it, but something, perhaps the skeleton chest, was holding it down. Her fingers ran its length and found a nearly pointed end with a rim at the edge and two small knobs raised from its slightly rounded side. She drew her fingers along it one more time to confirm its contour, which was the shape of a long, graceful leaf. It was not light; it wasn't bone or rock; it wasn't iron, though its surface texture was rough as though from corrosion.

When she was certain she couldn't remove it, she rested a moment, and then resumed her retreat from the cave. The wind hit her, then a wave. She hardly felt either. All her feelings were concentrated in her fingers which had traced a shape they had known in another time. She took the bronze man from her belt. She stood just under the opening in the cliff, one hand full, one hand empty, and yet not empty of sensation, of knowledge. Then another wave slapped her legs and stung her into the present, into a gray cold dawning on Thrumcap's islet.

Suddenly she was frightened. Her feet were planted on the ocean floor, not on any known land that people walked. Even as she stood on this bed of the sea, the water rushed in to claim its territory, and the next wave nearly knocked her down. Splashing and slipping, she stumbled around to the side of the cliff where she could reach the gentler slope. She tried to quell her panic. She remembered walking out here in the storm. But though it had been dark and wild, it had also been on the ebb. Now she felt pursued by the tide which rose to cover all things, living and dead.

Once she could see the shack, her panic subsided. She could tell that while the wind blew and the waves broke white over the gray chop, the storm was really spent. As soon as the water had risen sufficiently, Ernie's boat would be able to make it into the cove.

She found Mr. Colman sitting, his elbows on his knees, his face in his hands. At first she took it for a sign that he was feeling better. But after she had perked up the fire and set the pot on the stove, after she had put the bronze man away under the stone, she realized that he barely noticed her. She showed him her wet dungarees, as if to prove to him that she had done her best to find the crow, perhaps had risked drowning for him. Colman's pale eyes focused briefly on her close face during her animated description of the cave in the cliff that, but for this weird tide, they'd never have known was there. Encouraged by his brief look of comprehension, she kept up a stream of chatter about her discoveries.

She handed him a cup of tea, which he ignored, even when she held it to his mouth. She wanted to reassure him now that he seemed capable of understanding. "As soon as I warm up," she promised, "I'll go back for the crow." Surely it was right to make the most extravagant promises if it would give this old man hope. Soon Ernie and the others would be here, and the vigil would be over. If only she could keep Mr. Colman going till then.

"I looked for the crow on the cliff," she told him.

"I haven't tried the woods yet." She wiped her hand across her cheek, astonished to feel tears. Because she was lying? Because the crow was dead? She shook her head, baffled by the confusion of her grief. She couldn't even be sure that Mr. Colman's crow wasn't in fact alive somewhere on this island.

She talked faster, changed the subject again, telling him about the things in the cave that she had seen and felt. It was possible that she had touched the scabbard and blade of the sword of Culann. Hadn't Mr. Colman's father come here long ago looking for treasure or something? Wouldn't it be wonderful if it turned out to be true? If Mr. Colman went to the hospital and got all better, then maybe next summer they could all explore together. Next summer when it wouldn't be so cold and Mr. Colman would be feeling better, which he would very soon, very soon, because help was coming and modern medicine could perform marvels. "Wouldn't it be funny," cried Claudia, her tears streaming, "if it turned out that your father was right after all and not the way you said about losing his wits and—"

Mr. Colman didn't seem to notice that the torrent of words had been cut off mid-sentence. The burning turf crackled and hissed; Mr. Colman sat open-mouthed, wheezing unevenly; deep in the island woods the firs caught the sea wind in a long, unfolding sigh.

For a long time Claudia sat facing the old man, gazing into his face, trying to recognize him. But he was still and only the Mr. Colman Evan had found, already old beyond all imagining. Like Evan, she had believed what he had told them, though he had said little and they understood even less. This man, Colman, whose last name they could never remember, had warned

268

them not to go too far lest they be caught like his daddy who had followed the bronze man past reason itself. She knew little more, except that Colman's father had made a living fishing herring off Grand Manan, where he had come from far away. The place named by Mr. Colman bobbed on the surface of her memory. Two and a half years ago that name had meant nothing. Now it meant more than she could bear to admit.

Some day, she thought, she would be able to think about Mr. Colman, to imagine him not old and nearly empty. She imagined herself sitting beside him on a summer evening: Tell me how your father spoke of himself, of his past life in Birsay, of how he came to Grand Manan. If Mr. Colman recovered, she would ask him who his mother was and what his father had looked like when he first followed the bronze man to Thrumcap Island and found the Other Place through the mists and the half-light between night and day.

"Look," she said, pointing to the window, its ledge rotten with crow droppings, "it's nearly light. They're probably on their way. Maybe with a doctor."

Mr. Colman stirred, tried to rise.

"Wait. Have some tea. Look how light it's getting."

Mr. Colman lurched forward and stood rocking as if he were at sea. "Crow," he mumbled, weaving toward the door.

"All right. I'll go." She brushed past him and wheeled to face him. "You . . . you wait," she stammered. "You have to because . . . because it's morning. . . ." She meant: Because they had come through the night, had survived.

He looked at her, his mouth sagging, tiny bubbles of foam at the corners. She guessed that even if he had the strength to start looking for the crow, he wasn't likely to keep his balance for long.

She was afraid to leave him, but more afraid of being unable to stop him. His watery eyes went from her to the door. He shook his head, and though she knew he was protesting against being saved and taken away, she preferred to interpret his gesture as relating to the crow. She could handle the one lie about going out to look for it; she could only slide away from the other.

As soon as she started toward the woods, Mr. Colman came shuffling to the door of the shack. She waved to him and stepped along purposefully, though with some care, for the woods still held the darkness.

She tried to collect her thoughts, but all the impressions that had gathered around her were like the sea taking back its own: Ideas, half formed, were dragged from her consciousness, seized, and flung back in a jumble. She wandered in the darkness of the fir trees, the hanging moss like shadows of a summer green. When an animal crossed a fallen tree, she couldn't even trust her own perception enough to tell whether it was a deer or one of Mr. Colman's half-tame sheep.

After a while she found herself coming out of the woods near the beach where she had camped with her family. She hadn't meant to go this far. Probably Ernie Gray had already arrived. Mr. Colman would never be able to explain her absence. So she began to hurry, following the rocks till the wind carried the wet to her, then climbing up toward the inland path.

When she had reached the crest, something made her pause, someone moving, a man. From where she stood she could only see the top part of him; almost at once he disappeared around the far side of the islet. She tried to call to him: "Ernie, I'm here. I'm O.K. Ernie, it's me." He didn't reappear. Either he hadn't heard or it was someone else. Maybe Ernie was still in the shack and had sent another man to look for her.

She began to run. Even though Ernie would see that she had kept Mr. Colman warm and even got him to drink some soup, she needed to justify her absence. She burst through the door into the shack, shouting her breathless explanation. And then stopped dead. Where were they all? Loaded already? So quickly? She slammed out again, yelling at the top of her lungs, because even before she could see for herself that the cove was still empty, she knew that it was Mr. Colman she had spotted down along the edge of the islet, Mr. Colman following her clear and specific directions to the little cave.

Thirty-five

She kept on yelling, as if her voice could take her place and become for Colman a living presence demanding his attention. The sea was quieter than before, but much higher, and deceptive in its gentle surge.

When she plunged in, the cold took her breath away. She had to stop calling. Nor could she make it all the way around; already the water was too high.

Then where was Mr. Colman? He couldn't have waded much farther either. Only she had seen him

271

heading this way toward the cliff, heading for the cave.

She clambered back to the bar, not fleeing the waves as before, but cursing the relentless tide. Her only hope of reaching the cave was from the cliff itself, where once, at a lower point, she had tumbled unhurt onto the narrow shingle below.

Now on dry land her legs wouldn't perform for her. She couldn't run because her soaking dungarees were like clamps of ice. At the cliff, she turned from the highest precipice with its overhanging rock and collapsed on the turf from which she had first rolled laughing into the world of Culann's sword. This time she was without the hilt. Suddenly she realized this and understood what it meant. She didn't need to return to the shack, to turn up the hearthstone, to feel among the old man's accumulated rubble, to know that he had taken the hilt with him in his last and lasting quest.

She slipped down to the wet shingle. Then she got to her feet and, clinging to the face of the islet, edged her way toward the overhanging rock where she knew the cave to be. But she couldn't remain there. The tide was rising too fast. It struck her then that the only way Mr. Colman could have reached the cave was on the rising flood. He couldn't have dragged himself up as she had done. He had to have already been on a level with the opening and ledge. The sea had carried him in.

She considered diving under to the cave mouth. Only her memory of Thomas struggling with Mr. Lindsay made her realize the pointlessness of such an attempt. Besides, no one could survive that long in this frigid water.

The sea thrust her back from the overhang. Soon it would force her to clamber up to safety. She didn't worry about being cut off from Thrumcap; after all, Ernie Gray was coming. In fact she thought she could hear voices already.

She was almost certain there was someone calling. She listened. There was a voice, and it was quite near. She looked up, ready to cry with relief and regret, but also in triumph, because Mr. Colman had prevailed. But she made no cry, for it was Thomas who dangled above her like a specter hovering halfway between the land and the sea.

"I thought this would be the day." His voice was hushed. He held out the bronze man. "Still, I've brought it every time, just in case."

"You . . . kept it." But she knew that he had, that he would follow it, had followed it, for the rest of his life.

"Claudia, are you all right? You're different. Though I would know you anyhow, even in those trousers."

"I . . . ." Claudia glanced at herself. "No, they're just . . . . Thomas, where are we?"

"Right here in Birsay. I've been after the seafowl and over each cave I know of. The cliffs will soon be bare." He reached out with his long pole and caught two birds in its triangular net. Quickly he brought the net to him, broke the necks of the birds, and deposited them in the caisie on the ledge.

Three more fledgling guillemots tumbled down, one of them striking the rock at Claudia's feet and staggering on over that edge into the sea. Almost at once two adults swam to it and led it out to open water.

"Must you kill them?" Claudia appealed.

"Not all," he whispered. "There's hundreds already gone to sea. The tammie-norries too. Come back and I'll show you."

"I can't."

"You can. It's Lammas time."

"It's . . . too late."

"I'll give up the hilt if you come back. I promise." He chortled. "That man came, you know. The one to plot the church on Eynhallow. He couldn't find where the hole had been. Dr. Cameron blamed Mr. Lindsay for ruining the site. And Mr. Farrer took Mr. Lindsay to another digging to keep peace. I . . . . Claudia, I left my knife there for them."

"For Dr. Cameron? Why?"

"To keep him from blaming Mr. Lindsay about the bronze man too. Now Mr. Lindsay thinks Dr. Cameron has it, and Dr. Cameron thinks he has it too, only it's not what he was led to expect and he doesn't think it's very important. Just an old knife, maybe Eskimo. But he gave me a little money for it and said I should begin to save for my future. Mr. Lindsay has been too busy to talk about my future."

Claudia said, "I don't have the bronze man anymore. I'll never have it again."

Thomas fell silent. Then he asked, "Where is it?"

Claudia longed to tell him that it was with the blade and scabbard. But if she told him that, she would be denying what she had so fiercely maintained, that all was possible, not forespoken. She watched guillemots and puffins waddling to the edge of the cliff and plopping far below into the water. Blackbacks swooped

274

down; frantic parents swam after their young. Only the puffins had to strike out on their own, straight from their dark burrows to the pale, perilous sea.

"Claudia, it's getting light. They're going to pull me back up." Thomas tipped the pole against the cliff and swung out and then onto the narrow ledge. "Please," he urged, "quickly now, before they hear me and haul me up for being trowie this dawn. You can come with me if you take my bronze man. It brought you this far. It can lead you all the way." He stretched out and reached down; he seemed to be floating in gray mist.

She saw the familiar form, the small man-shaped hilt she would never hold again. She reached out to him.

"Try, try," Thomas implored. The cliff was bare. There was no place here to get a foothold. Thomas jerked at the rope, and from high above him came an exclamation of impatience. There was no more length to be let out. "I'll untie myself then. We'll get back somehow."

She shouted a warning, "No."

He froze. Above on the cliff the voices sounded alarmed. "Claudia," he whispered, "be quiet till we're safe."

Claudia shook her head.

"What is it?"

The whispered words broke away from her. "There is no safety. Don't . . . don't keep looking. . . . You have to live your own life."

Thomas was jerked sideways. A voice called, inquired, promised to have him up and safe in a moment. Claudia wanted to beg him to cast himself free, not of the rope, but of the hilt whose awful power he had only begun to discern.

"Stay with me," he implored.

She showed him her empty hands.

"Then it's true," he charged. "It's true what they said, all of them."

She knew that he was challenging her to deny that from the moment of birth a person could be lost. Only now she knew too much and she cared too much.

She said, "Someone who once carried the bronze man, the whole sword, told me that knowing what happens matters less than knowing . . . knowing what manner of folk you have dealt with." How could she make him understand that even the most certain things he knew of, the tides and seasons, had instants of uncertainty? She wanted him to believe that though the sea would fall as it had risen and the sun would light the summer sky and die each winter, there could be moments between the certain and the known when the sea held and the light flowed into the darkness. She said, "I didn't think when I wanted you to look at the crow . . . . I didn't realize you were holding Grima back . . . for the bronze man. When I went after Grima, I didn't mean to . . . trick you."

"I knew you would go," he told her.

"Knew?"

"Because the crow was dead. Sibbie told me. Told me when the crow was gone, you would be too."

They looked at each other, beyond comfort or promise. He kept holding the bronze man out to her as he was hauled up, until the rope spun him around and he faced the cliff.

276

Then there were exclamations again and he was lowered far enough down to retrieve the caisie. She wondered at his ability to perform this ordinary task, tying a rope, adjusting the weight. It was as if she hadn't appeared to him, didn't really exist.

"Thomas, Thomas," she shouted.

He turned to answer. Only he wasn't Thomas. He was Ernie Gray, and there were men with him, helping him scrape down to her. For a second she tried to fight him.

"Don't get hysterical," he drawled. "Like I said, we'll have you up in a bit."

Claudia flung herself sideways, pointing as she had pointed to the crow with its neck wrung. She wanted to show Ernie Gray the place under the cliff where Colman had chosen to die. She wanted a witness to the mystery of this dawn, to the crazy order that sent baby birds hurtling hundreds of feet to either life or death under the eyes of the ravenous gulls. But the sea had carried its summer fowl far from this winter shore. No living thing floated on the cold gray surface, which heaved and rolled and spread itself, inch by inch, to its absolute height.

Claudia allowed Ernie to drag her up. Someone had a blanket around her. They seemed to know, without having to be told, that the old man had gone off and fallen or been caught by the tide. It was assumed that she had tried to save him, as they themselves would have done. It had nothing to do with heroics, real or false, but with the tendency in people to strike out sometimes against a current they cannot match.

"A damn fool errand of mercy," Ernie grumbled, and

Claudia could tell from his voice that he would have done it all over again.

They gathered up what they had brought, and left the rest for summer cruisers and fishermen to pick over. A solid bank of cloud stretched to the horizon. It hardly seemed like morning. Still, when Claudia looked back from the wheel house of Ernie's boat, she saw that a sheep stood waiting out of habit in front of Colman's shack.

The door swung. She could hear it banging. Then it slammed extra hard and the sheep bolted. Ernie observed that they had neglected to shut the door; he guessed that it would pull itself off its hinges in the next storm.

Claudia wondered how long the sheep would keep returning. Maybe, after the door blew off, it would cross the threshold and next spring bear its lamb inside. And that lamb after it, till storms and time demolished the shack altogether.

She looked down at her hands. Her fingers ached from gripping. They held only memory, but its impression was still precise and hard. So had Thomas gazed at his hands, as though the shape of the bronze man might be seared into them.

Painfully her fingers began to unclench. She glanced up once more toward the empty shack. She could visualize sheep and picnickers there, but who would ever venture again beyond known bounds to the other threshold? Who would cross from dark to light and risk the thin transparency between?

AUThOR'S NOTE

ALL the Orkney and Greenland places and a number of "off-stage" characters in this book are or were real. The characters within the story are entirely fictitious, with the exception of Thorstein, Bjarne, Lik-Lodin, and Grima, who are named in Icelandic sagas and other medieval sources. Even Sibbie, whose name derives from a cottage that once stood on Hundland Hill (the cottage in turn taking its name from a Sibbie who lived there), has no intended prototype.

For the walker on that hill today, nothing that is seen or heard can be taken for granted. And more has changed than crofts and farms. One hundred years ago, for example, the bonxie (great skua) was still a rare visitor to Orkney, and the fulmar, now so evident on many Orkney cliffs, had not yet begun to breed there. *The Place Names of Birsay,* by Hugh Marwick, and Robert Rendall's unpublished map of Birsay (based on the 1903 Ordinance Survey) must be superimposed on the current scene to effect a sort of double exposure. With these invaluable references, the walker can begin to imagine Birsay in the 1860s.

Archaeologists and naturalists have always been attracted by the unspoiled nature of the Orkneys. An eighteenth-century account by the Rev. George Low, who was minister in Birsay, set a high standard for observing and recording all aspects of life there. But by the middle of the nineteenth century, in spite of the emergence of noteworthy antiquarians like George Petrie, a fever of barrow-digging was sweeping across all of Britain; everywhere amateurs were transformed into experts. Visitors to Kirkwall could purchase stereoscopic views of the antiquities of Orkney. Mounds were opened and ransacked without regard for method or preservation. Both treasure-seeking opportunists and high-minded blunderers took up their picks and spades the way so many naturalists set out, "well supplied with no. 4 and no. 8 shot, royal and green cartridges," as a member of the British Ornithologists Union put it. Without embarrassment, this ornithologist described (in *A Naturalist's Ramble to the Orcades,* 1866) how "quantities of plover" followed him in a "most obstinate manner" until he shot one "out of sheer aggravation . . . as an example to the rest of its species." It was in this spirit that many antiquarians pursued their quarry under the earth. A poem, written in 1845, testifies to the popularity of the sport:

> . . . [H]ither bring my trusty scratcher,
> 'Mongst barrow tools there's none to match her,
> And tread not heavily, because it
> May seriously affect deposit. . . .

The 1860s were years of notable discoveries in Orkney, beginning with David Farrer's opening in 1861 of Maes Howe, a prehistoric megalithic tomb, which revealed the runes of twelfth-century diggers and plunderers. Farrer also conducted the excavation in Birsay which produced, along with other finds, an early

Irish bronze bell. In 1866, the year Sir Henry Dryden plotted the church ruins on Eynhallow and the Brough of Birsay, a bitter controversy developed over Samuel Laing's published report of evidence in Iron Age sites of a "prehistoric race of degraded cannibals." Newspaper editorials and archaeologists of undisputed reputation (including George Petrie in a paper presented to the Society of Antiquaries of Scotland) debated Laing's methods and interpretation. Though his conclusions were thoroughly discredited, it was Laing who later that summer received permission from the Duke of Portland to carry on his excavations.

For those who lived off the land in Orkney, the mid-nineteenth century was a time of change. With the abandonment of the old "runrig" land system, with the decline of the kelp industry and straw-plaiting, and with the improvement of roads and transportation, many of the old practices died out. But life wasn't suddenly modernized. Farmers and fishermen still had words and place names and customs reflecting the beliefs and legends of centuries. There are extraordinary likenesses between the excavated farms from the "Norse" settlements of Greenland in the early Middle Ages and Orkney crofts of only a century ago when most of the technical advances of industrial areas were still unknown to the rural islanders. Their testimony before the Crofters Commission in 1886 shows people still struggling to maintain themselves at the simplest level of subsistence.

If they used stones from crumbled ruins to repair a wall or build a byre, they were not the first to do so. In this way, and through successive habitations on the same site, what was once an Iron Age hut might have become in turn a beehive cell or Celtic oratory, a smithy, an outbuilding for a Norse farm, and a nineteenth-century cru for sheep. The early and prehistoric objects most commonly found, like flint "elf arrows" or "elf shots," were believed to bring luck, but an impressive foundation or burial unearthed by a crofter could bring at least as much trouble as reward.

Tombs and graves and the stones of structures long covered by turf, middens and fragments of pots with pollen samples, artifacts plowed up by Orkney farmers, as well as objects sought and found through careful and careless excavations—all contribute to our increasing knowledge of northern Europe's history.

Some objects, however, remain inscrutable. The bronze anthropoid hilts recovered from bogs and rivers throughout Britain and Ireland are considered by some scholars to be dagger hilts and by others to be the hilts of votive swords. The bronze man, without its blade, is based on a hilt in the collection of the National Museum in Dublin. It is possible that it was buried either as an offering to a Celtic god or as a grave good. Literary evidence, as in the Irish poem quoted in the beginning of this book, suggests the fitting darkness of burial. And in Beowulf (lines 2247–2266) that theme is sustained:

> Take these treasures, earth, now that no one
> Living can enjoy them. They were yours
>   in the beginning;
> Allow them to return. . . .
>   No one is left
> To lift these swords, polish these jeweled
> Cups: no one leads, no one follows. . . .